FEMINIST FAIRY TALES

By Barbara G. Walker:

BOOKS

The Woman's Encyclopedia of Myths and Secrets

The Secrets of the Tarot: Origins, History, and Symbolism

The Crone: Woman of Age, Wisdom, and Power

The I Ching of the Goddess

The Skeptical Feminist: Discovering the Virgin, Mother, and Crone

The Woman's Dictionary of Symbols and Sacred Objects

The Book of Sacred Stones: Fact and Fallacy in the Crystal World

Women's Rituals: A Sourcebook

Amazon: A Novel

GRAPHICS

The Barbara Walker Tarot Deck

FEMINIST FAIRY TALES

BARBARA G. WALKER

Illustrations by Laurie Harden

HarperSanFrancisco
An Imprint of HarperCollins*Publishers*

HarperCollins Web Site: http://www.harpercollins.com

HarperCollins®, 🐧®, and HarperSanFrancisco™ are trademarks of HarperCollins Publishers Inc.

FIRST EDITION

Illustrations by Laurie Harden
Book design by Jaime Robles

Library of Congress Cataloging in Publication Data
Walker, Barbara G.
Feminist fairy tales / Barbara G. Walker.
ISBN 0–06–251319–2 (cloth)
ISBN 0–06–251320–6 (pbk.)
1. Women—Social life and customs—Fiction.   2. Man-woman
relationships—Fiction.   3. Fairy tales—Adaptations.   4. Feminism—
Fiction.   I. Title.
PS3573.A42516F46   1996
813'.54—dc20   95–39219

96   97   98   99   00   ❖   HAD   10   9   8   7   6   5   4   3   2   1

To Ishtar Hildachild Darkmoon

CONTENTS

INTRODUCTION

Traditional fairy tales are drawn from many sources, including ancient mythology, pagan religion, political allegory, morality plays, and orientalia. Most such tales have filtered through centuries of patriarchal culture and show little respect for women, except as young and beautiful "princesses." Only to be decorative is the customary female function in these old stories. Girls without beauty are automatically also without virtue, happiness, luck, or love.

For instance, in the old German tale of Puddocky (or Paddock, the toad-familiar of Shakespeare's three witches), a prince seeks the world's most beautiful girl to marry; wagonloads of less attractive candidates are casually thrown into the river and drowned, just to get rid of them.

The message that such stories convey to girls is plain: Your looks are your only asset. Whatever else you might be or do doesn't count. Female ugliness is a crime deserving the death penalty.

The following collection of tales turns such misogynous messages around. Some of them are obvious twists on well-known stories, like "Ugly and the Beast," "Snow Night," "Gorga and the Dragon," "The Littlest Mermaid," "The Frog Princess," "Ala Dean and the Wonderful Lamp," "Little White Riding Hood," "Three Little Pinks," "Jill and the Beanroot," and "The Empress's New Clothes."

"How the Gods Met Their End" is a version of the Teutonic Götterdämmerung. "How the Sexes Were Separated" is a retelling of the Greek myth about Zeus's jealous attack on the hermaphrodites of the Golden Age. "How Winter Came to the World" is another Greek myth, the familiar tale of Persephone or Kore (Corey) and her mother Demeter (Dea Mater), retold without the implied domination of Father Zeus and with a better appreciation of Mother Nature's cycles. Similarly, "The White God" features some of the best-known African goddesses in an appreciation of Nature. Three of them are chosen to remind the reader that the ancient Great Goddess frequently appeared as a trinity of Virgin, Mother, and Crone, representing the three stages of woman's life as well as the seasons of seed time, growth, and harvest; the tripartite world of heaven, earth, and underworld; the phenomena of birth, sex, and death; the spinning, weaving, and cutting functions of the Fates; and many other three-way cycles and divisions. Modern feminist spirituality has made this ancient trinitarian concept familiar to many of today's women.

Some stories in this collection are simply original fantasies couched in the language and form of traditional fairy tales. They are intended to be playful, sometimes funny, sometimes thought-provoking. A feminist message of some kind can be found embodied in each.

B.G.W.

FEMINIST FAIRY TALES

ONE

THE S HE-WOLF

Wolf worship can be traced at least as far back as the days of Europe's pagan clans, some of which revered the wolf as a sacred totem, as shown by the survival of "Wolf" as a family name. Wolf-clan members ritually transformed themselves into animal spirits by wearing wolf skins and performing wolf-mimicking dances. In Greek myth the heavenly father, Zeus Lycaeus, takes wolf form.

Having been diabolized by Christian authorities, wolf worship gave rise to medieval superstitions about lycanthropy (werewolfism). This in turn gave rise to fairy tales that made wolves the villains. This darker, wilder canine image probably owed less to the observed behavior of real wolves than to buried childhood fears of domestic dogs who looked formidable and might bite.

As a dog lover from my earliest years, I could never see anything especially scary about fairy-tale wolves, however big and bad they might be called. Why vilify an interesting and attractive animal? Members of the old wolf clans must have liked the basic premise of lycanthropy, which suggested that, through a magical transformation, humans might be able to experience the keen senses of smell and hearing, the agility, strength, and swiftness of the wolf. A certain envy of such animal characteristics has been found in nearly all human societies.

She squatted down and tenderly bandaged the wolf's leg.

*O*nce upon a time there was a poor widower who lived with his daughter, Lupa, in a wretched hut on a stony little farm. The land produced hardly enough food for them, and their only reliable source of nourishment was their one cow, who gave milk, butter, and cheese. The widower's only pleasure in life was watching his daughter grow up. She was both clever and kind, the apple of her father's eye.

One day disaster struck. The cow took sick and died. There was no more milk, butter, or cheese to be had. The widower had no money to buy another cow or even a chicken or two for eggs. He and Lupa cut up the dead cow and preserved her meat, which nourished them for a while. After the meat was gone, they had almost nothing left but the seeds put by for a new crop.

The widower's late wife had been an accomplished needlewoman and had left some beautiful tapestries behind when she died. Lupa's father took them from storage. "I had hoped to keep these in memory of your mother," he told Lupa sadly. "Now I have no choice but to offer them for sale. Tomorrow I must start the spring planting. While I do that, you must take this embroidery to market and get the best price you can."

Early the next morning Lupa set out with the tapestries rolled up under her arm. She had to travel many miles to town. Along the way, a fierce thunderstorm came up. Finding no shelter, she trudged on through the rain and became thoroughly soaked.

After the sky cleared, Lupa opened the soggy roll of tapestries to wring them out. To her horror, she found that all the colors had run together—her mother had not been able to afford colorfast dyes. The pictures were ruined.

Feeling hopeless and frustrated, Lupa sat down beside the road and cried. Not only did she now have nothing to sell, but she had even lost her mother's handiwork, which would grieve her father very much.

After a while she dried her tears and decided to go on to the market anyway, hoping to sell the canvas itself, or perhaps just beg for a few coins or a bit of bread to take home.

As she was passing through a thick forest, she heard a dismal howling not far away. It seemed the very expression of her own sorrow. Too depressed to feel frightened, she followed the sound and came upon a large, gray, yellow-eyed she-wolf caught in a trap by her right foreleg, howling with pain and distress.

"Oh, poor wolf," said kindhearted Lupa. "Can I help you?" To her amazed delight, the wolf replied.

"Get me out of this trap," begged the wolf. "I have babies at home in my den. They will die if they lose me."

Lupa picked up a stout stick and opened the jaws of the trap to release the wolf's leg. Then she squatted down and tenderly bandaged the lacerated limb with a strip torn from her petticoat. The wolf stood patiently for these ministrations.

"My cubs and I thank you," she said. "How can I repay your kindness?"

"Alas, my situation is so unhappy that no one can help me," said Lupa. She told the wolf all her troubles, beginning with the cow's death and ending with the spoiled tapestries.

"Never mind going to the market," said the wolf. "Go home and don't worry. All will be well."

With that, the wolf limped away on her bandaged leg and disappeared into the underbrush.

Lupa was puzzled, but she reflected that the word of a she-wolf magical enough to talk was probably a word to be trusted. She buried the tapestries, not wanting her father to see them spoiled. Then she went home empty-handed. She told her father a white lie, saying that she had sold the tapestries and had been robbed on her way back home.

Her father had worked all day and was hungry, but they had nothing to eat except a few roots and seeds. They went to bed with rumbling stomachs and slept badly. Both Lupa and her father were sporadically awakened by the howling of wolves nearby in the forest.

In the morning Lupa felt too tired to get up, but she hurried out of bed when she heard her father shouting.

"Look, look!" he was crying. "Here on the doorstep!" There lay a whole haunch of venison, freshly butchered, ragged at the edges as if it had been chewed from the carcass instead of cut. Father and daughter immediately roasted some slices for their breakfast and had their first good meal in a long time.

The next day they were startled to find a company of the king's guardsmen on the same doorstep. The captain of the guards pounded on their door with his sword hilt and roared, "Open up in the king's name, poachers!"

Lupa's father hastily opened the door. "I am no poacher, but a poor peasant," he said. "You have the wrong man."

"You have been poaching the king's deer in the royal woodland," bawled the captain. "Don't deny it. We followed a blood trail right to your door."

The guardsmen pushed their way into the hut and found the venison hanging by the hearth. The captain took one look and said, "You're both under arrest."

In vain Lupa and her father protested that the meat had been delivered to them by agents unknown, and they had no idea where it had come from. No one listened to them. They were seized, bound, and marched away to the king's castle to stand trial.

After a miserable night in the dungeons, father and daughter were dragged to the audience chamber where the king and queen sat surrounded by their courtiers. Even the twin infant princes were present, in their cradles next to the queen's throne. An imposing official in a gold-trimmed black velvet robe announced the accusations against various evildoers and presented the evidence.

When it was his turn to respond to the charges against him, Lupa's father knelt before the king and pleaded innocent. He explained that a person or persons unknown had somehow left a haunch of venison on his doorstep during the night. The king seemed bored by this story. The defendant himself realized how feeble it sounded and lapsed into shamefaced silence. The queen, however, looked interested.

She gazed intently at Lupa and her father. Lupa noticed that she had unusual yellowish eyes.

"You will pass no sentence on these two," the queen said firmly. "I will make them my servants."

"But, my dear," said the king, "the penalty for poaching is execution."

"I say these two will not be executed," said the queen, in a tone that brooked no opposition. "Guard, take them away to my quarters."

Lupa and her father waited under guard in the queen's drawing room until the queen appeared in person. She ordered their bonds removed and then dismissed the guardsmen. Lupa and her father fell at her feet and thanked her for her mercy.

"I am not merciful, only conscientious," the queen said. "I repay my debts. My former mode of recompense got you into trouble, and now it's up to me to repair the damage."

"I don't understand, Your Majesty," Lupa said timidly.

"Does this look familiar?" the queen asked. She rolled up her right sleeve. On her forearm was a bandage, slightly bloodstained. Lupa looked closely and recognized the strip torn from her own petticoat.

"Your Majesty is the she-wolf?" Lupa whispered in amazement.

"We will not speak of this again," said the queen. "You, Lupa, will become my handmaid. Your father will be a royal gardener. He will be well paid and well fed, as will you also. Your life of privation is over."

Lupa and her father wept tears of joy and kissed the queen's hands. They never returned to their poor hut but took up residence in the castle at once. Lupa served her royal mistress faithfully and well for many years. Her father tended the castle gardens with care and eventually rose to the rank of head groundskeeper.

Lupa dug up the tapestries her mother had made, rinsed out their cheap dyes, and gave them to the most expert of the royal needlewomen to be copied. The resulting work became known far and wide as the celebrated Lupine Tapestries. Years afterward they were still prized gems in the national museum.

People said that sometimes, on moonless nights, Lupa and her father both underwent a strange transformation and ran through the forest with the wild wolves, in a pack that was always led by a large gray female with yellow eyes and a scarred right foreleg.

TWO

PRINCESS QUESTA

"*A good man is hard to find*" seems to be the theme of Princess Questa's quest. Her disappointments begin with a father who fails her, and thereafter she learns several hard lessons about having to look after herself. The final message might serve as a feminist creed: Don't be sucked into the helper/nurturer role if it makes you suffer.

In any patriarchal society the principle of first taking care of yourself is implicitly followed by most men, but for most women it still needs to be consciously articulated.

Questa's cowrie shell, gift of the fairy godmother, is the primary worldwide symbol of female genitals, of the powers of birth and rebirth, and of the passages through the Gate of Life.

It was a cowrie shell with a round, polished back.

O nce upon a time there was a young princess named Questa. She grew up in a castle with her mother the queen and her father the king. Unfortunately, while Questa was still in her teens, her mother became sick and died. The grief-stricken king banished all the wisewomen who had tried in vain to cure his wife's illness. Then he plunged himself into affairs of state, ignoring Princess Questa and becoming more and more ruthless in his pursuit of glory for his kingdom. He began to make war on neighboring kingdoms, to seize more territory, and to destroy rivals. Within a few years' time he had become a cruel despot. Princess Questa could hardly recognize him, and she grieved for the father she had once known. He seemed to have gone mad.

As the king's displeasure brought terrible punishments, his fearful courtiers and servants all followed the king's lead in neglecting his daughter. Poor Questa was reduced to the status of an unpaid housekeeper. Her personal maid was fired. Her once-splendid dresses became shabby. The white stallion that she once loved to ride was taken from her and given to one of the king's generals. She was forced to serve meals to her father's knights, a rowdy collection of ruffians who pawed her, pulled her hair, spat on her skirts, and made her the butt of crude jokes. The nastiest of the knights, the king's champion, often hinted that she would soon become his personal plaything.

When she could manage to take time away from chores in the kitchen and scullery, Questa sometimes left the castle and went to a certain grove that she had loved since her childhood—a place said to be the haunt of fairies. It was a mossy mound surrounded by a thicket of willows whose lacy branches drooped like curtains around it. In the center of the mound stood a large upright stone that the peasants whispered about, saying that it had been sacred to an elder race and was imbued with mysterious powers. Questa never feared the magic stone. She liked to sit and lean her back against its sun-warmed roughness, feeling it as a support and a comfort.

One day when she was resting in the grove, she suddenly felt overwhelmed by the hopelessness and helplessness of her position. She began to cry bitterly, beating her fists against the upright stone. After a time, she heard a small rustling sound. She opened her eyes to see, standing before her, a beautiful lady in a shimmering silver gown.

"Why do you weep?" the lady asked.

"I am very unhappy," Questa said. "My mother is dead and my father has become a tyrant who treats me like the lowest of his servants. The knights harass me, and I think my father will soon give me to the fiercest and meanest of them, as a reward for his battlefield slaughterings."

"Then you must run away," the lady said.

A pang of fear touched Questa's heart. "But the castle is the only home I've ever had," she protested. "I have nowhere else to go. I have no money or possessions. I would starve to death, wandering the roads as an outcast."

"Don't be afraid," the lady said. "You are destined to undergo three trials before you find your rightful place in the world. Your present life is the first. Now it's time for you to move on."

From the silvery folds of her gown the lady withdrew an object the size of a child's fist and placed it in Questa's hand. It was a cowrie shell with a round, polished back and a front somewhat resembling a wide, slightly grinning mouth lined with small teeth.

"Here is an amulet to protect you. Listen to the sea's voice and be guided," the lady said.

Questa put the cowrie's mouth to her ear and heard the faraway murmur of the ocean. "Must I go to the seacoast, then?" she asked.

The lady made no answer. She only smiled and gently touched Questa's forehead with her finger. Then her outlines grew fainter and fainter, until she seemed to fade away into a dazzle of mist, absorbed by the sunlight.

"Surely," Questa said to herself, "I am favored by the fairy queen, who came to me in person. How can I not obey her instruction?"

Later that evening Questa made a bundle of her few shabby clothes, took food and a knife from the kitchen, stole a warm cloak that one of the knights had carelessly thrown aside, and crept unseen out of the castle.

The full moon lighted the roadway before her. She ran as fast as she could until she was deep into the forest, then she slowed to catch her breath. She walked all night in the direction of the seacoast. At dawn she lay down behind a haystack in an open field and slept.

During subsequent nights she traveled on foot in the same way, hiding during daylight hours, avoiding passersby, towns, and lighted dwellings. Her feet blistered, bled, and eventually toughened. When she ran out of food, she stole fruit from orchards, eggs from henhouses, bacon from smokehouses, and other provisions from sleeping farmsteads. Her solitary gypsy life made her alert and resourceful, but she was lonely and always afraid of being discovered and dragged back to face her father's wrath.

When she came to the seacoast, she listened to her cowrie shell. It said, "Here . . . here . . . here." She sat down on the beach, leaned against a fishing boat drawn up above the tide line, and fell asleep.

The next thing she knew, a hand was shaking her shoulder. She looked up and saw a handsome, curly haired young man with a coil of rope over his shoulder and a boat hook in his hand.

"You're sleeping on my boat," he said. "I have to launch now. Go home and be lazy there."

"I have no home," she murmured.

"Where did you come from?" he asked.

"From somewhere inland," she said. "I don't know."

"You don't know much, do you?" he snorted. "Well, maybe I can use you. Are you any good with nets? My net needs mending, and I can't handle everything by myself."

"I can sew and weave rope," said Princess Questa.

"All right, see what you can do with this." He pulled a large net from the boat and spread it on the sand. "If it's well mended when I come back ashore, I'll give you a good fish dinner."

The young fisherman launched his boat and rowed away toward the horizon, leaving Questa to pull together the broken meshes of his net. Though she was weary from walking, she worked all day under the hot sun. By late afternoon her fingers were stiff and she was hungry, thirsty, and gritty with sand.

The fisherman returned with a small net full of fish, saying that he needed his large net to catch more. He seemed pleased with Questa's repair work. True to his word, he took her to his little cottage behind the dunes and cooked her a fine meal of fresh fish, oat bread, and apple pudding. She ate ravenously.

Watching her, the fisherman asked, "You haven't had much to eat lately, have you?"

"No," Questa answered, gobbling the last spoonful of pudding.

"If you have no home, you could stay with me," he offered. "I can give you food and a roof over your head. You can keep my house, mend my nets, and maybe even warm my bed for me." He gave her an impish grin that made his cheeks dimple and his eyes sparkle attractively. "You're not bad-looking, you know."

Questa felt drawn to him. "You're not bad-looking either," she said. "Maybe I'll stay for a while."

She lived with the young fisherman and soon convinced herself that she loved him. For a while they were a happy couple, rejoicing in each other's company. Princess Questa thought she had never been so content in her castle as she was in the fisherman's cottage. But then things began to go wrong.

Autumn storms were unusually violent, and the schools of fish deserted their regular feeding grounds. Day after day, the young fisherman went out to sea for longer and longer hours, returning with only a sparse catch. There were fewer fish to eat and fewer to sell. Still the king's tax collectors came regularly for their accustomed tribute and would take nothing less. Questa and her fisherman had to sell some furniture and dishes to meet their demands. The cottage became less comfortable. "If I were on the throne instead of my greedy father," Questa thought to herself, "I would have more mercy on the poor people."

The young fisherman no longer laughed and smiled with her. All the merriment went out of him. He toiled grimly but fell more and more into debt. Questa suggested that he give up fishing and try some other line of work. At this he flew into a rage and slapped her, shouting that he was and would always be a fisherman, like his father and his father's father before him.

As time went on, he became more surly and morose. On several other occasions he struck Questa, blaming her for his bad luck, hinting that she might have cast an evil spell on the fishing. "That's ridiculous," she protested. "I'm not responsible for your troubles. The king's oppressive government is."

But because the fisherman dared not strike out or shout at the armed men who came for the tribute, he took out his rage on poor Questa. Soon she was living in fear again, slavishly hoping each day that he would catch enough fish to keep him from beating her when he returned from the sea.

Sometimes when he was gone she went out to walk the dunes in the wintry wind, weeping and bewailing her fate. One misty morning in the dunes she saw again the lady in the silver gown.

"Why do you weep?" the lady asked.

"Alas," said Questa, "I'm worse off than before. Now I am the servant of a man who has no gentlemanly manners at all and who abuses me whenever life frustrates him. How much lower can I fall?"

"Then you must run away," the lady said.

"I can't live on the open road in winter," Questa cried. "If I don't freeze, I'll starve."

"Trust your destiny," said the lady. "Listen to your amulet. This is your second trial." Then she disappeared into the mist.

Questa went back to the cottage and put her cowrie shell up to her ear. It whispered, "South . . . south . . . south." So, before the fisherman could return and stop her, she gathered up her clothing, her knife, some provisions, all the money she could find, and a good pair of boots. She left the cottage, heading southward along the coast.

Fortunately, the weather was not bitter cold. She was able to find shelter in empty barns, sheds, or shepherds' huts. After traveling a long way, she came to a town where large ships put in at busy docks. Her weary feet brought her to a waterfront inn. She found the warm, welcoming firelight and the smell of hot food irresistibly alluring.

The innkeeper looked at her shabby clothes and snapped, "No beggars allowed in here."

"I'm not a beggar," Questa said indignantly. "I have money." She displayed a few coins, and the man grudgingly gave her a piece of bread and a bowl of hot, thick soup. It seemed the most delicious thing she had ever tasted.

When she finished, she asked the innkeeper if he knew anyone in need of a willing worker. "You want to work?" he said. "We need a maid right here. A penny a day, free lodging, and all the soup you can eat. But you'd better not be afraid of hard work."

Princess Questa assured him she was not afraid of hard work and took the job at the inn. She was given an apron, a broom, and a tiny bedroom

up under the eaves. All that winter she worked long days, serving customers, making and remaking beds, cleaning rooms, doing laundry, scrub-
bing floors, washing dishes, helping the cook, and running errands. Her
once-pretty hands became rough and raw with chilblains. Her back and
legs often ached, and when she fell into her narrow bed every night she
was exhausted. But she was content to be supporting herself. Frequently,
men sought her favors and hinted that they would relieve her of drudgery,
but she rebuffed them all, wishing only to be left alone.

One flower-scented evening in spring, however, there came to the inn a
young man who aroused Questa's interest. He was a musician. He played
his guitar and sang sweet, plaintive ballads for the customers, who came
from miles around to hear him. The innkeeper was delighted by such volume of business and invited the musician to stay on and give regular per-
formances for a while. The musician agreed and was lodged on the floor
below Questa's garret. Sometimes at night she could hear him quietly prac-
ticing.

Questa came to know the musician as an easygoing person, with a
ready smile and a gentle manner. She succumbed to his soft charm, telling
herself that a man so sweet-natured would never turn brutish and violent,
as the fisherman had. She undertook to do the musician special favors: to
wash and press his costumes, polish his boots, darn his socks, and save him
tidbits from the kitchen, all out of what she thought was love.

When the musician decided to move on, she went with him. They were
happy together, free as birds, traveling from town to town, earning money
through their music. Questa learned to play the guitar and to sing duets
with him. They performed together for weddings, birthday parties, country
fairs, well dressings, and festivals. They were invited to stay at inns, manor
houses, farms, and community centers.

For a while Questa enjoyed the life. She didn't mind having to do all
the practical work while her gentle musician did nothing but sing, or sat
drinking wine and telling stories to his admirers.

As time went on, however, she became increasingly irritated by his
happy-go-lucky ways. He was never ill-tempered or impatient, but sometimes he was too indolent or too drunk to bother fulfilling one or another
of his engagements. The word got around that he was not reliable. People
became less eager for his services.

Questa worked harder and harder, creating new costumes, arranging bookings, collecting a crowd, making excuses for him when he was too drunk to perform. Sometimes she had to do an entire show by herself. She wasn't as accomplished a singer as he, so her audiences were disappointed. In addition, people had less and less money to spend on frivolities like music, due to the ever heavier taxes imposed by the king to support his wars.

In vain Questa tried to keep the musician away from wine and to hearten him to work more. He only smiled sweetly, kissed her, and went off to the tavern. He drank up most of their profits. Questa was especially concerned because she knew that she would soon become a mother. The responsibility of caring for a child seemed to make no impression whatever on her idle musician.

He was drunk when her baby son was born, and he was drunk most of the time afterward. He liked to play with the baby and sing lullabies, but he never helped with parental chores. Now that Questa was preoccupied with looking after her child, she couldn't look after the musician's career as she had before. Their audiences grew thinner and thinner.

The musician didn't seem to care whether he performed or not. He spent hours each day doing nothing at all. Questa grew angry and berated him for his indolence. He didn't mind. He only smiled, petted her, whispered soothing love words, and fell asleep.

They were living in a tent on the outskirts of a town where the musician had already worn out his welcome. Nevertheless, he went often to the tavern and left Questa alone with her baby. She sometimes wrapped up the child against the chill and went forth to walk the roads, begging a few coins from passersby and keeping herself warm by moving briskly.

One day, on a lonely roadside, she found herself weeping uncontrollably into her baby's hood. When she looked up, she saw the silver-gowned lady standing before her.

"Why do you weep?" the lady asked.

"I am penniless," said Questa, "and though the musician is gentle and kind, he is as irresponsible as this child here. I can't live like this."

"Then you must run away," the lady said.

"How can I care for my child as a homeless beggar?" Questa cried. "At least now he has a roof over his head, even if it is only a tent."

"You have passed through your third trial," the lady said. "It's time for you to remember that you are a princess. You have learned enough about your people. You know how weary they are of oppression and warfare. Instead of singing to them, you must tell them the things they need to hear." Then she disappeared.

Questa went back to the tent and listened to her cowrie shell. It whispered, "Speak . . . speak . . . speak."

She packed up all her belongings and went to the next town. There she used the skills she had learned to gather a crowd with music and song. Instead of entertaining, however, she made a speech. She told the people who she was and how she thought the government should be run. They cheered her seditious words.

Afterward, a tall rangy man in forester's clothing came to see her. He said he could gather an army of outlaws who were eager to overthrow the king but needed a legitimate heir to enthrone in his place. He proposed that Questa place herself at the head of his army and help prepare a people's revolution.

Questa agreed. She accompanied a growing ragtag army around the countryside, preaching her vision of a peaceful, equitable people's government. She became known to all as Queen Questa. She created a flag, showing a golden cowrie shell on a background of royal blue. Peasants flocked to her standard.

As it happened, the king had become ill and could no longer look after his affairs. Thinking that he had no heir, his rowdy knights were fighting among themselves for a chance at the succession. The government was neglected and corrupt, worse than ever. For such reasons, peasants and villagers were glad to join Queen Questa's army in the hope of better living conditions for themselves and their families.

When the outlaws finally completed their preparations and marched on the king's castle, the king was on his deathbed. The knights were demoralized by the sight of an army so huge that it seemed to spread to the horizon on every side. Some of the knights, who had been guilty of especially cruel oppressions and feared retaliation, crept out of the castle by secret gates and ran away. Others put up a token resistance, but in the end they were forced to surrender.

Questa entered the castle in triumph and faced her dying father, who recognized her and declared that she was the long-lost legitimate heir. She showed him her infant son, who would reign after her, and the old king died somewhat comforted.

Queen Questa had herself crowned twice: once at a splendid coronation ceremony in the castle, and once with a wreath of wildflowers in the old fairy grove. She established a shrine there and made regular oblations to the ancient standing stone.

Soon after she ascended the throne, Questa carried out all the reforms she had promised. She was merciful to the warlike knights, but she took away their lands and castles and made them take up honest trades. She also established strict compulsory reform schools for men who beat women or children. She sent palace guards to seek out offenders and compel them to attend such schools until their habits were changed. A few threats, as of grievous personal injury for noncompliance, went far toward helping such men take their lessons seriously.

Queen Questa was loved by her people. She reigned well for many years and trained the young prince to do likewise. She never took a husband and lived happily ever after.

THREE

NOW NIGHT

The wicked stepmother is ubiquitous in European fairy tales, whereas any father figure is usually given a good character. Snow White's stepmother seems to have been vilified because (a) she resented being less beautiful than Snow White, and (b) she practiced witchcraft.

One might suspect that female beauty was really a larger issue for men than for women, because male sexual response depends to a considerable degree on visual cues. Placing each "fair lady" (or anything else) somewhere on an arbitrary hierarchical scale seems to be a male idea. Women may recognize a thousand different types of beauty without having to make them compete.

As for witchcraft, the last bastion of female spiritual power fell when the church declared its all-out war on witches, the name they gave to rural midwives, healers, herbalists, counselors, and village wisewomen, inheritors of the unraveling cloak of the pre-Christian priestess. A queen who was also a witch would have been a formidable figure, adding political influence to spiritual mana. Snow White's stepmother therefore seems to me a projection of male jealousies. As re-envisioned in this story, she may seem more true to life.

Snow Night screamed and thrashed in a panic . . .

*O*nce upon a time there was a beautiful princess with skin white as snow and hair black as night, so she was called Snow Night. Her mother died when she was a baby, and her father remarried. Snow Night's stepmother was a noted sorceress, and also famous for her beauty, of a more mature type than that of the young princess.

Everyone at court watched with interest as Snow Night grew up to be a charming young woman. Particularly interested was her father's Master of the Hunt, who was called Lord Hunter. He aspired to improve his rank by marrying a royal princess. Moreover, he found Snow Night exceedingly desirable. Therefore he made every effort to woo her. He sent her the best flowers plucked from the royal gardens and very bad poems plucked from his own mind. He subjected her to long monologues about his hunting successes. He hovered at her elbow in every procession and tried to fill her dance card with his own name at every grand ball.

Snow Night, however, did her best to avoid him. Though he was arrogant and fancied himself a very gallant gentleman, she found his attentions unwelcome. His touch made her shudder. Lord Hunter was heavy, coarse, and greasy-haired. His breath stank, his fingernails were dirty, and his speech unrefined. Snow Night thought him repulsive. "If my father tries to make me marry a hideous old toad like Hunter," she confided to her maid, "I'll run away."

Lord Hunter also tried to make himself agreeable to the queen, hoping to become her confidant. The queen called him her huntsman and tolerated him with good grace. She was amused by his constant flattery and diverted by his gossip. Before long, he came to think of himself as the queen's intimate friend, not knowing that she held a rather different view of the matter.

One day Lord Hunter found Snow Night alone in a remote part of the castle gardens, and he seized the moment. He swept off his hat, bowed, and knelt at her feet (bumping down rather heavily), holding up a long-stemmed rosebud as an offering.

"Lovely princess," he said, hand on heart, "allow me to say what I have been yearning to say to you for a long time. You are the only woman

I'll ever love. You are my beloved, the lady of my heart. Do say you will let me court you, and perhaps one happy day to marry you."

"Marry!" cried Snow Night, appalled. "I'm not ready to marry. But when I am, I will certainly marry a handsome prince, not an ugly old huntsman. Lord Hunter, you presume far above your station."

Surprised in his turn by the vehemence of her rejection, Hunter snatched at her skirt with one hand and clamped her wrists together with the other. "You must not talk so to me," he exclaimed. "I'm a nobleman. Princess or not, you're only a young girl with little knowledge of the world. Maybe you should learn a lesson today."

Angry and frightened by his boldness, she struggled to free herself. "How dare you lay hands on me?" she demanded. "Let go at once!" When he did not, she wrenched a hand free and struck at his face with her fingernails, drawing blood.

At this, Lord Hunter quite forgot himself. He wrestled her down to the ground and clawed at her clothes, with some dim idea of ravishing her into submission. Snow Night screamed and thrashed in a panic, struck him with her fists, and finally kicked him in the crotch. As he curled up gasping for breath, she sprang to her feet and spat at him.

"Never, never come near me again, do you hear, you repellent monster?" she cried. "I hate and despise you, and I always will." She ran away, leaving Lord Hunter feeling that his ambitions—and other things—were thoroughly ruined.

Now Hunter's desire for the princess was replaced by hostility. He wanted to see her injured, even dead, in recompense for his humiliation. He sulked and brooded and awaited his chance.

One evening he found the queen alone in her anteroom, consulting her magic mirror, which always told the truth. He sat quietly while she asked the mirror several questions. Then, as she was turning away, he said, "I wonder if Your Majesty has ever asked the mirror who is the fairest lady in the land?"

The queen smiled. "I know the answer it would give, huntsman. Snow Night is the fairest."

"Doesn't that anger you?"

"No, why should it?"

"Surely Your Majesty's great beauty has always been fairest in the land. Wouldn't that make the princess a usurper and an upstart?"

The queen laughed. "We all go through our cycles, huntsman. The wise expect it. Younger life takes the place of the elder; it's the way of nature. Every mother of children feels it in her bones. To challenge nature is folly."

"But don't stepmothers always hate their stepdaughters?"

"That must be one of the ridiculous traditions about women invented by men. A stepmother has every reason to get along with her stepdaughter. Why cause unnecessary strife? In any case, I'm quite fond of Snow Night. She's a good-hearted little thing, if a bit slow in her wit. Why would I be so foolish as to mistreat her?"

"Your Majesty wouldn't undertake any such thing personally, of course," Hunter said, his obsession having deafened him to all her words, which he still believed were dissembling. "According to an old story, the royal stepmother sends another to act for her, such as her faithful huntsman. He is the one charged with killing the stepdaughter and bringing back her heart in a jeweled casket."

The queen gave him a shrewd glance. "You really are mad," she whispered. "Huntsman, that is an exceedingly obnoxious idea. Put it out of your head at once." But she saw from his slightly glazed look that the idea had already taken a firm hold on him. With a sudden chill, she realized that Snow Night was in mortal danger.

That night the queen went to her tower room and worked a spell to call a clever raven to her window. When the bird appeared, she censed it with herbal smoke and said, "Fly to the land of the dwarves and tell the queen that I need seven of her subjects, the ones most learned in techniques of concealment." The raven flew off.

Three days later the queen put on a white wig, a long putty nose, a black cloak, and a black broad-brimmed crone's hat. Thus disguised, accompanied only by her personal maid, she went to the village inn to meet with seven little men from the land of the dwarves.

They sat at a rough wooden table drinking flagons of ale. The queen produced a leather sack from the folds of her cloak and laid it before the leader, who opened it and poured forth a handful of glittering cut stones: sapphires, rubies, emeralds, and diamonds. The dwarves' eyes sparkled like the gems, which dwarves love above everything else. "Magnificent," said the leader. "For this we will do anything you ask, short of killing ourselves."

"I want you to watch the king's Master of the Hunt, whose picture I show you here," said the queen. "I want you also to watch over the Princess Snow Night, without letting yourselves be seen. Here is her picture. If she leaves the castle, follow her. If the Master of the Hunt ever approaches her in such a manner as to do her harm, you are to seize and bind him, carry him back to Dwarfland, and keep him a perpetual prisoner. Your queen, who owes me a favor or two, will see to it."

"We will obey you in every particular," promised the leader of the dwarves.

The queen arose and shook his hand. "Then it is agreed," she said. "From this moment on, let no one from the castle see you anywhere." She left the inn and returned by dark of night to her own quarters.

Less than a week later all the courtiers except Lord Hunter were gladdened by the news that a fine young prince named Charming was on his way from a neighboring country to woo Snow Night in person. The king's huntmaster kept to himself, avoiding his usual activities and his friends, who noticed that he was losing weight, seldom spoke, and never smiled any more.

Lord Hunter was obsessed by the demon of vengeance, which his violent nature could express only in violent terms. He never spoke to Snow Night, but he watched her always, even going so far as to hide in a cupboard near her chambers for many hours during the night.

On the day before Prince Charming was due, Snow Night took her lapdog and her maid, with a picnic basket, out for a greenwood lunch. Lord Hunter seized the opportunity to follow them. No sooner had they settled in a pleasant glade when he sprang from the bushes, grabbed the princess, and trussed her like a chicken, ignoring her shrieks and struggles. Her little dog yapped and snapped at him, and received a brutal kick that sent it flying against a tree. Her maid stood frozen with terror, until Lord Hunter commanded her to lie down on her face.

"No!" screamed Snow Night. "Don't stop! Run back to the castle and tell them! Run, you fool!"

But the maid was too long accustomed to habits of passivity and obedience. Her knees buckled. She sank down helplessly, and Lord Hunter trussed her too.

Then he turned his attention to the squirming princess. He drew out his long hunting knife and advanced on her, madness gleaming in his eyes. Realizing that she was at the mercy of a murderer, she gave herself up for lost.

Suddenly the seven little men charged from all directions around the glade, disarmed Lord Hunter, and bore him to the ground. Six of them sat on him while the seventh untied the princess and her maid. They used the same ropes to bind up Lord Hunter even more tightly than a trussed chicken.

The head dwarf then doffed his cap and bowed to Snow Night. "This man will never bother Your Highness again," he said. "We are under orders to return with him to Dwarfland, where he will be imprisoned for the rest of his life."

Ignoring Hunter's yell of protest, Snow Night said, "Excellent. How can I repay you for saving my life?"

"We have already been paid, Your Highness," said the dwarf (for dwarves are honest folk), "by your lady mother, the queen. With your permission, we will go now."

Six dwarves hoisted the tight-wrapped body of Lord Hunter to their shoulders (for dwarves are strong folk) and marched away after their leader, singing lustily to drown out his snarls and curses. As their noise faded into the distance, Snow Night and her maid collected their scattered picnic utensils and their wits. Snow Night carefully carried her little dog, whose ribs had been broken, home to a bed in her dressing room where he could rest until he was healed.

The next day Prince Charming arrived on schedule, and he proved to be charming indeed. He and Snow Night were delighted with each other. They soon became engaged and within a year were married in a magnificent ceremony. The queen was matron of honor. Snow Night never forgot her stepmother's wise forethought, which had saved her life. Both royal couples, elder and younger, lived happily ever after.

As for Lord Hunter, his reason quite gone, he lived confined for the rest of his life as the dwarves' prisoner. In later years he sometimes passed the weary hours by writing stories. It is said that he wrote an entirely different version of the story you have just heard.

FOUR

GORGA AND THE DRAGON

J. J. Bachofen said in Myth, Religion, and Mother-Right *that Gorgo was a title of the death-dealing Crone form of the Goddess Athene, who also appeared in Greek myth as Metis, "Wisdom," disguised as Athene's mother. Metis was the Greek rendering of Medusa, "Wisdom," eldest of the pre-Hellenic trinity of snake-haired Gorgons. The other two were Stheino and Euryale, "Strength" and "Universality."*

Before the Greeks mythologized her as the monster whose glance turned men to stone, Medusa was called a queen of the Libyan Amazons. It seems that Medusa-Metis and Gorgo-Athene were one and the same, for even the Greeks admitted that Athene came from Libya, not from the Greek city that bears her name. She was worshiped by Amazon tribes in northern Africa, where she wore the snake-haired Gorgon mask on her aegis, indicating her power to petrify men who intruded on her sacred mysteries. According to the myth, her ceremonial mask was carried to Athens by the culture hero Perseus, who learned its magic from Libyan warrior women.

The mythic fame of Gorgo's women warriors provides a startling point for the story of Gorga. She and her prince unite as equals in a vision of Utopia, an anagram for their nation. Would that the little wizards behind our modern technological dragons could be so well controlled by the Gorgas among us.

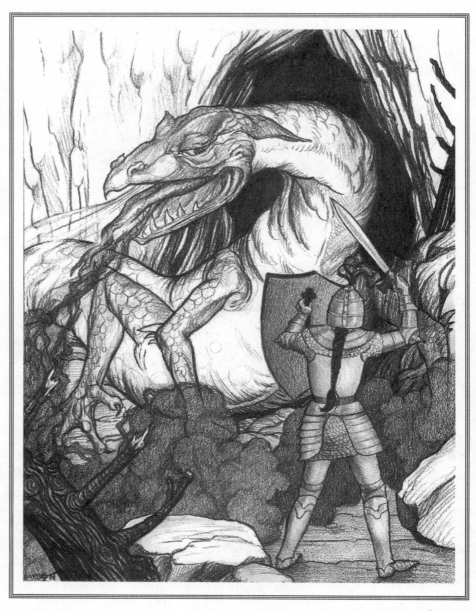

She advanced toward the creature . . .

nce upon a time there was an Amazon named Gorga, the daughter of a well-known wise-woman. Gorga was not beautiful, but she was renowned throughout the queendom for her great strength and skill in the martial arts. She was the undisputed champion in kick boxing, wrestling, javelin-throwing, archery, and swordswomanship. Every holiday, she invariably won the footrace, high jump, and spear-chucking contests. Her fame spread far beyond the borders of her own country. One day it brought her a noble foreign visitor, the prince of Poutia in person.

The neighboring nation of Poutia had been much troubled of late by the depredations of a fire-breathing dragon. The prince traveled all the way to Gorga's village just to beg her assistance in conquering the dragon. Laying aside his pride just as he removed his plumed hat, he fell to his knees before Gorga and pleaded with her.

"The soothsayers insist that the dragon can be slain only by a single adversary," he said, "but that no man alive can overcome it. Five of our mightiest heroes have tried and failed. They have plunged swords and spears right into its breast, without effect. I would make the attempt myself, but I am also a man. Besides, the royal succession must not be—ahem!—threatened, of course, you understand." Gorga gave the prince a wry glance. He was plump and out of shape, clearly in no condition to fight dragons.

"You are a woman," the prince went on, "as well as a great warrior. You must be the savior ordained for us. The dragon demands the sacrifice of a beautiful maiden every full moon. We are running out of beautiful maidens. Soon our young men will have no maidens left to marry except the ugly ones, begging your pardon, ma'am. Please, will you come with me to Poutia and slay the dragon for us?"

"What's in it for me?" asked Gorga.

"My lord the king says you can name your price, even to half our kingdom. I agree to this. If the dragon isn't slain, there won't be any kingdom left for me to rule, anyway. And sooner or later it may invade your country too. I know it's a great challenge. If you succeed, your fame will echo down the corridors of time forever."

Gorga liked this kind of talk. "I will consult my mother the wise-woman," she said. "Make yourself at home and take some refreshment."

She offered him home-baked gooseberry pie and fresh cider. While the prince sat down to eat, Gorga fetched her mother, who listened carefully to the prince's proposal.

At length her mother said, "I will advise Gorga to go with you, if she's willing. You may rest here until we're ready. We'll need to make some preparations."

The prince wept with relief and energetically kissed the hands of both Gorga and her mother. Gorga found this rather strange, as no man had ever kissed any part of her before.

Gorga's mother rummaged among her magic supplies and brought out a heavy silvery suit of mail, together with a helmet carved in the likeness of a nest of rearing snakes covering the whole head, plus a hideous mask over the face. "You must wear these in any encounter with a fire-breather," she told Gorga. "The suit is made of fiber of rock, and no fire can burn it. The mask carries a petrifaction charm, frightening enough to turn an opponent to stone. Take your sword, spears, and arrows. Dragon skin is usually impermeable, so remember to aim for the eyes or down the throat. Be bold, my daughter, and you will prevail where no man has yet succeeded."

Gorga hugged her mother and bade her farewell, receiving a protective blessing from her hand. Then she and the prince mounted their horses and rode away to Poutia. Following her mother's instructions, Gorga planned to stand in for the sacrificial maiden at the next full moon. The prince was dubious about this. He feared the dragon's displeasure when it noticed that Gorga was not beautiful. But Gorga assured him that by the time the dragon got close enough to examine her, it would be already half dead.

She was wined and dined for several days in the king's castle and treated like the greatest of honored guests, although some of the warrior heroes grumbled behind their hands and cast belittling glances at her. A few made sour comments, which she ignored with a bland smile. None were brave enough to pick a fight with her.

On the appointed day, Gorga donned her fireproof armor and girded herself with weapons, then covered herself completely with a voluminous white robe. Attended by the prince and a few warriors, she went to the front of the dragon's cave, where she was tied to the maidens' stake with false slipknots that would fall open at her touch. Then the Poutians fearfully withdrew and left her alone to face her fate.

Gorga calmly watched the sun set and the full moon rise. She also watched the black orifice of the dragon's cave. Soon she saw a dim orange flare in its depths. The dragon was coming.

Under her robe, she quietly loosened her sword in its sheath. The dragon emerged from its cave and came closer, making peculiar screeching sounds and occasional roars. At intervals, fire gushed from its open mouth with a windy crackling. It was indeed a formidable-looking creature, with thick brown scales all over its body and huge green eyes. It bent its head toward her and roared in deep, hollow, but humanlike speech, "This is not a beautiful maiden. Where is my proper sacrifice?"

Gorga whipped off her ropes and sent an arrow right into each of the dragon's eyes. "Now you won't care what I look like, Worm!" she shouted. The dragon paused momentarily but continued its advance. No blood came from its eyes, which Gorga found puzzling. Next she sent a spear down its flaming throat when it opened its mouth to roar. Again, there was no effect, and no evidence that it had been wounded.

She advanced toward the creature, putting on her petrifying snake helmet, walking boldly right into the ribbon of flame that gushed from its mouth. As her mother had promised, the rock-fiber suit was not even scorched. With all her strength, she gave the dragon a resounding blow on the nose with her battle-ax. Its head bent to one side and remained there, apparently stuck.

Then Gorga noticed something even more curious: The dragon's left forefoot didn't quite touch the ground but skimmed a few inches above it. She bent down and peered underneath to discover that within the structure of the foot, what rested on the ground was a wheel.

Her suspicions aroused, Gorga darted aside and down the length of the dragon's body. Near the tail she saw an oval-shaped crack in the skin. She seized a knob of one of the scales within the crack and tugged as hard as she could. It flew open like a trapdoor, showing a hollow darkness within. The dragon was no living creature. It was a machine.

Sword in hand, she entered and made her way through the dark interior toward the head, where she saw the light of a fire. She came to a round chamber, where an ugly little man stood by a bank of levers, working a huge bellows that sent flames and noises through the tunnel of the dragon's throat. He was peering through a series of lenses, trying to find out where Gorga had gone. She crept up behind him and put the point of her sword to his neck. The man turned, saw her terrifying serpent mask, screamed, and stood stock-still, petrified with fear.

"Just what do you think you're doing, little worm?" Gorga growled. The man's chin trembled, but he was too frightened to speak. Gorga pricked him slightly with the point of her sword, to encourage him to answer.

With blood trickling down his neck, shaking all over, the man fell to his knees and cried, "Please don't kill me, Monster! I meant no harm! I only wanted a few beautiful maidens, but they would never give me a second glance unless they were forced to do so."

"What did you do to them?" Gorga demanded.

"I didn't hurt them, honestly I didn't," he quavered. "They're locked up in my cave, perfectly safe. I gave special privileges and better food to the ones who let me make love to them, but I let the others alone, I swear. Please, Monster, let me go. You can understand, being so ugly yourself, that I'm too ugly to win a beautiful maiden by fair means. I promise I'll never do it again."

"Did you build this dragon?" Gorga asked. He nodded rapidly.

"You're a clever little worm," she told him. "Put out that fire. We'll go together to your cave and see about these maidens."

The man hastened to obey. He walked into the cave with Gorga's sword prodding his back. Torches were burning along the walls. In several chambers deep inside the cave, Gorga saw workshops with various kinds of machinery, fire pits, even rooms with rugs and bedding and cooking utensils.

Inside a large chamber at the heart of the hill, seven beautiful maidens sat despondently within an enclosure of iron bars. They jumped to their feet at the arrival of their captor and his captor, shrieking in horror at the sight of Gorga's mask.

"Relax, I'm only a woman like yourselves," Gorga said, removing her helmet. "This little worm here claims that you haven't been harmed. Is it true?"

"It's true that he hasn't injured us," one of the maidens said. "But he has kidnapped us, scared us, made us and our families very unhappy, and forced some of us to have sex with him. We have agreed among ourselves, though, never to reveal which ones of us are no longer technically maidens."

"Never mind about that," Gorga said. "The point is that now you can all go back to your homes. The dragon is officially dead—not that it was ever alive. And this little worm will be punished. What do you think his punishment should be?"

Some of the maidens immediately cried, "Kill him!" Gorga's intuition told her that those were the ones who had earned the man's "special privileges." Others said, "Lock him up in this cage to starve." One maiden, not quite so beautiful as the others, said, "Put him into the country's service as an inventor. He is very clever, and his intelligence shouldn't be wasted."

"We'll go back to the town, and you can tell your stories," said Gorga, pushing the inventor forward to open the cage. When the maidens had filed out, she shoved him inside the bars, took his key, and snapped the lock. "He can wait here until the king's guards come to get him."

Gorga and the seven maidens left the cave, passed the now silent, abandoned dragon machine, and returned to tell their stories in the king's castle. The maidens were greeted with tears of joy by their families, who had believed them dead, and by their sweethearts, who didn't seem to care whether they were still technically maidens or not.

The king's guards went to the cave to arrest the inventor but came back to report that he was not to be found. Somehow he had escaped the cage and fled, taking with him many of the workshop tools and provisions. In later years there were no further reports of dragons, so it was assumed that he never built another one. Much later, however, it was said that a very clever inventor had arrived in a distant country and had so pleased the king with his gadgets that he was allowed to marry the beautiful princess, even though he was only an ugly little man.

Gorga the Amazon received half of the kingdom of Poutia and became an intimate friend of its prince, whom she trained in martial arts, helping him build himself a fitter, stronger body. Eventually the prince got used to her homely appearance and came to realize that he had fallen in love with her, as she had with him. So they married, rejoining the two halves of the land of Poutia. They governed peacefully together because the prince was wise enough to defer to Gorga's greater wisdom. In this way they lived happily ever after.

The story of the snake-haired Gorga was told and retold down the corridors of time. In later centuries she was metamorphosed into a knight named George, because no one any longer believed that a woman could slay dragons.

FIVE

THE FROG PRINCESS

As a child I always liked frogs. They were lively, yet fairly easy to catch and play with. They couldn't bite. They were shaped something like tiny humans. They had the most beautiful eyes in the animal world. And their unique life cycle, with its strange fishlike, water-breathing tadpole childhood, was eternally fascinating. When I read the story of the frog prince, I couldn't understand the heroine's frenzied reluctance to kiss the frog. Personally, I wouldn't have objected.

Much later I discovered that frogs were once widely viewed as sacred to the Great Goddess, totems of Venus and Hecate, and consequently often characterized as witches' familiars in Christian times. Since female frogs are usually larger and stronger than the males—who, indeed, may sometimes change their sex—it seems that the frog may serve as a naturally feminist symbol.

*She hopped up on the moss and placed her snout
next to his lips.*

*O*nce upon a time there was a pretty green frog with golden eyes who lived on a pond in the deep woods. She was a lively little creature, always jumping for pleasure in the soft golden green sunlight of the glade, swimming quickly through the sparkling shallows in pursuit of a dragonfly or moth, or perching on a lily pad to wait for a mosquito to hover within range. Then, snap! her long tongue would whip out and pluck it from the air. She spent the slow, sweet summer days joining the croak chorus with her sisters and brothers, cooling her skin in the pond, and watching the insects darting above the glittering water.

It happened that her pond became a favorite fishing spot for the prince of the country, who sought relief from the cares of state by resting, with a casually held fishing pole, on its quiet green bank. Sometimes he caught a fish or two, sometimes not. He didn't care. His only real purpose was to be alone with nature for a while. Though he always came accompanied by his usual entourage of courtiers and servants, he would send them some distance away, out of earshot, to lay out the picnic lunch and entertain themselves with court gossip.

One day the little frog saw the prince leaning against a tree on the bank, his eyes closed, his fishing pole drooping in his hands. He was snoring gently. She felt pity on him for his weariness. She thought him very handsome. She thought about him all day, and the next day also. She became intrigued by this elegantly dressed human who seemed to appreciate her pond so much. Each time the prince returned, she watched him throughout his entire visit. Soon she began to feel that she was in love with him.

"How can I approach him?" she asked herself. "He is the prince. I'm a humble frog, not even of his species." But, like all frogs, she knew the classic story of the frog prince. Remembering this, she told herself that magic transformations between frog and human were not really so unusual. All she needed was the assistance of a fairy.

The frog knew that the nearest available fairy lived several miles away, in a dry part of the woods where there were no ponds. To travel in that direction, she would run the risk of dehydration, a very serious matter for a frog. Yet her love for the prince became so great that she determined to make the attempt.

She chose a rainy morning, hoping that her skin would stay wet so she could travel comfortably, and went hopping away from her pond toward the fairy's house. Unfortunately, the rain stopped before midday and the forest began to dry out. The frog halted a few times to cover herself with damp moss in an effort to extract a little moisture from it, but it was not enough. She began to feel the first dread symptoms of dehydration.

Hurrying onward, she prayed to the Amphibious Mother for a puddle, a spring, a small rivulet, anything to relieve her discomfort. She was beginning to weaken. Just when she believed herself near death from dehydration, her prayer was answered, after a fashion. She found a full canteen, apparently fallen from the kit of a passing rider. It was stoppered by a cork, through which she could smell fresh water within.

"Here's my salvation," she thought, "if only I can contrive to remove the cork." She pawed at it but couldn't get a grip with the soft webbed fingers of her forelimbs. Neither could she bite it with her toothless jaws. Despairing, she looked up into the dry, sunny air and saw a crow perched on a maple branch.

"Dear crow," she said, "please help me. I need water desperately. There's some in this canteen, but I can't open it. With your sharp beak, will you pry out the cork for me?"

"Why should I?" said the crow. "If you die on the forest floor, you will be one more nice bit of carrion for me to feed to my children. I would rather see you dead than alive."

Near despair, the frog raised her gaze and saw an owl resting on a higher branch. "Please, mistress owl, help me open this canteen with your hooked beak and your talons," she begged. The owl only laughed in a nasty way and groomed its feathers. "Go ahead and die, carrion," the owl said.

"The birds are too carnivorous," thought the frog. "I must find a vegetarian creature."

Soon, in answer to her wish, came a doe with a dappled fawn following her.

"Noble deer," cried the frog, "please help me. With your strong teeth, will you draw the cork from this canteen for me?"

"All right," said the doe. She held the canteen down with her hoof and bit the cork out. The water gushed forth, and the frog jumped into the puddle it made.

"Thank you, thank you, gracious lady deer!" she cried. "You've saved my life."

"Think nothing of it," said the doe, walking on.

"When I become a princess, I'll make permanent laws against deer hunting," the frog called after her.

The doe laughed. "Yes, and when I grow curly horns, I'll be a mountain goat," she said. "Good luck to you, Princess." She vanished with her fawn into the undergrowth.

The frog went on refreshed and soon came to the fairy's house, a dwelling made of shells, crystals, and colored feathers. She found the fairy washing her silver white hair in a trough of clear rainwater, into which the frog gratefully settled while she told the fairy her problem.

"You don't understand," the fairy said, wrapping a thistledown towel around her head. "I'm old. I've retired from active practice. I don't dance in the fairy ring anymore, or spin illusions out of moonlight, or work transformation charms. I'd recommend that you go to my younger sister, Maya of the Mountain."

"I can't climb mountains," said the frog sadly. "It was all I could do to get this far without dying. If you can't help me, I might as well kill myself, because I'll never be happy again unless I can marry the prince."

"Well, no one can call you an underachiever," the fairy remarked. "You don't lack ambition, that's for sure. Tell me, if I agree to get out the old tools one more time and see if I still have the knack, how will you repay me?"

"I will pay you anything within my power, whatever it may be."

"All right, all right. Promise me that, when or if you become a princess, you will place the largest diamond you can find for me on that altar stone yonder. Even old fairies never lose their fondness for jewels."

"I promise," said the frog.

"Now, then. Do you know the essential drawback in all frog-to-human enchantments?"

"No, what is it?"

"You have to be kissed. On the mouth. While still a frog. If that does-n't happen, there's no transformation. And if you return to the pond, the charm is canceled."

"I'll worry about that when the time comes," said the frog. "Go ahead with the charm."

So the fairy took out her dusty recipe books and paged through them, muttering. She assembled various crucibles and retorts, mixed her potions, recited invocations, gestured with her wand, and censed and bathed the frog with magical preparations. Finally she sat back and sighed, "There, it's done."

"Is it?" asked the frog. "I don't feel any different."

"Of course not. You won't be any different until you're kissed."

"Somehow I'll get the prince to kiss me, then. I thank you, and I will not forget my promise to you."

The fairy performed a simple wetting charm to keep the frog's skin moist on her return journey.

The next time the prince appeared with his fishing pole, the frog boldly hopped up on the bank and sat at his side.

"Well, hello there, froggie," the prince said. "Did you come to offer yourself as bait?"

Alarmed, the frog hopped a few feet farther away. The prince chuck-led, amused to see a frog apparently understanding his words. "Don't be afraid, little one," he said. "I wouldn't cut up so clever a creature for bait." Whistling softly, he turned back to his fishing pole.

The frog timidly hopped a little nearer, and a little nearer, until she was within one hop's length of the prince's knee. He looked down and saw her gazing earnestly up into his face with her gemlike golden eyes.

"You *are* a bold froggie," he said. "I wonder, would you let me touch you?" He stretched out a finger. The frog allowed him to stroke the top of her head, though she was trembling with the effort to hold still and keep herself from bounding away. After all, he was a human and therefore a tra-ditional enemy of her kind, even though she found him so attractive.

The prince's touch was gentle. Somewhat reassured, she allowed him to scratch her back. Then she even dared to hop up on his thigh. The prince chuckled again. "It seems I have tamed me a wild frog," he re-marked. "How many rulers in this world can make such a claim?"

Each time the prince came to the pond after that, the frog hopped right up and sat beside him while he fished. He came to expect her. They would sit together companionably on the bank, the prince taking an occasional fish and the frog taking an occasional fly. She was eager to perform her transformation, but she couldn't think of a way to get the prince to kiss her.

Then one drowsy summer afternoon the prince fell asleep at the pond's edge. The fishing pole dropped from his hands. His torso sagged slowly sideways and settled to the ground, the side of his face resting on a mound of moss. The frog noticed that he worked his lips now and then in his sleep. She hopped up on the moss and placed her snout a millimeter away from his lips. The next time they moved, the kiss was accomplished.

The frog began to feel very strange. She was expanding, as if her little body was blowing up with air, like a bubble. Her nose was growing, her mouth was narrowing, her forelimbs were lengthening. Her skin prickled, dried out, and metamorphosed into human skin covered by a beautiful green silk gown. Her flesh became warm. Her gums sprouted teeth. Her head sprouted soft blond hair. In a matter of moments, she was fully trans-formed into an attractive human maiden with only one froggy feature re-maining: her sparkling golden eyes.

She waited quietly until the prince awakened from his doze. He stared at her in disbelief. "Beautiful lady, who are you? Where did you come from? Are you one of the woodland fairies?" he asked.

"My name is Rana," said the frog maiden, speaking the first words that popped into her head. "I'm not a fairy, but I've come to be your loyal companion, dear prince."

At this, the prince graciously kissed her hand. His fishing quite forgot-ten, he talked for the rest of the afternoon to his new acquaintance, Rana. She had, he discovered, wondrously deep and detailed knowledge of na-ture, especially the hidden lives of forest-dwelling animals, birds, insects, and even smaller creatures. She told him things about the habits of fish that not even the most experienced fishermen in his kingdom had ever heard of. She knew astonishing facts about algae, crayfish, snails, water-treaders, dragonflies, and mosquito larvae. She knew how the water spiders kept their air bubbles, how the bats fed, and how the wild ducklings learned to swim.

The prince was so fascinated by her knowledge that he invited her to accompany him to his castle and be his guest for as long as she wished to stay. Of course, Rana eagerly accepted.

She was quite overwhelmed by the magnificence of the prince's castle, and the elaborate ceremony by which he lived. The prince was king in effect, governing jointly with his elderly widowed father, who was in failing health. Despite the many demands on his time, however, the prince found hours to spend with his beautiful guest. He soon fell so deeply in love with her that he wanted to be with her constantly. Accordingly, he asked her to marry him. She said she would.

The decision caused a stir in the court. The old king and his counselors objected to Rana, on the ground of her propertyless state, her lack of antecedents, and her obvious unfamiliarity with courtly manners. They deemed the prince besotted by a landless stranger, a nobody. As tactfully as they could, they advised against the match, saying that Rana was not a suitable choice for the role of future queen.

The prince, however, was too much in love to listen to them. He ignored their advice and went ahead with the wedding. Soon afterward, he was delighted to learn that Princess Rana was expecting a child. He believed that when it was born, all objections would be silenced forever.

Rana was happy to be the new princess, but she couldn't help being embarrassed sometimes by her own mistakes in etiquette and protocol. She often failed to use the right fork, or to address visiting dignitaries by their correct titles. She yawned openly during their long, boring speeches. She didn't understand the conversation of aristocratic ladies. She didn't know the court dances. She disliked having to stand still for hours at a time during state receptions and diplomatic functions. She couldn't get used to waiting each morning and evening while a bevy of handmaids dressed or undressed her, arranged her hair, and laced her into agonizingly confining corsets. She hated being weighed down by heavy, embroidered, bejeweled clothes with their stiff sleeves and multiple skirts. To comfort herself, she often spent hours at a time lying in her bathtub and dreaming of her past life.

Sometimes she escaped to the garden alone, threw off her dress, and *hopped* across the grass, releasing her pent-up energy in great bounds. She thought herself unobserved at these exercises, but in a court nothing is ever unobserved. She was seen, and tongues wagged.

Even worse things were observed. The courtiers noticed that the new princess sometimes *ate flies*. When a fly buzzed near her, she would instinctively snatch it with a lightning-fast hand and pop it into her mouth. The gossip about this habit increased a thousandfold after a particularly memorable incident in the kitchen.

On this occasion, Princess Rana was discussing a formal menu with the head cook. All at once, a cockroach scuttled across the floor. Quick as a flash, the princess grabbed it up and ate it. After that, even her personal maids treated her with cool distaste. Her only escape from the atmosphere of general disapprobation was her habit of taking day trips into the forest. Like her husband, she often left her attendants and went on deeper into the woods by herself.

Princess Rana made herself ever more unpopular by meddling in the affairs of state. She insisted that the prince outlaw deer hunting throughout his domain. To please her, he did so, against his better judgment. As a result, many of the forest peasants were left without a reliable source of meat. There was much grumbling among the people.

Then came the incident of the crown diamond. The princess had appropriated the largest diamond in the royal treasury, a world-famous gem that backed a sizeable portion of the country's coinage. After it had been missing for some time, the prince tactfully asked her how she was planning to have it set. A necklace? A tiara? A brooch? Surely it was too large and heavy for a ring?

"I'm not planning to have it set at all," said Rana.

"Then why not put it back in the treasury?" the prince asked. "It isn't safe to leave the crown diamond knocking around loose in your jewel box."

"It isn't in my jewel box."

"Then where is it?"

"I no longer have it."

"What!" the prince shouted. "You've lost the crown diamond?" It was the first time he had ever raised his voice to her.

"I took it to pay an important debt," Rana said. "A matter of honor."

Of course this was insufficient excuse. The prince, the king, and all the counselors badgered her for hours to tell the whereabouts of the diamond.

She refused to answer them. The prince pleaded with her: "Rana, please, you are risking criminal prosecution for thievery, and worse. To steal one of the crown jewels is high treason. Don't you understand? You could be executed, and I'd be powerless to save you."

She remained silent.

The counselors demanded that she be imprisoned at once. The prince countered that, in view of her expectant condition, she should only be placed under house arrest, and her case could not go to trial until after her child was born. "Remember, this is no ordinary child," he said. "We're talking about the heir to the throne. Surely his or her mother deserves every consideration, no matter what crime she may have committed."

So Rana was allowed to remain in her royal quarters. Every day the prince begged her, with tears in his eyes, to save herself and reveal what she had done with the diamond. Though she loved him and was moved by his unhappiness, she said nothing. The counselors made plans to try her and find her guilty immediately after she gave birth. The broken-hearted prince had to agree to this, because it was the law.

When the time came for Princess Rana to give birth to the royal heir, matters went from bad to much worse. The child was horribly deformed. It had a large head with gill slits, and instead of legs, it had a broad, flat tail that tapered to a point. For a few moments after birth it gasped frantically like a fish out of water. Then it died.

The prince was doubly distressed. His heir had proved to be a monster, not human enough to live. His beloved princess was a criminal, almost certainly doomed to formal execution. Nearly out of his mind with sorrow, he sat weeping at her bedside while Princess Rana tried in vain to comfort him.

"I'd hoped to live with you to a ripe old age," the prince told her. "Now it seems we must be forever parted. I can hardly bear to think about it."

Princess Rana contemplated the vision of many future years of court life, and suddenly realized that she couldn't have put up with it anyway. She loved her husband but couldn't adapt herself to his lifestyle. She had tried and failed.

"Yes, we must be parted," she said. "It's too bad, but some people simply are not meant to stay together. Dear husband, will you grant me one last request?"

"Anything," said the prince.

"Let me go back once more to the pond where we first met."

"You're still under house arrest."

"I know," she said, "but you can contrive a way. I will never ask you for anything else again."

The prince agreed. In the small hours of the night, he slipped out of the castle with Rana, both of them muffled in black cloaks and masks. He took two horses from the stable and passed the guards by showing them his face and saying he was engaged on a secret mission.

The prince and princess rode until dawn, when they arrived at the pond and dismounted from their puffing horses. Rana kissed her prince tenderly and said, "Now leave me alone here for a little while." The prince thought she was planning to escape, and he was willing to let it happen. He stroked her hair, looked into her golden eyes one last time, and led the horses away into the forest.

As he was walking, he heard a great splash behind. He hurried back to the pond. There were ripples still spreading across the water. Princess Rana's clothing lay abandoned on the bank, but there was no sign of her.

Desperately, the prince tore off his cloak and dived into the pond. Though he searched to the very bottom, until his lungs were bursting for air, he found nothing. At last he had to admit to himself that she was gone. He didn't notice a small, green, golden-eyed frog watching him from a lily pad.

The prince decided that she had committed suicide to save him from further disgrace. In time, he came to accept this view. His grief gradually softened. Some years later, he remarried. His new bride was a gracious, well-trained, wealthy princess who became an eminently suitable queen, and they lived happily ever after.

So did the frog, even though she never saw her prince again. Busy with affairs of state and his growing family, he lost interest in fishing.

SIX

GLY AND THE BEAST

On first reading the original version of Beauty and the Beast, I was puzzled by the apparent inconsistency between the Beast's kindly nature and his threatening hostility toward Beauty's father. Then I decided that the story was in part a homily on the subject of honesty. The merchant was well treated until he showed dishonest tendencies. Even then, he was given a chance to redeem himself by keeping a difficult promise. Can a merchant be truly honest?

Lack of honesty in appearances is a common theme in all stories of transformation. I thought the heroine might have been more admirable if she had less beauty and more character and I feared that the Beast's transformation into a handsome prince might turn him into a less likable creature, perhaps conceited or selfish, as handsome princes are sometimes known to be. The illustration in my fairy tale book showed him with a trunk, tusks, and large ears like an elephant. I continued to see him that way, despite Walt Disney's later lionlike version. It seemed more honest to leave him as he was, so his kindliness could shine through to match that of the ordinary, human, unattractive maiden.

He addressed her quietly, "So, you meet the Beast at last."

*O*nce upon a time there was a merchant who had seven sons and seven daughters. All of them were very handsome except the eldest daughter, who was hunchbacked, bowlegged, pigeon-toed, overweight, coarse-skinned, and lank-haired, with small piglike eyes, a bulbous nose, crooked teeth, and a deformed jaw. The poor girl was so hideous that everyone called her Ugly. Nevertheless, she took it in good spirit, knowing that it was a fair description. Despite her appearance, she had a sweet, warm, generous nature. Consequently her handsome siblings loved her dearly and shielded her from public ridicule.

The merchant had a successful career until he suffered a series of disasters that wiped out almost all his assets in a single year. Two ships carrying his goods were lost at sea, then river floods destroyed his inventory in three warehouses. In addition, his own house caught fire and burned to the ground, the family escaping with only the clothes on their backs. They were forced to move into a gardener's cottage that was their only remaining property, and the merchant started from poverty all over again.

The children worked to help their father, but they often became discouraged, especially when there was not quite enough to eat. Only Ugly faced every setback with unfailing courage and cheerfulness, heartening her brothers and sisters, comforting them when they were sorrowful, raising a laugh when things looked bleakest. She always knew how to say the right thing and to give events an optimistic twist.

The merchant had to travel a great deal to rebuild his business. One winter evening he was returning home from a distant city, having sold all his goods and packed his mule with the money he earned. It began to snow. By the time the merchant reached the loneliest stretches of road, a raging blizzard had developed. As he passed under a wall of beetling cliffs by a river, suddenly an avalanche came crashing down and killed his pack mule, toppling it and all it carried into the icy torrent below.

Bruised, battered, lost, and half dead with cold, the merchant stumbled on alone for hours through the blinding snow. He wanted nothing more than to lie down in the snow and go to sleep, but he knew he would never get up again; so he struggled doggedly on, until suddenly he bumped into a tall iron gate.

Feeling too weak to change direction and keep walking, the merchant clung to the bars of the gate and gasped for breath. Then he felt the gate swing open. A broad avenue lay before him. It seemed that the snow fell less thickly there, so the merchant walked down its length toward a large palace that could be seen dimly in the distance. As he advanced, the snow ceased to fall. The temperature grew warmer and warmer. When he arrived in the palace gardens, he found a lush paradise with many green plants, fruit trees, and flowers enriching a soft, warm breeze with their delicious scents.

The bronze doors of the palace stood open. The merchant entered and found himself in an elegant hall, richly furnished, lighted by a thousand candles in crystal chandeliers. A cheery fire burned on the hearth. Before it stood a table laden with delicate foods and fine wines in golden vessels. No servants or other persons were anywhere to be seen, so the merchant didn't wait for an invitation. He sat down and helped himself to the refreshments.

After he had eaten, he wandered through other rooms of the palace and was astonished by all the wonders he found there. Being a merchant, he knew the value of the furnishings, paintings, and ornaments that he saw. Most were virtually priceless, and all were arranged with exquisite taste. He marveled greatly to see all these treasures lying unguarded; yet he encountered no one. The palace seemed completely uninhabited.

He came to a bedchamber where a huge bed was beautifully made up with blue satin sheets and a soft peach-colored quilt invitingly turned down. The weary merchant climbed into the bed for what he told himself would be just a catnap. But it was so deliciously comfortable that he immediately fell fast asleep and didn't awaken until the following afternoon.

As he sat up, he saw a blue velvet bathrobe laid out for him on the foot of the bed and heard water running in the adjoining bathroom. There he found a square, sunken marble bathtub filled with scented water of exactly the right temperature, with perfumed soap and thick towels laid ready; but no servants were to be seen. After bathing, he returned to the bedroom and found a little table set up by the window with a dainty breakfast laid on an antique lace cloth, and fresh flowers in a crystal vase. All was done without the slightest sound, by unseen hands. The merchant felt uneasy about this mysterious service, but he enjoyed everything that was offered to him.

After breakfast he roamed again through some of the rooms, looking at their treasures. In a hall of art objects he came across a small pedestal supporting a bunch of seven roses, exquisitely sculpted and cast in pure gold.

"If I had this object alone," he thought, "I'd be rich enough to renew all my business. Perhaps the seven roses are meant for me, symbolizing my seven daughters." In such manner he reasoned, convincing himself that because so much else in this magic palace seemed to be free, he might take a bit of treasure for his own.

He picked up the golden roses from their pedestal and tucked them into his coat. Immediately, there was a great thunderclap. All at once a terrible Beast stood before him, seven feet high and nearly as broad, with a snout like a wild boar, protruding tusks, tiny porcine eyes, and huge hands with long claws. The merchant fell on his knees, crying, "Have mercy, Beast! Don't kill me! I have a large family dependent on me! I didn't mean to take your gold—see, here it is, I'll put it back."

"Of course you meant it," growled the Beast. "And because you touched it, you can't put it back. Thievery is a poor way to repay my hospitality."

"What can I do to make it up to you, then?" asked the trembling merchant.

"Take the golden roses for the sake of your dependents, and in return send me one of your daughters. I'll lend you a magic carriage that will take you to your home, and bring her back here within three hours of your arrival. I am lonely and I long for a female companion. Remember, you must place one of your daughters in my coach before three hours pass, or I will come down on your house and fetch you."

"Yes, yes, Beast, I promise to do exactly as you ask," quavered the merchant. "You have my word as an honorable man of business."

"See to it, then," snarled the Beast, "and I will overlook this one occasion when you have seemed not to be an honorable man of business." Another thunderclap, a sizzle of lighting, and the beast disappeared.

The merchant ran to the entranceway and found a closed carriage waiting there, drawn by a pair of black horses with silvered hooves. Holding the reins on the coachman's seat was a strange figure entirely muffled in black, the face masked, even the hands covered. As soon as the merchant

stepped into the carriage, it set off at great speed. As there were no windows, he could see nothing of his progress.

When at last the carriage halted, he opened the door and found himself
in front of his own cottage. His children rushed out to meet him, amazed
at his rich equipage, the silent, black-swathed coachman, the magnificent
horses, the beautiful golden roses that he held in his hand.

"We're rich again!" one of the boys cried.

"Father, have you made a new fortune?" Ugly asked.

"Alas, my children, I have brought you prosperity, but at a terrible
price." While the silent carriage waited and the clock ticked the hours
away, he told them the whole story.

When he had finished, Ugly said, "Well, there's no question about who
must go to the Beast. I will be the one."

The others raised a chorus of protest, for Ugly was much loved. Yet
not one of the other girls offered herself.

"It makes sense," Ugly said. "I am the one who will never win a husband and so will bring no assets into the family. Here is my opportunity to
contribute to our prosperity." This was how merchants' children were
taught to think.

"But the Beast will probably tear you limb from limb, then cook you
and eat you!" cried the youngest brother. This was how youngest children
were taught to think.

"If that's so, then I must face it bravely," Ugly said. "I'll go and pack
my clothes now." She went to gather her few belongings. All the family
burst into tears, including the merchant. They clustered around Ugly as she
boarded the Beast's carriage, kissing and petting her between sobs, telling
her how sorely she would be missed. The merchant secretly hoped the
Beast would find her acceptable and would not come rampaging after him
to punish him for not having sent a prettier daughter.

Ugly wept throughout most of her journey but eventually dried her
reddened eyes, thinking that she should prevent any additional uglification.
When the carriage stopped at last, she timidly opened the door. She saw a
magnificent palace soaring before her eyes into a soft summer-blue sky,
even though she had left her home in winter.

She entered the great bronze doors and looked around, expecting at
any moment to be seized and torn limb from limb by the hideous Beast.

Instead, a delicious dinner was laid for her on the table. No living creature appeared. She ate, then explored the palace. She found each room more beautiful than the last, and equally empty of life.

When she felt unutterably weary, she chose a bedroom hung with white silk, with an ivory bedstead and green satin bedding. She got into the bed and fell into a dreamless sleep.

When she awoke, her bath was ready, beautiful new garments were laid out for her, and her breakfast was provided by unseen hands, as her father had described. She spent the day playing games in the game room, wandering in the gardens, looking at the views from various windows, and skimming some of the books in the library. Always she anticipated the terrifying appearance of the Beast, but it didn't happen. She began to relax and enjoy herself.

Not until a week had passed did the Beast decide to reveal himself. He appeared at first in the garden, some distance away from her, swathed in a red velvet cloak and hood that partly concealed his form. He stood still and allowed her to approach him gradually, as one might attract a wild forest creature through its own curiosity.

When Ugly came close enough, he addressed her quietly. "So, little lady, you meet the Beast at last. Are you frightened?"

"A little," said Ugly.

"I must say you frighten me a little, too," said the Beast. "You're not the most attractive lady in the world, are you?"

"I have always been called Ugly, because that's what I am," she answered. "I hope this won't anger you. I can see by your possessions that you have a taste for beautiful things."

"Beauty is in the eye of the beholder," said the Beast, "or so I've been told. Do you mind if I walk along with you?"

Finding the Beast so polite and gentlemanly, Ugly felt somewhat reassured. As they strolled along, the Beast pointed out to her some of his rarer plants and offered her some exotic fruits to taste. She began to think his company rather pleasant, though she couldn't yet bring herself to look directly at his frightful face.

At sunset the Beast left her alone, promising to meet her in the garden again the following day. This time he appeared without his hood and cloak. She began to get used to his ugliness. Each day he returned to join her, and she found herself eagerly looking forward to his company to relieve her solitude.

After a while they began to eat meals together, play games or read together in the library. Ugly found the Beast a charming companion. She became sufficiently comfortable with him that one day she finally dared to ask him how he came to have such an unattractive exterior.

"I knew that would come up," the Beast sighed, "so we might as well get it over with. You're expecting me to say that I'm under an enchantment, and I'm really a handsome prince, and your love will bring forth my real self."

"I had thought about it," Ugly said. "But I also thought that if you were changed into a handsome prince, you would no longer have any pleasure in my company. I'm far from being a beautiful princess, so I could never hope to keep you. As much for your sake as for my own, for the first time in my life I really wish I were a beauty."

"I had a beauty once," the Beast said. "She was very sweet, but she so wanted me to be a handsome prince that to please her I created the illusion for her by magic. As you can see from all the charms around my palace here, I'm a competent magician. But it was a strain, keeping up the illusion. In the end I couldn't manage it anymore. I had to tell her the truth, and she left me. The truth is that I'm a Beast. This freakish appearance is the real me."

"Oh, Beast, I'm so glad," Ugly cried, embracing him. "I don't mind being Ugly and I don't mind your ugliness either, as long as it brings us together. I've never been so happy as I am here with you."

The Beast was so pleased that she didn't want him to be a handsome prince, and Ugly was so pleased that he didn't want her to be a beautiful princess, that they agreed to marry at once.

Ugly's family came to the wedding and received rich gifts, though they were no longer needy because her father had made wise investments with the golden sculpture. The palace was opened to guests, and there was much festivity. Ugly and the Beast became known far and wide as a warm and beneficent couple. They loved each other truly, because they were free of the narcissism that often mars the relationships of beautiful people; and so they lived happily ever after.

SEVEN

THOMAS RHYMER

This story is an almost straight retelling of the famous bard's affiliation with the pagan Goddess (fairy queen), who was his teacher and muse. According to Celtic legend, the fairy queen came to Thomas of Erceldoune and took him away to her mystic land "beyond the river of lunar blood." She became his teacher and muse, and since, as folk belief would have it, time spent with the fairies was time greatly contracted, Thomas's seven-year apprenticeship seemed very brief to him.

Like Orpheus and the worshipers of Mnemosyne before them, Celtic poets believed that true inspiration lay in this Goddess's underworld Cauldron, symbol of the universal womb of Mother Earth. She also received the dead in her various guises of Cerridwen, Mab, Brigit, or the Morrigan. She appeared in Arthurian legend as Morgan le Fay (Morgan, the Fate or the Fairy), who was originally described as a Goddess from the olden time. Her symbol was a pentacle. Her priests served a seven-year apprenticeship.

He was almost too tired to hold on to the stirrup anymore.

*O*nce upon a time there was a young lord named Thomas, heir to the earldom of Erceldoune. Young Thomas was raised in a manner befitting a gentleman, that is to say, he was trained to fight and kill, to exploit the land and its creatures, to be duplicitously charming, and to become a ruthless seducer of women. He learned his lessons dutifully enough, but the life of a country lordling didn't really satisfy him. His deepest yearning was to become a poet.

Unfortunately, his talent for poetry was so meager that his friends learned to stay away from the "poetic evenings" that he regularly scheduled for readings of his latest works. He was reduced to reading his poems to the servants, who had no choice but to listen to him; but they did so with gritted teeth and escaped as soon as they could.

His poems were so bad that even he occasionally caught some glimmering awareness of their shortcomings. He would say, "I guess that line could scan a bit better," or "That's not the best possible simile, is it?" His suffering listener would agree. Then Thomas would work on the poem some more and make it worse.

One soft day in the merry month of May, Thomas was resting alone on Huntlie Bank, pondering a new poem (worse than any yet), tapping his teeth with his pen, happily perceiving himself as the gentleman bard in the throes of creation. All at once, a troop of ladies on horseback appeared before him, seemingly out of nowhere. Every one was dressed in green from head to foot. Their leader, the tallest and most beautiful of them, wore a crown and rode a pure white horse caparisoned with silver.

Thomas politely rose to his feet and bowed. "Dear ladies, I bid you welcome to my lands of Erceldoune," he said, doffing his hat. "Whom have I the honor of addressing, and whence come you?" That was how Thomas talked, when he was in a poetic mood.

The leader said, "We come from a place unknown to you, to tell you that these lands are not yours. They're mine. Since the world began, this place has been known as Ursel's Down. You should know that Ursel is one

of your ancestors' names for the fairy queen. You occupy this territory only by my sufferance."

"Then you, madam, are the same fairy queen?"

"Yes. And I have been told that you're misusing my gifts of inspiration and visualization on this land that the fairies have favored and tended through the centuries. I have come to remedy the situation."

Thomas was astonished. "Misusing? How, madam?"

"You write abominable poetry," said the fairy queen. "You are ignorant of the true poetic soul, which lies in woman and in man's relationship to woman. You have no muse. You illustrate the saying of our foremothers, that a fool is most foolish when he attempts to appear wise."

"It's true that people don't seem to want to listen to my work," Thomas admitted rather sheepishly.

"There, you have taken the first step toward learning: that is, a little dose of humility," said the fairy queen. "Do you want to become a better poet?"

"More than anything," said Thomas.

"Very well. I will assume for the moment that you're worth training." She dismounted from her horse and tethered the animal to a tree. Then she came toward him, waving her hand at her companions, all of whom disappeared as abruptly as they had come.

The fairy queen sat down on Huntlie Bank with Thomas and invited him to lay his head in her lap. When he had done so, she drew from under her skirts a flask of claret wine and offered it to him. "Drink, it will give you strength," she said. He drank. The claret seemed oddly salty. He felt a mysterious tingling throughout his body.

"Now you must come with me to Elfland, or as you call it, Fairyland," said the queen. "You must run beside me and hold my stirrup, and never let go. Do you understand?"

"Yes."

She mounted her horse and set off, with Thomas holding her left stirrup tightly in his right hand. His fingers seemed to clamp shut of themselves. His body felt so strong and fit that he had no trouble keeping up with the horse's pace, even at a smart trot. They traveled over hill and dale, to a wild country that Thomas had never seen, full of dark glens and rocky cliffs.

They came to a river that ran red as blood and followed its bank up-
stream. The river valley narrowed between two long ridges that gradually
converged, until it was blocked off at the head by the steep wall of a huge,
rounded mountain. At the base of the wall there was an opening into a
dark cave, out of which the red river ran.

"Now you will wade," said the fairy queen. Her horse splashed into
the river and walked into the cave, Thomas following. He found the water
oddly warm, and not much over knee-deep. The horse went steadily on
into darkness, drawing Thomas along. Blinded by the total blackness of
the cave, he felt nothing but the stirrup clutched in his hand and the liquid
around his legs. He heard nothing but the sloshing footsteps of the fairy
queen's mount.

He thought he had traveled thus for many hours, and he was almost
too tired to hold on to the stirrup anymore, when the horse stopped suddenly. The fairy queen held up a glowing wand. In the wand's faint bluish
gleam, Thomas saw that the way was blocked by an oval wall of rock, narrowed at the top and bottom, under which the red stream ran out. In the
wall there was a curiously rounded iron door.

"This is the central place of the earth," said the fairy queen. "Only
three mortals before you have passed through that door. You would recognize their names if I told them to you. Now you will enter the realm of fulfilled desires."

The door opened of itself, slitting down the middle and folding back to
either side. Within, Thomas saw three corridors leading in three different
directions. One was illuminated by a white light. The second was bathed in
a red glare. The third was dark.

"These are the three roads of ultimate choosing," said the queen. "The
first leads to heaven, the second to hell, and the third to fair Elfland. Do
you choose to come with me?"

"Oh, yes," said Thomas.

They set off down the dark corridor, which gradually became lighter as
a greenish glow brightened the way. Presently the passage opened out at
the top of a hill, and Thomas saw a vast countryside spread out below,
under a greenish yellow sun.

It was the most beautiful countryside he had ever seen. Streams
sparkled like molten diamonds among banks of velvety green grass and

flowering shrubs. Little ponds flashed like emeralds, reflecting the sky, supporting waxy white water lilies. Fruit trees glittered with red apples, golden
peaches and pears, garnet cherries, apricots and oranges like flames among
the green leaves. White marble benches and little pillared temples were scattered about the lawns, cloaked by white and purple blossoming vines.
Fountains tinkled in silver basins. Colorful birds sang in every tree. Richly
dressed people moved over the scene, some walking quietly, some dancing,
some singing in groups or listening to musicians. Lovers sat whispering together. Deer, rabbits, squirrels, foxes, and other woodland animals, all as
tame as house cats, allowed themselves to be petted and hand-fed. A perfumed breeze cooled the air, which was also warmed by the tinted sunlight,
so it was neither too hot nor too cold but perfectly comfortable.

"This is the paradise of long ago," the fairy queen said. "It was created
by the dreams of your ancestors, in the time when they worshiped the
earth. Now only a few are privileged to see it. You have been chosen because Ursel's Down was one of our sacred places, and you wish to become
its bard. We want you to be worthy of the tradition."

"I am deeply honored," Thomas said humbly.

The fairy queen took him into her palace, a graceful structure of marble and glass, with delicate colonnades and large airy rooms, opening on
terraces set with flowers. Gauze curtains moved softly in the gentle breeze.
Satin-covered couches invited the visitor to rest. Jewel-inlaid tables were
set with crystal bowls of ripe fruit and delicious cakes. In this place, time
passed for Thomas in a dream of delight.

The fairy queen loved him and taught him all manner of secrets about
loving. She also brought other teachers, male and female, who made him
understand how to make the kind of poetry that would keep listeners spell-
bound. He learned old stories to retell in rhyme. He learned to play the
harp with exquisite expressiveness. He learned to sing in a voice so pure as
to seem that of a heavenly spirit. He learned how to use words and music
to create enchantment, even to make his hearers dream once more of the
paradise of long ago. After all, as he often remarked, he was inspired by
the greatest muse the world had ever known.

When he had been fully instructed, the fairy queen summoned him to
her sweet-scented, cedar-paneled audience chamber for a final examina-
tion. The fairy bards, his teachers, gathered together with other listeners to

judge his ability. Thomas was nervous but confident. He knew that what he had learned was good, and he was no longer a bumbling tyro. He played well. He sang sweetly. He told stories in rhymes of such grace as to bring tears to the eyes of even fairy people.

"You have passed your test," said the fairy queen. "I now name you True Thomas, as a man true to the old ways and the old faith. Now you can go, and be a bard worthy of Ursel's Down."

"Dearest lady, are you sending me away?" Thomas cried. "I have only been here a few weeks, and I would be happy to spend the rest of my life at your side. Do let me stay a little longer."

"You think you have lived here for only a few weeks? True Thomas, I tell you true, it has been seven years since we met on Huntlie Bank. Your father is dead and your mother has need of you. It's time for you to go."

Thomas was astonished and chagrined to learn that so many years had passed while he lived in the dream of Fairyland. Weeping, he kissed the fairy queen and embraced his other teachers and friends, bidding them not to forget him. The queen gave him a magic drink in a golden goblet. It was a delectable sweet wine that he had never tasted before. As soon as he drank it, his head began to buzz, his limbs turned limp, and he fell down unconscious.

When he awoke, he was lying on Huntlie Bank, dressed in the green uniform of Fairyland, with his head pillowed on the long hair that had grown down his back. His harp lay beside him. He got up and rubbed his eyes. The trees seemed larger than he remembered them. The stream seemed muddier. The view was subtly different.

When Thomas returned home, his mother and sisters greeted him with tears of joy, having given him up for lost many years ago. He tried to explain that he had been with the fairies, but they paid little attention to this. His mother secretly believed that he had suffered some strange mental breakdown that was now cured. She told him all that had happened in the seven years of his absence. She opined that he had come back in the nick of time, as the crown was about to annex his lands for a monastery, in default of a male heir. True Thomas soon straightened out the legal intricacies of his inheritance.

In subsequent years, he became one of the most benevolent and beloved landowners in the country. He never hunted or killed again. He was genuinely fond of, and respectful to, women—especially his wife, a forthright and good-hearted heiress from a neighboring county, whom he loved dearly. He practiced conservation of the land. He was as honest as the day, and fair in all his dealings with the peasantry. In short, he never again behaved like a gentleman.

He also became a bard so renowned that his fame spread even across the seas. People came on pilgrimages from many foreign lands just to hear him. His poetry provided all his listeners with beautiful dreams of olden times, dreams so rich that people wished they would never end. They called him Thomas Rhymer, and some even compared him to Homer, Virgil, and Sappho. To this day he is known as Thomas Rhymer, the man who visited Fairyland and lived to tell about it, and who then lived happily ever after.

JILL AND THE BEANROOT

The tale of Jack and the Beanstalk is here reversed, not only to present a feminine protagonist but also to send her in the opposite direction: not up, toward the heavens, but down, toward the womb of Earth, once said to be the true source of life, inspiration, truth, death, and rebirth. Jungian psychology speaks of a spiritual journey downward into the darkness of the unconscious as a prerequisite to mystical enlightenment, often symbolized as a return to the womb. It was also the underworld, traditional realm of dwarves, with their notorious affinity for rocks, metals, gemstones, and minerals in general.

Like Osiris, Jack climbed the ladder of heaven, met the giant (jealous father), and boldly stole the goose that laid the golden egg, which recalls Egypt's Hathor as goose-mother of the sun. In this new story, Jill climbs down into darkness and conquers her own fears for the sake of her mother. White, red, and black, the colors of her beans, are also the traditional colors of the triple Goddess as Virgin, Mother, and Crone.

She wanted to climb down at once . . .

*O*nce upon a time there was a poor widow who lived in a small cottage with her daughter, Jill, a good-hearted, cheerful, but rather scatterbrained girl. Times were hard for Jill and her mother. The day came when they had nothing in the cottage to eat, except a little milk from their only remaining cow.

Jill's mother said, "We can't live on nothing but the cow's milk, and besides, she will soon go dry. Tomorrow you must take her to the market and sell her for the best price you can get, and buy us some staples."

So Jill set out the next morning with the cow. On the way to the market, she met an old woman who drew her aside, promising to show her something wonderful. The woman opened her hand and showed Jill three beans, one white, one red, and one black.

"They're only beans," Jill said.

"Ah, no," said the woman, "they are magic beans. They have powers you can hardly imagine. Few things in the world are more precious than these beans."

Jill believed her and decided that she must have the magic beans. "I have nothing to offer but this cow," she said, "but I'll trade her for your magic beans."

"Done," said the old woman. She put the beans into Jill's hand and went off leading the cow.

Jill danced home again and joyfully showed her mother the magic beans, for which she had traded the cow.

"Alas," cried her mother with alarm, "these are only three beans, and we can't live a day on that. Where are the bread, salt, meat, potatoes, cheese, and honey that I told you to buy?"

Crestfallen, Jill murmured, "I guess the old woman was a wicked witch who made a fool of me, Mother."

"Well, don't cry, daughter. It's not your fault that you are too innocent yourself to be suspicious of others. You'll grow older and learn better. Though we go to bed hungry tonight, perhaps tomorrow will bring better luck."

After her mother retired, Jill sat by the tiny fire gazing at the three beans. "It's hardly worth keeping them for food," she reflected. "I might as well plant them." She went out into the garden and planted the three beans. Then she went sorrowfully to bed and tried to sleep away her hunger pangs.

In the morning, Jill told her mother that she had planted the beans.

"There was an old story about a giant beanstalk that grew up overnight," her mother said. "Let's go see if any such miracle has happened here."

They went to the garden and saw that a bean plant had indeed grown up overnight and was already bearing white, red, and black beans. It was no taller than any other bean plant, but Jill and her mother considered it miracle enough. At least they could eat beans.

Jill went closer and saw that alongside the bean plant there was a deep hole, about three feet wide, going down into a shaft of blackness. The bean plant's root went down along the side of the shaft. Moreover, the root was knobbed with ladderlike projections that looked easy to climb down.

"Look, Mother," said Jill, "the magic beans have made a ladder into the earth."

She wanted to climb down at once, to see where the hole led. "Perhaps there are treasures," she said excitedly. "I've heard that there are treasures underground. The old woman was a good witch after all."

Jill's mother was cautious and a little frightened by the black shaft. She warned Jill to be very careful and to climb back up immediately if she sensed anything wrong. She gave Jill a candle to illuminate whatever she might find at the bottom of the shaft.

Jill climbed down and down. As she proceeded, the hole at the top of the shaft dwindled down to a tiny star of daylight. Soon she was enveloped in total blackness. Unable to hold her candle while climbing, she progressed by feeling her way. The beanroot with its convenient footholds seemed to go on forever.

After what Jill thought were hours of descent, her feet found a floor. Cautiously she let go of the beanroot and lighted her candle. She saw that she stood in a rocky chamber with a tunnel leading off horizontally. She entered the dark passage with her candle held high.

Before she had gone a hundred yards, she saw a pale glow of light coming toward her. As it approached, she saw that the light consisted of two long beams, emanating from two brilliantly shining eyes about three feet from the floor. "Oh, I'm dead," Jill thought. "It's some terrible animal with eyes glowing like sunlight, and it's going to eat me up." She wanted to run back to the beanroot, but she stood paralyzed with fear.

When the creature came closer, she saw that it was not an animal but a dwarf, whose brilliantly shining eyes lighted his surroundings like a miner's lamp.

"What's this?" the dwarf exclaimed. "One of the airy-fairies has come down from the aboveworld to visit me!"

"Oh, no, I'm not a fairy," Jill quavered. "I'm only a human girl. I didn't mean to intrude. Don't harm me. If you want, I'll climb back up right away."

The dwarf snickered. "We dwarves don't do harm to humans," he said. "Mischief perhaps, but nothing murderous. Murder they do to themselves. Now that you're here, human, perhaps you'd like to see some of the underworld."

"That would be nice," Jill said uncertainly. The dwarf was very ugly, and his harsh, croaking voice was anything but reassuring. She remembered her mother's advice to be more suspicious of strangers. Nevertheless, when the dwarf turned about and headed away down the tunnel, lighting the way with his brilliant eye-beams, Jill scrambled after him.

They passed several dark side passages. Jill counted three of them on the right and two on the left. Then the tunnel forked. The left-hand way was illuminated by a fiery orange glow. The dwarf went steadily toward the glow, bringing Jill out on a high ledge overlooking a huge, noisy cavern. Below, the cavern was filled with fires and forges where many dwarves were busily working.

"This is one of the workshops where we make treasures for the airy-fairies," the dwarf told her. "As you must know, dwarves are the best craftsmen in the world. The airy-fairies are good at making mere illusions of treasure, that melt away in daylight. They don't have the skill to make their own genuine crowns, necklaces, wands, pots of gold, and so on. They hire us to do it. Real fairy treasure comes not from the air but from the earth. Everything good comes from deep in the earth."

He sounded angry, so Jill said soothingly, "I'm sure you're right."

The dwarf next led her to what he called a nursery of vugs. All around the cave walls were shallow pockets filled with many kinds of crystals, all glittering in a pale light that came from luminous patches on the ceiling.

"This is one of the mature nurseries," he said. "These crystals are full grown, no longer bathed in their natal fluid. You couldn't stand the heat of that. These are dry, and filled with mature mineral spirits."

Suddenly he addressed one of the crystals in a loud tone. "How are you feeling, tourmaline?"

To Jill's astonishment, an eight-inch, cranberry-red crystal answered in a thin but clear voice, "Very triangular, dwarf. There's some nameless dirt clogging my striations. Wipe me off, will you?"

The dwarf bent over and polished the crystal with his sleeve.

Jill exclaimed, "You *talk* to crystals?"

"Of course. It makes them grow better. Don't you talk to plants to make them grow better?"

"Sometimes," Jill admitted. "But they don't talk back."

"The gemstones are our garden flowers, except that they live forever instead of for just a week or two. These crystals are older than the mountains. They have plenty of time to learn speech. They speak to those who understand them, such as the dwarves."

"Can I talk to them?" Jill asked.

"Go ahead and try."

Never having addressed a rock before, Jill felt a little nervous. She said to all the crystals generally, "You are all very beautiful."

"Who is this person, dwarf?" demanded a green sapphire in a high, rather petulant voice. "She is too big. She will have too many inclusions. Her structure is rather loose and friable."

"What right have you to talk about inclusions?" a nearby aquamarine said sharply. "You're not so perfect yourself. Your green is too yellow, whereas I have the more desirable blue tinge."

"Oh, be quiet, aqua," snapped a pink beryl. "You're altogether too common to have any opinion. I, on the other hand, am much rarer and will fetch many more pounds of gold."

"How conceited they are," Jill muttered to the dwarf.

He shrugged. "Every creature that has a lot of money spent on it is going to be conceited, inevitably. That's the way of both worlds. Ounce for ounce, these may have more money spent on them than anything else in the universe. Besides, they are immortal. Their beauty never fades. Who in the world has any better right to be conceited?"

"Take her away, dwarf," piped a citrine crystal. "We don't want to talk to anyone so ephemeral and so opaque, let alone listen to her ignorant criticisms."

"If you have lived so long, you should have learned more wisdom," Jill said indignantly. "All of you should be above petty backbiting, jealousy, and rudeness. You should be like the Earth Mother herself, strong, calm, wise, and tolerant. Your beauty should be matched by largeness of spirit."

"You know, she may be right," said a pale rose quartz, faintly. A small, flat crystal of ruby agreed. Soon the gemstones were discussing the matter animatedly among themselves, ignoring Jill and the dwarf.

"This is the most amazing thing I've ever heard," Jill said to the dwarf. "I never dreamed that gems could speak."

"Those now in use as jewelry are listening, not speaking," he said. "They are storing up history to teach the next dominant race, which will be silicon-based and therefore much stronger and hardier than your species. We dwarves are learning to create that race. We will be its gods."

"What will happen to the humans?" Jill asked.

"Of course, they will all be killed," said the dwarf. "Those few that manage to escape the humans' own planetwide mutual massacre will succumb to starvation and disease. Your race isn't good enough, physically or mentally, to occupy a leading position on this planet."

"Oh, no?" Jill cried angrily. "And do you think people like yourselves, who live underground and never see sunlight, grass, or trees, can understand the living earth any better?"

"We know the earth's very bones," said the dwarf solemnly. "We love her as you humans never will. That's why we are the gods of the future."

"I think you're just as conceited as your crystals," Jill said, terrified by his vision of the future. With a spasm of revulsion, she shoved the ugly dwarf as hard as she could. He fell on his back, squirming helplessly. In the same instant, Jill grabbed the red tourmaline, snapped it off its matrix rock, and ran. The crystal emitted a high, thin wail of protest in her hand, summoning other dwarves from various chambers and tunnels.

They moved too slowly to catch Jill, who raced desperately along, trying to remember the route she had taken and counting the entrances to side passages. She found her way back to the base of the beanroot shaft and began to climb, pushing the tourmaline crystal into her pocket.

All the way up the shaft, the shrill little voice of the crystal was crying, "Thief! Thief!" Jill paid no attention to it. She heard a clamor of dwarves below and climbed all the more frantically. She was panting, trembling, gasping for breath. Several times she almost lost her hold on the beanroot projections and her heart seemed to jump into her throat. After what seemed an eternity of terrified exertion, she scrambled out of the top of the shaft and fell at her mother's feet.

"Quick, cut down the bean plant," she gasped.

Her mother lifted her to her feet. "Jill dear, these beans are all we have to eat," she protested. "We mustn't destroy our food source."

"Mother, trust me, our lives may depend on closing that magic root shaft, right now!"

Her mother trusted her, picked up a hoe, and chopped the bean plant down. Instantly, the root shaft closed and became solid ground again.

Jill took the now silent tourmaline crystal from her pocket and showed it to her mother, whose eyes bulged. "I never saw anything so beautiful," she said. "A dozen egg-size gems, fit for a queen's crown, could be cut out of that."

"This is the bird that will lay golden eggs for us," said Jill.

She and her mother borrowed travel expenses from a neighbor and carried the tourmaline to the queen's castle. After days of negotiation, they sold the crystal to the queen's gem cutter for a medium-sized fortune. On returning home, they were able to buy a more commodious cottage with a barn and a small herd of cows. They prospered and lived happily ever after.

Gems cut from the tourmaline never spoke again. But they listened.

NINE

BARBIDOL

The ever-popular, impossible-shaped Barbie and her numerous clones surely have helped train American girls to be forever dissatisfied with themselves and to think of the ideal female form as one that almost no female ever achieves. Barbie is the unattainable ideal produced by the latter half of the twentieth century. In other times women's self-image has been mocked by the eighteen-inch waist of the hoopskirt era; the huge padded rear of the bustle; the Chinese bound foot and its Western approximation, the high heel; the romantic painters' fat nudes, in times when most women suffered from malnutrition; and even the impossibly parthenogenic medieval Virgin Mary, whose maternal purity remained always unreachable by any mortal woman. We still have adolescent girls falling victim to anorexia and other eating disorders, partially because they despise themselves for not being more like Barbie.

At the same time, Barbie has become a symbol of the beautiful bimbo with the overstuffed closet and the empty plastic head. Similarly, GI Joe symbolizes mindless, ceaseless military aggression, in a world that needs peace above all. Together, these dolls say a lot about our culture. Their messages are not lost on our children.

She slapped his face as hard as she could.

*O*nce upon a time there was a toy shop where the dolls came to life at night, after dark. A half-forgotten genius named Mikimaus had taught them long ago to open the seals on their boxes and emerge for the nightly revels, then reseal themselves in at the first sign of dawn. Children sometimes noticed that the dolls bought in this shop looked a bit worn, but their elders seldom paid attention.

Aside from the baby dolls, who did nothing but cry and wet and were excessively boring, by far the most popular doll in the shop was Barbidol. She looked grown-up enough to have lived about eighteen human years, and she wore costumes enough to have lived about eighteen human lifetimes. She was a fashion model, rock star, astronaut, cheerleader, nurse, beach bunny, princess, showgirl, artist, ballerina, actress, dream date, prom queen, gymnast, and beauty-contest winner, of at least eleven different nationalities. She had far more clothes than any other doll, and that put her at the top of the toy shop social order.

Barbidol had nothing but contempt for the human females, both large and small, who came to the shop. Not one of them had ever even approached her own perfect proportions. Their waists were too wide, their busts too small or droopy, and their feet were monstrously huge. Barbidol showed them the proportions they should desire but never achieve, so they could learn to despise their own appearance. She dreaded the day when some loutish adolescent would buy her and take her away from the shop where she was queen.

Barbidol had several female associates whose proportions were exactly like hers, and also a male consort named Kendall. He looked a bit more like a human being, in a prep-school sort of way. Kendall's only mission in life was to escort Barbidol in her various roles and activities, so he was allowed to wear tuxedos, swimsuits, and ethnic or theatrical costumes but no work clothes. He never worked. He looked down particularly on those humans who had to scrimp and save money that they earned by working in order to buy him. Like Barbidol, Kendall was a snob.

One night, Barbidol noticed a new grown-up male doll on the premises. His name was Gijo, and he wasn't interested in female dolls at all. He seemed to care only for uniforms, helmets, guns, grenades, bombs, and other battlefield hardware. He liked to kill enemies and blow things up. He knew nothing of proms, parties, fashions, cruises, or any of the other civilized frivolities that preoccupied Barbidol and Kendall. He dwelt only in the all-male, generally working-class milieu of war.

Barbidol found herself more and more fascinated by Gijo, especially because he didn't seem affected by her charm. This was a novel experience for Barbidol. She was used to being the center of attention at all times. She began to see Gijo as a challenge to her powers of attraction. Besides, as she remarked to Kendall, he was kind of cute.

Kendall didn't think so. "He's shorter than you, and built like an outhouse," he sniffed. "Besides, he's Not Our Sort. He probably doesn't even know how to dance. Wouldn't you be embarrassed if your friends saw you dating an ape like him?"

"I don't think he's quite an ape," Barbidol said meditatively. "He's kind of sexy. Maybe with him I could do things I haven't done before."

"Maybe, but I'll bet you wouldn't like them," Kendall grumbled. He was feeling pangs of jealousy, because he had never seen Barbidol cast that speculative look upon anyone but him. "Gijo is nothing but a crude, low-class, stupid grunt, without a particle of breeding. I know, trust me."

"Oh, I do trust you, Kendall," she said, batting her eyelashes, which were real nylon and generally considered one of her best features. "But it's always broadening to meet new kinds of people and have new experiences, don't you think?"

"Yes, if you want to become nothing but a broad," Kendall snapped irritably. He didn't often make puns, because Barbidol never caught on to them anyway, but he was fuming.

Barbidol ignored Kendall's objections and began to flirt with Gijo. Following her perennial guide, the "How to Be Popular" advice column for girls, she pretended to be intensely interested in whatever he liked. Consequently, she found herself listening to hours of his monologues about automatic weapons, handguns, assault rifles, ammunition (which he called "ammo" or "rounds"), explosive devices, minefields, barrages, air cover, foxholes, and beachheads. She was severely bored by all this, but she liked watching Gijo's eyes light up when he expounded on notable battles and famous generals. The fact that she couldn't understand what he could possibly think so fascinating about all these matters made him seem all the more exotic and unusual.

She tried to attract Gijo by becoming less frivolous. She neglected her customary activities. She didn't even talk about going to the mall. She lost interest in pool parties, luncheons, fashion shows, and shopping expeditions with her friends. She sometimes forgot to put on her makeup and style her hair properly. Her best friend Midj told everyone that Barbidol was turning into a frump. "The next thing you know," Midj said maliciously, "she'll be spreading that hourglass waist into a jelly glass."

Barbidol's conversational skills deteriorated also. She was no longer able to discuss the latest designer jeans or this month's eyeshadow color ("Tahitian apricot"). Instead, she talked of air strikes, tanks, and nukes. She let her clothes become shabby and unwashed. Her friends found her boring. Kendall started dating Midj, though his heart wasn't in it. He missed the old Barbidol and hoped to bring her to her senses by making her jealous.

She didn't notice.

Gijo seemed to enjoy Barbidol's rapt attention. However, on the few occasions when she did some of the talking, he would gaze into space, fiddle with his sidearm, or push his cap over his eyes and go to sleep. Barbidol had an uneasy feeling that his interest in her talk was minimal at best. Still, she chattered on while his eyes glazed over or closed altogether. Piqued by his indifference, trying to become more interesting, she began to do some unprecedented thinking.

Gijo talked so much about enemies that Barbidol thought about them too. One day in a fit of inspiration, she wrote a poem that she entitled "Against the Enemies." Triumphantly, she hurried to read it to Gijo.

"Listen!" she cried.

AGAINST THE ENEMIES

They tell you to hate,
Those devils to break,
But when the war ends,
They say, "Oh, now wait—

> *We made a mistake;*
> *Those devils are friends."*

She sat back and waited modestly for his praise, but Gijo only glared at her in a silence that went on too long, until Barbidol began to feel uneasy. "Don't you like it?" she asked. "It tells about enemies. See, it rhymes and everything."

"What kind of stupid kapok is that?" Gijo snarled. "What are you, some kind of crazy pinko bleeding-heart parlor liberal or something? Take your silly poem and get lost."

Such unexpected rejection of her first literary inspiration infuriated Barbidol, but she swallowed her anger and tried to smile. Remembering the "How to Be Popular" advice column's recommendation for getting a boyfriend to "open up," she inquired about what the column called his Personal Life Goal.

"What's your Personal Life Goal?" she asked.

"My what?"

"You know—what you want to be, your ultimate ambition."

"Got no ambitions," said Gijo. "Take out the enemy, that's all."

"If you could be the kind of person you most admire, what would you be?"

"A hero, I guess."

"Don't you want to be *my* hero?" Barbidol asked, fluttering her nylon eyelashes provocatively.

Gijo snickered. "You don't hand out no medals," he said. "You ain't nothing but a dumb broad."

"How dare you!" Barbidol cried. Her anger welled up, and she slapped his face as hard as she could. Gijo grabbed her and shoved her up against the side of his box.

"Listen, doll, don't try to give me no hard time. I'm pretty sick of your airhead chatter. Broads like you should be seen and not heard." He shook her shoulders for emphasis.

"You're being totally nasty," Barbidol exclaimed. "You don't really like me at all."

"I like you all right, as long as you keep your mouth shut. You talk too much, and you don't know nothing important."

Barbidol burst into tears. "Let go of me, you moron!" she yelled. "Why did I ever think you'd make a decent boyfriend? You're a bloody-minded pig with nothing between your ears but plastic explosive!"

At this Gijo slapped her face in return and pushed her away. Barbidol ran off crying.

It was the end of her flirtation with Gijo. She never went near him again. She never again spoke of military matters. She returned to Kendall, declaring that he was the escort with whom she shared a true, profound philosophy. Kendall was glad to hear this, though he hadn't been aware that they shared any philosophy, profound or otherwise.

One day Barbidol asked him, "Kendall, are you patriotic?"

"Sure, why not?"

"What's your patriotic Personal Life Goal?"

"What any patriotic guy wants, I guess. To have lots of friends, parties, a house with a swimming pool, a condo in the Bahamas, a wide-screen TV, a wall-size stereo, and a three-car garage with a BMW, a Porsche, and a Ferrari."

"I can relate to that," said Barbidol. "Do you want to be a hero?"

"No."

"Why not?"

"Heroes are guys who get destroyed."

"Oh."

Presently, Gijo was sold to a small boy who liked to stage battles with real fire and serious mutilations. He tore off one of Gijo's arms, stuck an ice pick through his body, interred him in a plastic body bag, and finally burned him severely in a fireworks explosion. Gijo was forcibly retired, a wounded veteran, permanently scarred and half melted. He spent the rest of his days doing nothing at all in a dirty, jumbled, neglected toy box.

Barbidol and Kendall were sold to a little girl who loved them, treated them well, and provided them with many new clothes. They lived happily ever after.

TEN

SIR VIVOR AND THE HOLY CAULDRON

The Holy Grail of the medieval Christian myths—the quest stories of the Arthurian cycle—actually originated in European pagan tradition, in the form of the sacred Cauldron, another blood-filled vessel signifying death and rebirth. Although the Christianized Grail legends represented a patriarchal world, even in these the Grail was housed in a temple of women and revealed only to suitably gallant or woman-friendly knights. Joseph Campbell has pointed out that the lost Grail really represented the lost religion of pagan ancestors, whose ideas of life after death were quite different from those of Christian theologians.

Unlike Sir Galahad, Sir Lancelot, Sir Bors, and the rest, my Sir Vivor seeks not the Christianized transformation but the Cauldron itself, as a symbolic survivor of the older, earth-centered religion. Thus his story reverses the reversal and returns to the ancient concept of the world-creating womb.

"I am Sir Valance, guardian of the Holy Cauldron."

Once upon a time there was a young squire named Vivor, apprenticed to one of the king's knights, the notorious Sir Render, who was known for his wild, roistering ways. Sir Render loved wine-bibbing, wenching, gaming, and jousting, more or less in that order. He would begin drinking wine on first rising in the morning (or early after-noon) and would continue all day, becoming surly and truculent by evening. He would pick fights with other knights at the table round. He would crudely paw ladies and serving maids alike. He would kick dogs or serfs out of his way. He sometimes showed up at tournaments too drunk to hold his lance steady. Sir Render was not an easy master, but young Vivor tried to serve him faithfully.

Vivor was a conscientious lad with a serious turn of mind. Unlike other young squires, he actually knew how to read. During long hours of waiting for Sir Render to sleep off his stupor, Vivor read books instead of playing at dice or quarterstaves with other apprentices.

Vivor sometimes tried to engage his master in philosophical discussion, hoping to learn about the world from an older and presumably wiser per-son. Usually, Sir Render only slapped him on the back hard enough to make him cough and shouted cheerily that too much thinking would shrivel his private parts. Sir Render's remarks nearly always were delivered at shouting volume.

Vivor also listened to the quieter voices of old beldames and serving women about the royal castle, when they told ancient stories by the fire on winter evenings, or when they sang ancient narrative songs over the wash-tubs and embroidery hoops. From such sources he learned about the Holy Cauldron, so secret and so magical that folk hardly dared to speak of it.

It was, so the whispers went, the true source of all life and death. To look upon it was to become a god. But it was hidden in a fairy castle far away, where only one person had ever dared to venture. That was the fa-mous knight Sir Valance; the great warrior had vanished on his quest for the Cauldron and was never seen again.

Vivor resolved that when he became a knight, he would find the castle of the Holy Cauldron. He asked the oldest of the court ladies where the castle was, and she told him that the directions could be had only from the Witch of the North, who had been a great priestess and had since retired to her forest home. He kept this information in mind.

As Vivor's patron knight sank deeper into wine sickness, he suffered bouts of indigestion, jaundice, and befuddlement. Eventually Sir Render became too ill to accompany his liege lord on raiding expeditions into neighboring kingdoms. He stayed in bed, drinking, groaning, and puking, while the other knights trotted gallantly forth in quest of gold, girls, and glory. Vivor remained with his master, dutifully holding his head over the basin, privately dreaming of his own glory to come. He imagined that he would outshine all other knights because of the great worthiness of the high quest he had chosen.

In due course, Sir Render succumbed to a final overdose of malmsey and died in his bed, a half-empty flagon clutched in one hand and a maid-servant's corset in the other. The king condescended to fill his place in the ranks by knighting young Squire Vivor.

His Majesty advised Vivor to go forth on his first quest—the duty of a newly initiated knight—as soon as possible, the better to heal his grief for his late master. Actually, Vivor was not at all grieved to see the last of the bibulous Sir Render, but he bowed to the king and said he would obey.

"What will your quest be, Sir Vivor?" asked the king.

"Sire, I intend to search for the castle of the Holy Cauldron."

There was a collective gasp from the assembled knights, then a loud burst of laughter.

"Surely, Sir Vivor, this is a fruitless quest," the king said. "That castle is but a fable from the olden time. No one even knows in what direction it lies."

"There is one who knows," Vivor persisted. "The Witch of the North will tell me."

Again the knights laughed.

"You're a foolish boy," said the king. "But you're officially a knight, and even the youngest, most callow knight has the right to choose whatever quest he fancies. Therefore, go with Our blessing, and may you return twelve months wiser at the end of your maiden year."

Overjoyed, Sir Vivor saddled his new horse and girded on his new sword. Within a few days he had prepared for his journey, and he set out on a fresh spring morning, feeling that he owned the world. The birds sang for him, the grass grew for him, the sun shone just to warm the cold metal of his armor. After a few hours, it grew altogether too warm, and Vivor sweated profusely inside his metal shell. But this discomfort failed to dent his confidence.

A chill fell over his spirit, however, when he entered the forest that was the dwelling place of the Witch of the North. It was deep, dark, and dank, with huge trees whose roots ran everywhere and made his horse stumble. Through the upper branches of the forest canopy the wind spoke in strange tongues. A hawk flew screeching past his head. A dark, indistinct animal flitted across his path. He was startled by a serpent hanging from a branch, staring at him with lidless topaz eyes.

By the time Sir Vivor reached the witch's house, in a gloomy ravine, his ebullient mood had vanished altogether. He knocked on the door with the hilt of his sword. When the door silently swung inward without visible human agency, he stood still, disconcerted.

"Well, are you going to come in, or are you going to stand there dithering?" a voice said.

Vivor entered and stood looking around a dim, empty, stone-floored room. One cresset burned on the wall.

"What do you want?" the voice demanded.

"I've come to ask the Witch of the North the way to the castle of the Holy Cauldron," Vivor said.

The unseen questioner laughed. "Go away, boy. Go somewhere else and dream some other dream."

"I have sworn it on my honor as a maiden knight," Vivor said firmly. "It's my quest. I won't leave here until I've seen the Witch of the North face-to-face."

"Well then, look at her!" said the voice. A door suddenly opened in what had seemed a blank wall. There stood a fantastic figure dressed in a thousand fluttering rags, with an ankle-length cloak of wiry red hair falling from under her pointed hat. Her face was dead white, distorted, and startlingly ugly. It gave Sir Vivor a pang of fright, until he realized that it was a mask.

"Let me see your real face," he said.

"No one sees my real face."

"No matter if it is ugly," he responded. "It can't be any worse than your mask."

"Enough. What will you give me for the information you seek?"

"I have nothing but my horse, my weapons, and my armor. If I give you any of those, I will be disabled. What do you want me to give?"

"Give me your sacred word that if you find the castle of the Holy Cauldron, you will never reveal its location to any other human being."

"Gladly," said Vivor. "You have my sacred word."

"All right then, listen." She explained the route that he must follow, through the quaking bogs, over the Mist Mountains, along an abandoned stretch of the Highway of the Ancients, to the Stone Seacoast. There, she said, in a place where the sun never shines, he would find the castle of the Holy Cauldron. "Once you reach the castle, you're on your own," the witch said. "I have no knowledge of the enchantments they may use to repel unwanted visitors."

"How can there be a place where the sun never shines?" Vivor asked.

"I don't know. I haven't been there. I tell you as it was told to me."

Sir Vivor thanked the witch for her help and set off toward the quaking bogs. His horse balked at the edge, being wise enough to want to avoid such unsteady earth. Sir Vivor managed to prevail and drive it forward, but the poor animal trembled almost as much as the semiliquid ground. By keeping strictly to the witch's directions, Vivor found the firm path. Only once did the horse misstep and slip down, one leg engulfed almost to the knee, but on the next step the hoof was safely snatched out of the sucking mud.

As Vivor emerged from the bogs, the Mist Mountains rose before him, shrouded in their perpetual cloak of vapors. Night was drawing on. Vivor reflected that the trails through the mists would be difficult enough to find in daylight, let alone in the dark, so he camped and slept by the roadside. His sleep was disturbed by thin, wailing dream specters. He awoke chilled and stiff.

The Mist Mountains proved harder to negotiate than he had expected. The mist was cold but stifling, with a sour odor that made him cough. Several times his horse wandered from the path, which was found again only after much trouble. The mist was so thick that, from the saddle, Vivor couldn't see his horse's feet. In the end he had to dismount and lead the horse, so as to feel the way with his own feet.

All day he toiled in choking white clouds, until the dimming light showed him that night was coming again. Beginning to despair of ever emerging from the mountain fogs, he camped and again slept badly.

He awoke thoroughly wet with condensation that had penetrated under his armor. To make matters worse, his trail rations were running low. Though his horse had no difficulty in finding forage, he himself had nothing left but some cheese that was going moldy, a few strips of leathery dried venison, and a chunk of bread so stale and hard that he had to break it with a rock. He had neither seen nor heard any game in the silent mountains. Not a bird called in the mist.

Another day passed among the fog-enshrouded ridges. Toward dusk, Vivor sensed a thinning of the mists as the trail began to descend. Now and then a fitful breeze blew aside the curtains of vapor. He glimpsed a dim valley below. Somewhat encouraged by these signs, he and his horse pressed on with renewed hope. They arrived on the valley floor just as the last rays of the fallen sun were staining the dark clouds' edges with a sullen red.

The scene was bleak, but Vivor was glad to see clearly again. He saw a barren landscape, walled on one side by the Mist Mountains and on the other by a range of stony hills. The Highway of the Ancients ran through the center of the valley, along a small, sluggish stream. Here he watered his horse and camped for the night.

The highway had been built during the lost dream time by people whose very name was long forgotten. It was a road of huge dressed stone blocks, laid with such skill that hardly any of them had crumbled or upheaved in centuries. No one knew how to build such a road anymore. People believed that it had been done with the aid of dark magic and so avoided the highway out of superstitious fear. Adding to this fear was the fact that all along the side of the road stood mysterious stone figures, like images of ancient, unknown deities, exuding who knew what dangerous influences. Their shoulders were hunched, their hands tense but empty, their faces half rubbed away by wind and weather. They seemed malignant in their immensely old age.

Trying not to look at these glowering effigies, Sir Vivor arose in the morning and directed his horse northward along the road. He traveled for days through this empty, monotonous landscape, where wind sang over the low scrub. At night he seemed to hear faint, jeering voices in the wind. Having run out of food, he grew hungrier by the day. He managed to kill a moorhen with one of his arrows, but after that meal he saw no more game.

By degrees he became faint and semidelirious, wavering in the saddle while his horse plodded stolidly on. The highway, which seemed to have no end, shimmered before his eyes. Several times he thought he saw the stone figures move, or he thought he heard their voices addressing him. From the corner of his eye he saw one particularly grotesque figure make a sudden bounding leap toward him, with claws held menacingly aloft. But when he looked at it directly, it stood still.

When Vivor came to the end of the highway, he was no longer sure whether his eyes saw reality or fever visions. Two tall pillars marked the curb where the stone blocks ceased. Beyond them there seemed to be nothing at all. Coming up to the brink, Sir Vivor saw that the road ended on top of a steep cliff. A switchback path led down into a very deep, very dark, narrow gorge or canyon that opened out northward into an arm of a dim, cold sea. Looking over the edge, Vivor saw a castle at the very bottom of the gorge, shaded by high beetling rock walls to the east, south, and west. "A place where the sun never shines," he said to himself. "On the Stone Seacoast. This must be the place."

He urged his reluctant horse onto the switchback path. Though it protested, the animal was surefooted enough to pick its way down slowly and carefully, with only a few slips. At the bottom, in deep shade, stood the castle. It was built of dark basalt, with very thick walls and squat turrets at each corner. Banners, bearing the image of a round, black, three-legged cauldron, fluttered on the battlements. No other movement could be seen. There was no sound but the gnashing of the restless waves, slowly chewing away at the seacoast rocks.

Vivor rode up to the castle gate and rang the bell that hung there. Presently a knight appeared, dressed in black armor, riding a black horse.

"Who goes there?" he shouted.

"I am Sir Vivor, on a quest in search of the Holy Cauldron. Who might you be, sir?"

"I am Sir Valance, guardian of the Holy Cauldron. You can't pass unless you fight me."

Vivor was weaving in his saddle, squinting because he saw two or three figures of the opposing knight, sliding in and out of one another. "The famous Sir Valance?" he cried. "Your name is known everywhere. You have become a legend, sir."

Sir Valance lowered his lance. "Are you going to defend yourself, or not?"

Sir Vivor picked up his lance but was too weak with hunger to hold it steady. The point described wobbly circles in the air for a minute or two. Then Sir Vivor toppled slowly sideways, fell off his horse with a great metallic crash, and lay still.

When he next regained consciousness, Sir Vivor found himself lying alone on a narrow cot in a narrow room illuminated by one candle and a dim square of daylight from the single window. As he was looking around this celllike chamber, the door opened and a white-gowned lady entered, bearing a bowl of soup. The smell of it made his mouth water. "You're looking better," she remarked.

"What is this place?" Vivor asked.

"You are in the castle of the Holy Cauldron, the most sacred place in the world, the center of the earth. Now eat." She sat down on the edge of the cot and began spooning soup into his mouth, which embarrassed him. He tried to take the bowl from her, but his hands trembled so that he gave up and let her feed him. With each swallow, the soup seemed to restore a little more strength to his limbs.

"The knight said I couldn't pass until I fought him," Vivor said. "Did that happen?"

"No. Sir Valance is not a brute like many other knights. When he saw how weak you were, he brought you through the gate. He too once came here starving."

"I'm grateful," said Vivor.

"Rest now. I'll bring you more food later." She went away, locking the door behind her.

"I am being taken care of," Vivor thought, "but it seems I am also a prisoner. I must find a way to escape, but later. Much later." He fell asleep again.

Over the next few days several different white-gowned ladies brought him nourishment. Several different white-robed male servants brought him basins and towels for washing and removed his waste pail. All were un-communicative. When he became strong enough to walk around the room and exercise his arms, he thought of shoving the next visitor aside and getting out while the door was unlocked. However, his next visitor was a great personage, whom he knew could not be shoved. He saw that she was a great personage because she wore a silver crown set with diamonds and a robe of white velvet embroidered with silver crescent moons.

"I am the high priestess of the Holy Cauldron," the personage said. "I have come to offer you a choice of futures."

"What choice would that be?" he asked.

"In the past, outsiders who found their way to this place were put to death, and their blood was added to . . . a secret something. Recent years have brought a more humane policy. The first choice open to you is this: We will let you go back where you came from, provided you first submit to a procedure that will obliterate your memory. You will believe that your journey to this place was nothing but a fever dream or a random vision. You will never be inclined to repeat it. The second choice open to you is to remain here and become like Sir Valance and a few others, a guardian of the Cauldron in perpetuity."

"If I choose the second, will I be allowed to see the cauldron?" he asked.

"Yes."

"Then I so choose," said Vivor. During his recent days of solitude he had thought back on his past and had decided that it didn't amount to much. He had no family. The knightly life of hanging around the king's castle, engaging in trivial pastimes like Sir Render's, while waiting for the next battle, with its risk of severe injury or death, seemed not so attractive anymore. Sir Vivor had come close to death and had found it inglorious.

The high priestess nodded, touched his forehead once, and left the room. The place between his eyebrows where her finger touched him tingled strangely for hours afterward.

The next day Sir Valance himself appeared, bringing a white robe for Vivor to wear. "I'm here to begin your initiation," he said.

He led Vivor out of the room and through a maze of corridors to a dim, vaulted chamber whose walls were broken by a series of niches, each containing shelves of books, statuary, crystals, and other mysterious objects. In this chamber Vivor met an aged woman who was introduced as his teacher. For weeks he spent many hours each day with her, learning the lore of the olden time and mastering various techniques and disciplines too secret to be divulged.

When his teacher declared him ready, he was directed to prepare himself for the revelation of the Holy Cauldron. Preparation involved the performance of certain rituals, a night of vigil, and fasting. At last the appointed day arrived.

Filled with anticipation, Sir Vivor met the high priestess and a small entourage, who conducted him through many levels of the castle, downward through basements and subbasements, to the very foundations of living rock that lay at the bottom of the dark gorge. Here they entered a vast cavern, deep beneath the castle walls, dark and filled with the sound of rushing waters.

"What you are about to see," the high priestess said, "is the world's holiest symbol, the Cauldron, which encompasses the endless cycles of life and death on Earth. All that lives must die and be reabsorbed into the churning mass from which all forms arise. This philosophical principle of the Cauldron teaches us that no entity can be immortal. Only the Cauldron is immortal, redistributing every part of everything in a mixing that goes on forever. Therefore as the eternal giver of birth and taker of life, the Cauldron is not an it, but a she."

Her assistants lighted torches around the periphery of the great cavern. Then Vivor saw that the whole floor was shaped, partly by nature and partly by artifice, like a huge woman lying on her back, facing up to the high, dim, arched ceiling. The woman's body was perhaps two hundred yards long, with a clearly carved face, rippled mounds of hair, upthrust breasts, and long limbs touching the cavern's walls. The most remarkable feature was her belly mound, which rose to the rim of a huge, round, natural well sunk into the floor. From within this shaft rose the sound of ceaseless, restless waters sloshing and churning.

"That is the Holy Cauldron," said the high priestess. "Its waters are as salty as blood, and they rise and fall with the tides of the northern sea. The cauldron illustrates the fact that all life proceeds from the female principle, not from any god. The Cauldron was revered by the ancients, time out of mind. It is revered today by those of us who hold this place in sacred trust."

Sir Vivor fell on his knees and clasped his hands in wonder.

He became a convert to the philosophy of the Holy Cauldron. He remained at the castle for the rest of his life, learning and meditating. In time, he became a great adept. Sir Valance became his close friend. He married one of the priestesses and lived happily ever after. In the country of the king, he was never seen again and so became a legend.

Eventually, in view of the outer world's increasing violence, the high priestess decreed that the castle of the Holy Cauldron should be even less accessible to random adventurers. She cast magical spells to enclose it forever in dense mists and to provide in its place the illusion of an uninviting, uninhabited seacoast. All paths leading to it were enchanted to twist back on themselves and leave travelers lost in confusion.

Stories about the Cauldron were altered as they were repeated over centuries. At last the symbol was changed from a natural vessel of seawater representing the female principle to an artificial vessel of a holy man's blood. Knights sometimes went in quest of it, but it was never found.

ELEVEN

ALA DEAN AND THE WONDERFUL LAMP

Feminizing Aladdin puts a surprising twist on the old Arabian tale. When I began, I didn't know what Ala Dean would require of her genie. She took over the story on her own, so to speak, and followed a feminist route to her happy-ever-after, which entailed happiness not only for herself but for others too. There's much to be said for her approach, as opposed to the personal fortune, rank, and power demanded by the typically selfish heroes of traditional stories. The social changes that she brought about represent one of the wish-fulfillment fantasies commonly expressed in feminist groups.

All at once a thick mist poured out of the lamp . . .

*O*nce upon a time, in an old-fashioned feudal kingdom, there lived a poor widow named Ganga Dean, otherwise known as Mistress Dean the dressmaker. Day and night she toiled with her needle to eke out a living for herself and her daughter, Ala. They lived in a tiny, mean hovel in an alley behind the king's palace.

Ganga Dean looked up at the high walls of the royal domicile with considerable distaste. She complained constantly to her daughter about the king's exorbitant taxes, which took bread from the mouths of poor women and children to help finance his foreign wars, fought to bring more riches to the king and his courtiers. "War is a game that rulers play," she told Ala bitterly, "at the expense of the ruled, who are killed or ruined so the game can go on."

Like her neighbors, Ganga Dean hated the tax collectors and their escorts, the armed guards who often took even more than the collectors did. They would casually pick up the odd piglet, hen, family heirloom, young girl, or young boy, which would be taken away and never seen again. Any taxpayer who objected to the loss of a possession or a child would be hurt or killed, and the king's men would walk away laughing. "They're worse than vultures," Ganga Dean would say in a fearful whisper. "They steal and rape and kill. We common people exist only to feed their greed, which is bottomless." As Ala began to grow into handsome young womanhood, her mother always hid her from the tax collectors, lest she should be taken away to service the soldiers' lusts.

Ala Dean was a carefree sort of girl, determined to enjoy life as much as her poverty would allow. She ran wild in the streets, played tricks on merchants, took part in ball games with the boys, and defied authority whenever she could. Her mother begged her to wear modest dresses and adopt ladylike airs and graces, so she might attract a rich husband and save them both from their life of want. But Ala refused to change her hoydenish ways. She didn't mind concealing her beauty with a dirty face, tangled hair, and unkempt garments.

One day a street magician came to Ganga Dean's house, slyly claiming to be the long-lost brother of the widow's deceased husband. The widow hastened to entertain him as well as she could, opening her last bottle of cider and killing her last chicken for his dinner. As he ate, the magician studied Ala, remarked on her beauty, and said he could train her to become the richest courtesan in the land. Eventually, he declared, she could marry a lofty aristocrat, perhaps a duke or a prince.

Ganga Dean clasped her hands in delight. "My Ala, to become a duchess or a princess?" she cried. "Bless you, sir. Let her take up the useful trade of courtesan, for heaven knows she does nothing particularly useful now."

"But Mother, I don't want to become a courtesan," Ala protested.

"We must be practical, dear," her mother said. "Given our circumstances, it's the best life you could make for yourself. It would put you in touch with the Right People as nothing else could. Remember, only courtesans can influence the heartless men who rule us. You could do much good. And here is your own uncle, offering to train you. It's a golden opportunity, Ala."

"I don't think so," Ala grumbled, instinctively mistrusting the visitor's ingratiating manner.

"Just imagine," her mother burbled on, lost in a dream of affluence, "someday we might even live in the palace, and look down from that balcony on our old hovel here. You're a beautiful girl. Your looks could take you to the very heights of society."

Ala Dean only hunched down in her chair and sulkily picked at a hangnail on her thumb.

"No more for tonight," the magician said cheerily. "Tomorrow I'll take her to a friend of mine, a very great lady, to begin her apprenticeship. For now, let us rest."

He retired to Ganga Dean's own bed, which she had freshly made up for him, while she slept on a straw pallet on the floor. Like most men of his time, the magician firmly believed that every woman should be happy to serve him and deprive herself for his benefit, especially if she was (or believed herself to be) his relative by marriage or by blood.

Ala sat up for a while, staring at the fire, wondering whether she should run away from home before the magician took her. Because she loved her poor naive mother and didn't want her to worry, Ala decided to go along with the magician and wait for an opportunity to take advantage of the situation.

In the morning she set out with him, carrying her few possessions bound up in a sack. They walked far, toward the mountains. Ala Dean became very weary. She saw around her only a rocky wasteland, without a sign of habitation where a great lady might live. "How much farther, Uncle?" she asked.

"We're almost there," he assured her. She was not reassured.

Soon they entered a stony canyon. The magician took a shovel from his pack and began to dig in the gravel. Presently he uncovered an iron ring set in a granite block. "Pull that ring," he ordered Ala. She did so. The granite block moved aside, groaning grittily, to reveal an open trapdoor with stone stairs leading down into the earth.

"You must go down those stairs and through the caves below," the magician told her. "Touch nothing that you pass, for one touch could be deadly. At the end of the large cavern you will come to a niche containing a common brass lamp. Bring me the lamp. Remember to touch nothing else." He gave her a lighted candle and pushed her toward the trapdoor.

Ala Dean went down the stairs willingly enough, for this felt like an adventure. Her candle showed her a dry cave filled with dusty wooden boxes and chests. Soft, powdery dust lay on the floor and swirled up around her feet as she walked. She touched nothing, although she was itching with curiosity to know what the chests contained.

The cave chamber led to a narrow passage, which in turn led to another chamber, much larger than the first. This one too was nearly filled with wooden boxes, one of which stood open. Ala Dean leaned over it with her candle. She was thrilled to see that it contained just what she expected: treasure. Golden beads, cups, and bracelets; jeweled tiaras and necklaces; rings, anklets, and breastplates all glittering with precious metals and gems.

The eye-level niche on the far wall of this cave contained nothing but a small, dirty, tarnished lamp of common brass. Ala couldn't imagine why her purported uncle would want this article above all the other riches in the cave. Neither could she imagine why he didn't come down and see for himself what was hidden here. Her suspicion of him grew apace.

As she returned with the lamp in her hand, she found the granite block drawn back again over the hole, nearly covering it, except for a gap of six inches at one side. Through the gap she saw the magician's face.

"You took long enough about it," he grumbled. "Hurry, girl, pass the lamp up to me. Then I'll move the stone back and let you out."

Ala Dean laughed. "What kind of a fool do you take me for, Uncle?" she said. "You let me out first, then you'll get your lamp."

The magician flew into a rage and demanded with many curses that Ala relinquish the lamp immediately—all of which made her refusal even firmer. The magician stuck his arm, then a stick, through the hole, trying to reach her. She took the lamp and retreated to the foot of the stairs. "Why don't you come down yourself, Uncle?" she called. "What's wrong with this place?"

Seeing that it was useless to try to persuade her, the magician shouted: "Stupid girl! Go ahead, then, and enjoy your treasure—forever!" With that, he closed the doorway completely. The heavy stone cut off all sound. Ala Dean was left alone in tomblike silence.

At first she went up the stairs and tried to move the granite block, but it weighed tons and couldn't be budged without the aid of the magic ring on the outside. For a while she tried to entertain herself by singing and talking, hoping that the magician would relent and release her from her underground prison. Time passed. She grew hungry and thirsty. Little by little her spirits fell, as she realized that in all probability her false uncle had left her to die.

She gave way to a fit of hopeless weeping. Her tears fell on the old lamp that she still clutched in her hand, smearing the dirt on its surface. Automatically she rubbed away the damp patch to expose the metal.

All at once a thick mist poured out of the lamp and coalesced into the shape of a huge genie with a bald head, pendulous earrings, and voluminous silk trousers. "What a relief!" cried the genie, to Ala's astonishment. "I've been cooped up in that lamp for two hundred years. It's about time somebody found me. Now, little mistress, you have the slave of the lamp at your command. What is your wish?"

"I wish to be out of this cave," Ala said promptly.

"No sooner said than done, little mistress." The genie picked her up in his arms, took several strides through a strangely thick, dark medium, and deposited her on the ground above the granite slab. She looked around. Dusk was falling. A chill wind whined among the rocks. There was no sign of the magician.

"Now I wish for some food and drink," Ala said.

The genie snapped his fingers. At her feet appeared a beautiful rug spread with plates of fruit, flagons of water and wine, loaves of bread, cheeses, and sweet cakes. Ala ate until she was more than full. Then she ordered the genie to take her home.

"But what about the treasure?" he asked slyly. "Don't you want to take some gold and jewels along, to buy yourself a new life?"

"I don't think so," said Ala, sensing a trap. "I'm not sure about that treasure. Maybe my false uncle was right to tell me it shouldn't be touched."

"Wise girl," said the genie. "The fact is, that treasure was obtained at the price of much bloodshed and never gave any of its owners more than momentary satisfaction. Had you touched it, you would have been infected with the insatiability disease, which can be crippling or even fatal. Entering the cave is fatal to anyone other than a pure maiden, which is why your companion sent you down where he dared not go himself."

The genie cleared away the dishes with another snap of his fingers and seated Ala with the lamp on the rug. Ala gasped as the rug rose from the ground and flew through the night air at great speed, carrying her back to her home and depositing her gently before her mother's door.

"There, little mistress," said the genie. "You're home. Now what about a real miracle or two? I haven't exercised my powers for much too long a time. How about a nice fifty-room white-marble palace with a hundred Circassian slaves, a stable full of racehorses, a dress spangled all over with diamonds? What's your pleasure? Wouldn't you like to become a rich aristocrat, maybe even a princess?"

"No. I don't want to be a princess. Aristocrats do nothing but oppress and steal from the poor to finance their own frivolous pleasures and unnecessary extravagances."

"My, you're a sententious bore," the genie said. "Where do you get off, with such a holier-than-thou attitude? Every master I ever had has gone for the palace and the slaves and all the ruling-class perks."

"I want something more useful. I want to eliminate war. I want you to vaporize every single weapon in this entire country and in all of the neighboring countries, so that men will have no more means to fight and harm others."

The genie rolled up his eyes. "I'm not used to this," he complained. "My masters always wanted me to kill some enemy or other, and set them up as top dogs. Peace is a little out of my line."

"Well, if you can't manage it—"

"Bite your tongue, little mistress! I am the genie of the lamp. I can do anything." The genie clenched his fists, squeezed his eyes shut, gritted his teeth, and strained. "There. It's done. What's your next bizarre behest?"

"Turn all the tax collectors into sheep, and their escorts into sheep-dogs."

Again the genie strained, then told her it was done.

"Turn all the aristocrats' jewels into loaves of bread, and distribute them among the poor."

That, too, was done.

"Now turn all the palaces and all the hovels alike into modest but comfortable middle-sized houses, so that all the country's wealth is fairly distributed among its citizens."

"You're asking a poor genie to change an entire society," the genie protested. "It's an immense job."

"Well, if you're not up to it—"

"Never!" he cried. "I can do anything!" With that, he strained more than ever. His eyeballs popped, his tongue stuck out, his face turned purple. Ala saw her mother's wretched hovel change before her eyes into a pleasant white-painted cottage with a flower garden and picket fence. Other houses along the alley underwent similar changes, while the towering walls of the king's palace suddenly shrank out of sight.

The genie sank panting to the ground. "I'm exhausted," he said. "You have taken my last ounce of strength. I can do nothing more for a long while. Dismiss me, mistress; I have no more magic left."

"Go, then," said Ala Dean.

The genie slowly inserted himself back into the lamp. As he disappeared, she heard his voice saying faintly, "If you want anything, just rub."

The next day, chaos reigned. The nobles were terrified at the magical disappearance of their palaces and jewels. They screamed for the soldiers, who tried to arm themselves with pitchforks, rakes, and hoes, but there were not enough of these to go around. The king's counselors feared a people's revolution, or else a campaign of retaliation from surrounding kingdoms that had been looted in the past. Everyone breathed easier when it was found that none of the neighbors had any weapons either. In time, military leaders found nothing left to do and took up new lines of work.

Fear of revolution dissolved when it was found that the people's resentments had been soothed by their new circumstances. Common folk even extended neighborly assistance to former aristocrats, showing them how to till their fields and take care of their modest properties. Previously divergent classes adjusted themselves into a classless nation, where people didn't feel obliged to put others down for their own aggrandizement.

Ala Dean and her mother were honored by their neighbors. Ganga Dean was no longer forced to sew day and night for her living. She worked a comfortable eight-hour day and enjoyed putting thought and creativity into her designs. Ala went to work on a dairy farm, run by a man who had formerly been a duke. Eventually, she married the dairyman's son and lived happily ever after.

Nearly everyone in the kingdom lived more happily ever after except the genie, whose powers had been so overstrained by changing a whole society that he never created another palace. All he could do was entertain at children's birthday parties and pull live pigeons out of hats. Sometimes he tried to harangue people with tales of the wonders that he used to perform in his glory days, but no one really wanted to listen. In the end, he retired into his lamp and learned to be content with making just a little light in a dark world.

TWELVE

THE DESCENT OF SHALOMA

This tale recalls the descent of Babylon's goddess Ishtar (Sumerian Inanna) to the underworld to resurrect her lover, Tammuz (Sumerian Dumuzi), who may have been biblically reincarnated as doubting Thomas. Ishtar gave up a garment at each of the seven underworld gates, met her dark twin sister, Ereshkigal (here combined with Kali, India's dark Goddess), and was hung from a hook to be reduced to bones. The priestess's dance depicting these events apparently descended to the biblical story of Salome and her mother, Herodias (Arodia), who may have been the elder priestess or priestess-queen ceremonially mated to the king (Herod). We know that the worship of Ishtar and Tammuz was prevalent in Palestine, and women annually wailed for Tammuz in the Jerusalem temple (Ezek. 8:14).

Page 104

Still she danced . . .

*O*nce upon a time there was a beautiful priestess named Shaloma, who loved a prince named Thamus. In those days it was the custom for a man of royal blood to be chosen by lot, each year, to go underground to the Land of Death, so that crops would grow well from the earth and the people would be saved from a season of dearth.

When spring came and the lot was drawn, Shaloma was appalled to learn that it fell on her lover. "You mustn't go, you mustn't," she pleaded with Thamus.

"It's my duty," he answered. "How can I not go? My only other choice is to flee into exile and live like a peasant in a foreign land. Princes must be above such cowardice."

Shaloma wept and raged, but Thamus was adamant. Others had gone before him, he said, and were honored like gods for their willing self-sacrifice. He too wished to be honored like a god. "Is that more important than being with me?" Shaloma asked him.

"It's more important than anything," said Thamus. "As a holy woman, you know that very well. I must do my duty for the people, and in return they will worship me forever."

Seeing that nothing could change his mind, Shaloma went to her mother, Arodia, a powerful fairy queen, and laid the problem before her. "Thamus is determined to go through the sacrificial ceremony and enter the underworld," she said. "What can I do to prevent it?"

"Nothing," Queen Arodia told her. "You should not prevent it. After all, the people believe they would starve without it. Let the ceremony be performed, then go after him yourself and bring him back."

"How can I do that?"

"I'll tell you, but I must warn you that it won't be an easy task."

"I don't care, I'll do anything."

"Then listen carefully. After the ceremony, you must go into the temple wearing seven of your very best jeweled robes, one over the other. The outermost one must be red, the next orange, the third yellow, the fourth green, the fifth blue, the sixth purple, and the innermost one black. In the central chamber of the temple, before the deities, you must dance until you fall into a trance. In this state you will pass through the seven gates of the underworld. Each of the seven gatekeepers will demand one of your garments as payment, so you will arrive naked in the land of death. You must also carry coins to pay the ferrymen of the underground rivers, of which there are three. You must meet Kgali the queen. She will tell you what to do to retrieve Thamus. More than that I can't say, because I haven't been there myself. I tell you only what is written in the secret books, which only those of fairy blood can read."

Shaloma thanked Queen Arodia and hastened to her wardrobe to choose seven of her lightest, filmiest robes, which would least hamper her dancing. When she tried them all on, one over the other, she felt like one enveloped in a cloud.

The fatal day arrived. Prince Thamus was dressed in royal purple and mounted on a white mule. He was conducted to the temple enclosure by a splendid procession, with much banging of cymbals, blowing of horns, and waving of palm branches. In the center of the enclosure stood the giant tree, shorn of its boughs, where he was hung up by his hands and made to bleed.

He endured everything bravely and made the correct verbal responses to the ritual questions while Shaloma wept at the foot of the tree. So did her maidservants and other women, because the tradition said women's wailing was necessary to help waft the prince into the underworld.

After Thamus had not moved for a long while, the ritual leaders announced that his spirit had gone to the underworld. He was removed from the tree and carried to a shiny new tomb. At the conclusion of the ceremony, Shaloma went to the central chamber of the temple. In the space surrounded by towering, frowning statues of the deities, before the royal throne, she began to dance.

She danced until her feet were tired, her breath came in gasps, and she was covered with sweat under her seven filmy gowns. Still she danced, until blackness grew at the edges of her perception. The outlines of the temple chamber began to flicker and fade before her eyes. In their place, she saw fitful glimpses of a vast abyss opening at her feet, an unfathomable deep into which a path went spiraling downward. Her dancing feet took her onto the path, while the rest of her went along almost reluctantly, unable to stop the rhythm of the dance.

At the first gate she was halted by a red-skinned creature dressed entirely in scarlet, with long red-lacquered claws on his hands and crimson horns on his head. The gate itself was painted as red as fresh blood and studded with red stones: rubies, garnets, carnelians. The rocks around it were rusty red sandstone and cinnabar.

The gatekeeper stood in her way and said, "You are of the living. You can't pass into the land of the dead without paying a price."

"I can pay the price," Shaloma said. She took off her outermost robe and held out the thin veillike material embroidered with its gems. The gatekeeper took it and opened the gate. She passed through and found herself on the bank of a thickly flowing red river—a river of blood.

A small ferryboat was drawn up to the bank. A hooded figure, draped in crimson, stood with one skeletal hand on the oar and the other reaching out, palm up. Shaloma suppressed a shudder, entered the boat, and placed a coin in the skeletal hand. Immediately the ferryman pushed off and rowed her across the blood river. She endured the trip, trying not to breathe the overwhelmingly cloying smell of blood.

On the other bank, the sands were orange and hot. She followed a curving path through rock walls to the second gate, which was painted bright orange with the likeness of flames and studded with fire opals. Torches burned on each side of it. The gatekeeper wore a saffron robe and a crown of burning candles. He stopped her by waving a burning brand before her, saying, "You are of the living. You can't pass into the land of the dead without paying a price."

"I can pay the price," said Shaloma, taking off her second garment. The gatekeeper took it and opened the gate. She passed through and was almost suffocated by the heat. She was in a land of fire. Small fires burned in holes in the rock all around her. She stood on the bank of a river of red-hot lava. A rusty iron ferryboat was drawn up on the shore, manned by an artificial creature made of metal in the shape of a man. It held out its hand, and Shaloma gave it a coin. It ferried her across the burning river. During the trip, the iron boat became too hot to touch. Shaloma might have been burned, had not her five layers of clothing protected her skin. As it was, she breathed the hot air only with difficulty.

The other bank was ocher yellow mud from which grew huge, rank, buttery gold sunflowers that nodded their heads at her and squirmed on their stems as if sentient. The third gate, made of yellow gold, was emblazoned with the rayed image of the sun and surrounded by fluttering clouds of brilliant yellow butterflies. The gatekeeper's yellow robe was covered by more of these insects, so he seemed a tower of rustling, flickering yellow wings.

Again Shaloma was challenged, and she gave the butterfly-covered gatekeeper her third garment. She was beginning to feel a little freer in her movements as she passed through the golden gate into a landscape made entirely of sulfur (brimstone), brilliant yellow in color and quite beautiful but raising such a stench that Shaloma could hardly breathe. Holding her nose, taking shallow breaths through her mouth, she followed the curving path between stinking sun-yellow pinnacles and giant crystals of pure sulfur.

The next gate was a towering monument made entirely of rich green malachite, studded with emeralds. The gatekeeper was a green giant clothed entirely in vegetation, his bearded face peeking out of a spreading corona of green leaves. This green man informed her that she must pay the price to enter the land of the dead, and received her fourth garment.

She passed through the gate into a lush jungle. Green growth sprang up so thickly that the path was obscured in many places. She found her way with difficulty, pushing aside the fronds. She had to cross a sluggish, shallow stream covered by a coat of poison-green algae. There was no ferry, but she found stepping stones made of the bright green feldspar that her teachers had called Amazon stone.

The fifth gate was made of the stone she had learned to call heavenly: brilliant blue lapis lazuli, gemmed with sapphires and aquamarines glittering like blue stars in an azure sky. The gatekeeper was a benevolent-looking blue-haired elf in a robe of ink blue satin. He gazed on her with a pitying expression as he issued the usual challenge and received her fifth garment. "Why would one of the living go voluntarily into death?" he asked.

Shaloma paid no attention. She hastened through the gate into a blue land, giving the impression of open spaces covered by bright blue sky and floored by steel blue rocks, in whose crannies grew clumps of bluebells, cornflowers, and blue gentians.

The sixth gate seemed to be carved from one enormous translucent crystal of amethyst, glowing in a dim purplish light. Its keeper was an unnaturally tall, slender figure muffled from head to foot in purple velvet, except for a thin hand with faintly lavender skin, silently extended to take her garment. The purple gatekeeper said nothing. He opened the gate to show her a landscape of permanent dusk, violet mists, and small streams meandering between banks of purple flowers.

There was nothing overtly menacing about the scene, but somehow Shaloma felt more reluctant to enter this purple gloom than she had felt at any of the other gates. She advanced timidly, looking about with wary glances, as if she expected the mists to solidify into terrifying shapes at any moment. Nothing appeared to frighten her, yet an unshakeable depression settled on her spirit as she followed the curving path.

Her despair intensified at the sight of the seventh gate, soaring up against a night sky like a wall of black obsidian, polished to a dark mirror-like gleam. Set into pitch black rocks, it looked forbidding, impenetrable. She halted before it, seeing no gatekeeper.

Her pale body was visible now through the dark veiling of her last garment. Its thin folds did nothing to repel the chill that afflicted her—an icy, unearthly cold, as of outer darkness, utterly alien and far from all that was sunny, cheerful, or familiar. Shaloma involuntarily hugged herself and tried to rub the chill from her arms, with little success. She stood shivering before the gigantic black gate, waiting for what seemed an interminable time.

Suddenly the black soil in front of her rose up in a man-shaped column, developing a shiny, pitchy surface as it took a humanlike form. Its face was featureless, its arms and hands only roughly shaped. With one half-articulated limb it reached out toward her. Though she could see no mouth, it spoke, saying, "You are of the living. You can't pass into the land of the dead without paying a price."

"I can pay the price," Shaloma whispered, not trusting herself to speak aloud lest her voice quiver too much. She removed her black veil and handed it to the black creature. Now she was naked, having nothing but her last coin held in her hand.

Ponderously, slowly, the huge obsidian gates parted just enough to admit her to the central abyss of the underworld. On the other side of the gate she came to a black river, widest and swiftest of the underground streams, slipping silkily along between its banks like an immense, silent black snake. A ferry stood on the shore, manned by a person so withered and gray with age that he resembled a giant spider. His skinny limbs were hardly more than twigs, yet when Shaloma paid him her last coin, he propelled the ferry with almost superhuman strength across the swift, oily black waters.

Once on the other shore, Shaloma paused in confusion. All around her drifted the dark, tenuous shades of the dead, sighing in thin voices, saying words that she could not quite understand. They seemed human, yet not human. They were like forms made of black smoke, or like shadows slipping silently over all obstructions, flitting back and forth, whispering about her among themselves.

She summoned up her courage and announced into the air, "I am here to see Kgali, queen of the underworld." Her voice cracked a little but sounded strong against the background of hisses and whispers. The shades flicked aside to open a path before her. She went on, in the direction they indicated, until she came to a vast hall surrounded by crystal pillars on all sides.

In the center of the hall, on a throne of black onyx, sat an enormous woman with four arms and black skin. She was crowned, dressed in gold and scarlet, and wearing many jewels. Her long hair flowed upward as if blown by ceaselessly upwelling vapors. Her appearance was intimidating enough in itself, but on looking closely at her black face, Shaloma discovered something truly startling. Aside from their ebony color, Kgali's features were exactly like her own.

She took a deep breath, bowed, and addressed the entity on the throne. "Your Majesty, I am here to retrieve the shade of Prince Thamus," she said.

"Are you indeed?" said Kgali. "And are you willing to pay the required ransom?"

"I have nothing left to pay," said Shaloma. "I have come naked into your presence, as I was instructed to do."

"Yes, the dead must come naked from the world above, just as they come naked into it at birth. Even though you follow the convention, however, you are not dead. You must become more than bare-skinned to fully reproduce the condition of the dead. You must also put off your flesh, and be naked down to your bones."

Shaloma shuddered. "How then can I be joined to Prince Thamus, who loves me after the manner of the flesh? Bones can't make love."

"Whosoever gives up flesh in the realm of the dead may also put on flesh when reborn in the realm of the living," Kgali said. "That is the way of nature."

"Are you saying that I can get my body back?"

"I say that all bodies are one in the cauldron of being. Don't you see that I am your shadow twin, the oneness of your living and your dead selves? So I am to every creature, for I am queen of them all."

Shaloma had little time to ponder the meaning of these cryptic remarks because she was suddenly seized by two leathery-winged trolls and carried up to a hook in the ceiling of Kgali's hall. There she hung while her flesh rapidly melted from her bones and reduced her to a skeleton. Then one of the trolls flew up before her, bearing the shade of Prince Thamus.

"Look, king-victim," Kgali called to him. "Do you recognize these bones?"

Thamus looked closely. Then he started. "Yes, I see the lovely white teeth of my sweetheart, Shaloma. I'd know them anywhere, even without the shapely lips that covered them."

"Congratulations," said Queen Kgali with a trace of irony. "You have proved yourself an unusually observant lover and have earned the life her sacrifice buys for you. One thing I charge you to remember always. Her sacrifice was made for love, whereas yours was made for pride. Never again be so foolish as to think you can love all humanity, unless you are capable of loving one person above all. Learn from woman how to be a man."

Thamus hung his head and said, "I should never have doubted her wisdom."

"Now begone, the two of you," the queen commanded. "We'll meet again in another time of shadows, because no one ever leaves the land of the dead for good."

The trolls removed Shaloma's bones from their hook. Her flesh quickly grew around them again, leaving her as whole as before. Thamus hugged her with delight, then she led him away from the queen's hall, back through all the gates and levels of the underworld. As it was for those coming to earth to be born, for them all gates were freely opened and all rivers freely passed.

When the happy couple returned home to the palace, they were greeted by cheering well-wishers and honored by a great feast. Not only was Thamus revered as a god, but Shaloma also was revered as a goddess, assimilated to the same heavenly Mother whose shadow twin was said to live deep underground and govern the world of the shades.

She never told anyone—not even Thamus—about the mysterious resemblance between herself and Kgali. But she often pondered it, ultimately reaching certain conclusions about the connections between the human and the divine. These conclusions she wrote down in a book, which was kept in a secret place in the temple and was never read lest it upset the naive faith of the people.

When Prince Thamus and Shaloma became king and queen of their country, they did away with the annual sacrifices, proclaiming that the salvation of the people had been achieved for all time. And so it seemed, for the crops flourished each year with no more than normal agricultural care.

The couple lived happily ever after, until the time came for them to return to the underworld together. Eventually they were placed at the head of the people's pantheon as the most important and most beloved deities. Every year, for many centuries afterward, a royal maiden formally performed Shaloma's dance of the seven veils as a special charm for continuing life.

THIRTEEN

THE WEAVER

In classical Greek myth Arachne was a mortal maiden so skilled at weaving that she aroused the jealousy of gray-eyed Athene, Goddess of all handicrafts, who ill-naturedly turned her into a spider to teach her that she must not compete with divinity. This was a revised myth, intended to belittle the Goddess herself in her aspect of fate-weaver. In this guise, Arachne was earlier manifested on Earth as her own totem spider. Our spinning and weaving ancestresses must have been mightily impressed by the delicate skills of spiders and naturally attributed them to the Goddess's influence.

Another Greek name for the fate-weaver was Clotho, whose magical blood-red thread entered into the web of every life to bring about events in the earthly world. Centuries later, many Europeans still believed that women's weaving, knotting, and threading charms could make things happen, to bring about the results of both blessings and cursings. Spiders remained sacred to the fairies, who were often said to wear garments of spider silk.

*Rich ladies brought her skeins of fine silk, damask,
and cashmere.*

*O*nce upon a time there was a poor widow with a talented daughter named Rosette, who was known throughout the countryside for her expert spinning and weaving. Though they owned little, Rosette was able to provide for her mother by means of her skill. Rich ladies brought her skeins of fine silk, damask, and cashmere, and paid her to weave beautiful fabrics and ribbons for their dresses. Local farmers paid her to spin sturdy wools and weave them into tight, weatherproof cloaks and trousers. Dealers in tapestry bought her products to resell for many times her prices. "Like a Rosette cloth" became a byword of praise for any fabric that was exquisitely made and full of colorful figures.

Rosette's mother often recounted how Rosette, from her earliest childhood, had been fascinated by spiders. She would sit for hours to watch a spider making its web, and afterward she would try to imitate the web with bits of string. She was always very solicitous of spiders. She would never kill a spider found in the house, making its web in an inconvenient place. Instead, she would take the creature carefully outdoors and place it where it could spin undisturbed.

Spiders seemed to trust her. They would hop up on her fingers without fear and gaze into her face with their eight tiny beady eyes while she carried them to safety. She used to say that any common garden spider had more skill at spinning and weaving than a hundred of the finest human artisans, and if she could do half as well as a spider she would be perfectly content.

When she came of age, Rosette was betrothed to her childhood sweetheart, a shepherd lad named Rambow. Inspired by Rosette, Rambow had taken to breeding sheep for especially fine, long-staple fleeces to be spun into soft but durable wools. All the villagers believed that when they were married, Rosette and Rambow would be forever prosperous because of their complementary skills.

Rosette's village was part of the estate of the Baron Wrathchild, a cruel master who held the power of life and death over all his serfs. One day the baron happened to be passing Rosette's cottage as she was spinning in the sun on her doorstep. Seeing her, he stopped and dismounted from his horse.

"I'm thirsty; fetch me a cup of beer," he commanded. Rosette left her spinning and hurried to obey. As she handed the beer to him, the baron gazed keenly into her face.

"You're a remarkably pretty wench," he said. "What's your name?"

"Rosette, milord."

"Well, Rosette, come tomorrow to my castle. I'll make you one of my baroness's ladies-in-waiting. It'll be a big step up for a peasant girl like you."

Rosette curtsied and said nothing. Like everyone else on Wrathchild's estates, she knew well enough that the baroness's ladies-in-waiting were nothing more nor less than the baron's private harem slaves, waiting perforce not for his wife but for him. The baroness herself knew it and welcomed a situation that helped relieve her of the baron's cruel, often violent sexual attentions. Each time a new recruit joined the harem, Wrathchild would concentrate his brutalities on her for a while, until she was thoroughly spiritbroken and eager to obey any command in order to avoid further pain.

When the baron rode away, Rosette burst into tears and ran to tell her mother what he had said. "It's the end of my life," she sobbed. "Now I'll never be able to marry Rambow. I'll never spin again. I'll never be free. I'll be a prisoner in that castle until I die. *His* prisoner—that ugly monster!"

"Hush, you mustn't speak so," her mother said, looking fearfully around as if she expected one of the baron's guards to be listening. She too was in despair. She could think of no way to save her daughter. She petted Rosette and kissed her, saying faintly, "But you'll be able to wear fine gowns and jewels."

"Yes, with bruises and blisters under them!" Rosette cried fiercely. "I can't stand it, Mother. I'll run away."

"Then you'll be a fugitive serf, subject to a summary death penalty whenever you're caught," her mother said. "Oh, dear, what have we done to deserve such misery?"

Rosette and her mother wept themselves into a state of exhaustion and went to bed, hoping to find a solution to their problem in the light of a new day. During the night, Rosette was awakened by a mysterious glow beside her bed. She opened her eyes and saw a strange lady standing there. She was tall, with clear silver gray eyes, long silky gray hair, and very long fingers. She wore a filmy white gown that seemed to float in the air around her.

"Who are you?" Rosette cried.

"I am the fairy Arachne, patroness of weavers," the lady said. "My servants, the spiders, have heard your distress and summoned me to help you. I can save you from Baron Wrathchild."

"Oh, tell me how!"

The fairy gave Rosette a skein of red silk that had an unusual iridescent shimmer. "Don't go to his castle tomorrow. Instead, sit at your loom and weave a picture of a man dressed like the baron, falling from his horse into a ditch, with his leg bent at an unnatural angle. Weave this red thread into the figure."

Rosette did as Arachne instructed her. At the same time that she was weaving her picture, Baron Wrathchild's horse happened to stumble and threw him into a ditch, where he suffered a broken leg.

For some months thereafter, the baron was laid up, waiting for his leg to mend, cursing and berating his doctors and attendants, making life burdensome for all around him. Rosette hoped that he had forgotten her. Unfortunately, when he had recovered and could ride again, the baron turned up at her door, demanding to know why she had not presented herself according to his order.

"Come tomorrow without fail," he told her. "I'll give you a new satin gown. That should be incentive enough for any peasant."

He rode away, leaving Rosette and her mother again in tears.

During the night, the fairy Arachne reappeared at Rosette's bedside.

"Help me, dear fairy," Rosette cried. "The baron is determined to have me."

"Don't be afraid," said Arachne, giving her another skein of red silk. "Instead of following his order, sit at your loom tomorrow and weave a picture of a nobleman in bed, pale with sickness, and doctors hovering about. Weave this red thread into the figure."

The next day, while Rosette was weaving, Baron Wrathchild suddenly fell sick with a disease that none of his doctors could identify. He became too weak to rise from his bed, almost too weak to eat or drink. Most of his attendants secretly hoped that he would die. His wife certainly hoped so.

He didn't die, however. After some months had passed, he slowly re-covered and regained his strength. By the time spring came again to the world, he was up and around.

Rosette and Rambow, assuming the baron would not remember his de-mand for Rosette, were planning their wedding, which was to take place in the greenwood and be attended by all the village swains. The couple wan-dered happily together over the meadow, hand in hand, as Rambow tended his sheep. Rosette had told him what had come of her encounters with the baron. "Kindness to spiders certainly pays off," Rambow had commented. "Who'd have thought it?"

Meanwhile, a tapestry dealer visited Rosette's cottage and saw the two pictures she had woven with the magic thread.

"These are the most magnificent things she's ever done," he said to Rosette's mother. "I'll give you five gold sovereigns apiece for them."

The poor widow was stunned by such a munificent offer. It was enough to buy her bread and beer for several years. She accepted at once. The dealer wrapped up Rosette's pictures, greatly pleased, sure that they would fetch at least fifty gold sovereigns apiece.

Actually, he sold them a few days later for sixty-five gold sovereigns apiece, to none other than the Baroness Wrathchild.

The pictures were hung in the baroness's drawing room and soon caught the eye of the baron. Looking closely at them, he recognized un-canny likenesses to himself, the trappings of his horse, the hangings of his bed, and other details associated with his recent misfortunes.

He stormed into his wife's bedroom and dragged her out of bed, shout-ing, "Where did you get those tapestries?"

When she told him, he went off at once to the dealer and learned that the weaver was Rosette. Wrathchild immediately summoned the inquisi-tors and told them that Rosette was a witch who had cast two spells on him. The first spell made him break his leg, the second made him sick. To prove it, he showed the pictures.

The inquisitors arrested Rosette and tied her to the ducking stool to subject her to trial by water. The theory of ducking-stool justice was simple enough for anyone to understand. If the defendant drowned when held under the water, she was proved innocent. If she didn't drown, she was proved a witch and must be executed. Either way, the inquisitors won and earned a hefty proportion of her worldly goods.

They ducked Rosette in the village pond, while Rambow and her mother stood with the crowd, looking on and wringing their hands. Rosette was held under water for a very long time. Everyone was sure that she must have drowned. But dozens and dozens of water spiders gathered around her, each hauling its little silken bell filled with air. They covered her nostrils with silk and gave her the air to breathe.

When she was drawn up and found to be still alive, the inquisitors convicted her of witchcraft and sentenced her to be executed the next day. The baron instructed the inquisitors to imprison her overnight in the tower room of his castle. He still craved her, and intended to ravish her during the night as she awaited her death.

Poor Rambow was devastated. He helped Rosette's weeping mother home to her cottage, then went and sat alone in the meadow where he had so recently walked with his sweetheart. As he dabbed at his tears, thinking of one desperate plan after another, he was startled to see a tall lady standing beside him, having appeared without making a sound. "Who are you?" he cried.

"I am the fairy Arachne, patroness of weavers. I will tell you how to save Rosette."

"How, how?"

"Wait in the bushes at the foot of the baron's tower after midnight, with traveling provisions and two horses. Be sure you're not seen by anyone. Rosette will escape from the tower, and you will ride away together. Go to the eastern country, and don't return. You will meet a good destiny."

Rambow trusted the fairy and hastened to make his preparations. He informed Rosette's mother but told no one else of his plan.

As dusk fell, anyone who might have been looking would have seen something very curious on the baron's tower. A strange, dim, pulsating column was forming, from the ground all the way up the wall to the single window in the high turret. An observer at closer range might have realized (just before darkness obscured it) that the pulsating column was formed of thousands of spiders climbing the wall together. They were making something, but the mat of little legs and bodies was so thick that their work could not be seen.

In the turret room, Rosette sat drooping on a wooden bench, feeling desolate and hopeless. The night drew on. She supposed it to be the last night of her life. She was regretting all the years she would never have, the love she would never feel, the children she would never bear, the works of art she would never weave.

She was roused from these sad reveries by the sound of a key turning in the lock. The door opened, and there stood Baron Wrathchild, a leather whip in his hand. A guard locked the door behind him.

"So, weaver, we meet again," he sneered. "This time you'll obey me, I think. I've come to take my own revenge for your witchcraft, before the holy men take theirs. You have no thread to weave me another catastrophe. Tonight the catastrophe will be yours."

She jumped up from the bench and cowered against the wall. He advanced on her, struck her once with the whip, and threw her down on the floor. As he was bending down to tear off her skirt, her terrified eyes looked past him at the window. There she saw the face of the fairy Arachne, scowling like a thundercloud.

The fairy seemed to shrink and darken, folding herself up on the windowsill. She turned into a huge black spider wearing a blood-red hourglass sign on its round belly. The spider darted across the floor and up Baron Wrathchild's back to his bare neck, where it sank its fangs into his flesh.

The baron screamed, fell down, and tore at the spider, which adroitly eluded his clawing fingers and scrambled over his writhing body to Rosette's side. "He is a dead man," said the spider's tiny voice in Rosette's ear. "Go to the window now and climb down. Your lover awaits."

Rosette hurried to the window and found a silken ladder firmly attached to the windowsill, reaching all the way to the ground. Being made of spider silk, it was light but very strong. She climbed down safely. When she reached the ground, Rambow clasped her in his arms. They mounted the horses he had brought and rode away.

In the morning, when Baron Wrathchild was found dead in the tower, the baroness and her ladies-in-waiting held a little private celebration in her drawing room. They decorated Rosette's two tapestries with garlands of flowers and drank a few toasts with the baron's best wine. Afterward the baroness arranged marriages for most of her ladies-in-waiting, bidding farewell to those who wished to leave and assigning better quarters to those who wished to stay with her.

Having inherited all her husband's estates, the baroness proved to be a wise and kind administrator. She lowered the taxes, encouraged thrifty management of the farms, treated the peasants fairly, and earned the respect of all. Though she had many suitors, she declined to remarry, remarking that one visit to hell in a lifetime was more than sufficient. She lived long and died at a good old age, well mourned by the whole country.

Rosette and Rambow settled in another country far to the east and made a good living for themselves by raising sheep, spinning, and weaving. Rosette's mother went to live with them. In time their marriage was blessed with children, the eldest of whom was a girl with clear silver-gray eyes, named Arachne. It is usually agreed that they lived happily ever after. Some say Rosette never died but at the end of her life was transformed into a spider. To this day, every garden spider wears rosettes on its body.

FOURTEEN

THE SEA WITCH

Imperfect sightings of manatees or dolphins seem to have figured largely in the creation of mermaid legends, but there were also very ancient precedents for that perennial favorite, the story of a young man taken by a sea fairy or a sea witch. Since antiquity a recurrent fantasy of sailors has been the love affair with a sea nymph or with the piscine Goddess herself. She was classical Aphrodite with her fish tail and pearl necklace; Themis or Eurynome, the all-embracing ocean womb; the Sea Goddess of the Romans, Mater Cara (Mother Carey); or Tiamat of Babylon, representing the primal waters from which all life arose in the beginning. Drowning at sea was sometimes romanticized in sailors' lore as a retreat into the eternally loving arms of an immortal sea fairy, an angel of the abyss. Men who spent much of their time at sea—an essentially hostile environment for humans—inevitably developed wonder tales to humanize and even sexualize the intimidating forces around them.

A pair of dolphins frisked gaily around each other . . .

*O*nce upon a time there was a poor young man named Devi, who lived alone in a ramshackle cottage by the sea. Though a handsome enough fellow, he had a withered arm and a lame leg and couldn't support himself at any local trade, which required heavy physical labor. He eked out a living by picking up seashells, which he polished and made into jewelry, or by solitary fishing, crabbing, and clamming to help supply the local innkeeper. He never knew who his parents were; he had been a foundling, given the generic name of Jones at the orphanage in which he grew up.

When he felt lonely or downhearted in his isolated cottage, he would cheer himself up by limping into town and joining the company at the inn. The local fishermen accepted him, in a condescending sort of way, and let him sit at their table. They would tease him, pretending that the innkeeper's pretty daughter Beersheba was flirting with him.

In reality, Beersheba flirted with every man in the room except Devi. When a customer jocularly paired her with the cripple, she would wrinkle her nose and say, "Do you think I can't do better than that poor excuse for a man? Such a wretched creature would be of no use to me!" She would toss her head and move on, never speaking so much as a word to Devi himself.

Devi good-naturedly endured the teasing. He had grown up expecting it, all his life. None of the local girls would have anything to do with him. Sometimes he yearned for a straight, strong body that would attract the right kind of feminine attention. But he knew this was a hopeless dream. Crippled as he was, he looked forward to nothing but growing older and lonelier until he became a demented old hermit who talked to the wind and listened to the voices of the ocean.

One day there was a fierce storm that whipped up the surf and made very high tides. Devi knew this weather would bring many shells onto the beach and went out to gather them. As he was limping along, dragging his sack, he saw a man-sized object thrashing about on the sand. He hurried up to it and found a dolphin that had been beached by the storm, struggling to get back to the water.

Devi was fond of dolphins. He often admired their agility as he watched them playing beyond the breakers. They seemed to him the very spirits of the waves, full of the joy of living. To see this poor creature trapped, out of its element, touched his heart.

He whistled softly to the dolphin, thinking that this might sound a little like its own language. It ceased thrashing. He reached out and gently stroked the dolphin's head, and the frightened creature seemed to relax.

"Don't worry, I'll help you," Devi said. The dolphin lay still. Devi took the rope from his sack and passed it around the dolphin's body, behind the flippers. Slowly, painfully, he dragged its dead weight over the sand toward the water. The dolphin made high-pitched noises, and Devi whistled to it in reply, hoping that it might find the sound reassuring.

When he got the dolphin into two feet of water, he took off the rope and steered it with his hands. The dolphin began to swim on its own. Suddenly it leaped from the surf, circled around Devi's body several times in what seemed an expression of gratitude, then took off out to sea. A little sadly, Devi watched it jumping the waves, leaving him behind. For a few moments he had felt that he had found a friend.

The next evening, at dusk, he was walking the same beach when he saw a lone dolphin frolicking close inshore. "Could this be *my* dolphin, about to beach itself again?" he asked himself. He stopped to watch. It held its position until gathering darkness obscured his view. As Devi was turning away, he heard a whistle that sounded human. He looked back. There was a naked woman walking toward him out of the surf.

She was beautiful, with a pale, sleek body and long bluish gray hair streaming down her back. As Devi stood rooted with astonishment, she walked straight up to him and took his hand. Her skin was warm and damp, like the skin of the dolphin.

"I am a sea witch," she said. "You may have heard of us. During certain seasons I can live as a sea creature by day and as a human by night. I've come to thank you for saving my life."

Devi was flustered. He could think of nothing to do but take off his shirt and put it around her to conceal her nakedness, which both attracted and embarrassed him. He told himself that she might be cold.

She accepted this and took him firmly by the elbow. "Let us go," she said.

"Go where?"

"To your home, of course."

Devi led her along the beach to his cottage, thinking that this must surely be a dream. Once indoors, the sea witch threw off the shirt and took him in her arms. She taught him to make love to her and stayed with him all night. Devi was so happy that the hours seemed to pass like minutes.

At the first light of dawn, the sea witch kissed him and left, promising to return the next night. She walked out of the cottage, across the beach, and into the sea. Devi watched with his heart pounding. He saw her dive under a wave and disappear. A few moments later, he saw a dolphin leaping away beyond the breakers.

Devi passed the day in a haze of delight, hardly able to wait for sunset. At nightfall, the sea witch came to him again, and they spent the night in lovemaking and intimate talk. Devi could hardly believe his good fortune. He was head over heels in love and thought himself the happiest man on earth.

The sea witch told him that she would continue to visit him every night through one cycle of the moon. After that, she would have to return to the sea and eventually migrate with other dolphins to a distant ocean. By the end of the lunar cycle, she had told him many things about life in the deep: the wonders of the submarine caves, the treasures of sunken ships, the social customs of the great whales and the dolphins. "Many dolphins believe that humans are degenerate dolphins," she said. "They think the humans left the sea thousands of years ago and lost the use of their swimming muscles, so they can only stump along on land with two legs and swim even more awkwardly than a newborn calf. Some dolphins have seen humans do terrible things to one another. They think this comes of their having forgotten the rules of right behavior, which the sea mothers teach."

"It's true that some humans do terrible things," Devi admitted. "But not all do. Some have kind hearts."

"Yes, like you, my love," she said. "I've noticed that you move even more awkwardly than most humans. Why is that?"

"I'm crippled."

"Why? Were you shark-bitten?"

"No. I was crippled from birth. I don't know what it's like to move easily. That's one reason why I like to watch the dolphins. They are so graceful and seem to take such joy in moving."

"Would you like to be able to swim like a dolphin?"

"Oh, yes."

"Since the time has come for us to part, I'll tell you that there is a charm for that—but it's a fearsome one."

"I'd do anything to live like a dolphin and stay with you."

The sea witch stroked his cheek sadly and took a deep breath. "First, you must eat nothing but fish for three weeks. Second, you must swim a mile every day. Third, you must give up the use of your hands. At the exact moment when the setting sun touches the horizon, you must have someone chop off both your arms at the elbows and throw you into the sea."

"Wouldn't I bleed to death?"

"Not if the charm has been properly prepared."

"Could I live like you? Would we be together?"

"Forever, my love."

"I'll do it," Devi declared. "I don't care how painful it is. Life without you would be even more painful. I can't bear to think that I'll never see you again."

"But you need an assistant—a strong person with an ax."

"I'll find someone."

When the sea witch left him in the morning, she kissed him with special tenderness. "I, too, would like us to be together in the sea," she said. "You have no idea how pleasant it is, making love in green depths while you are bathed and cushioned by the water. Good-bye for now. I hope we'll meet again when the charm is completed."

Devi determined that he would endure the charm at all costs. He went to the inn, hoping to find someone to help him. The fishermen were surprised to see him.

"Where have you been, Devi?" they asked. "We haven't seen you around here for weeks. We thought maybe you and your shack washed away in the storm."

Devi told them the whole story of his affair with the sea witch, while they looked at one another in wonder. The eldest fisherman slowly shook his head and touched his temple, signifying that Devi's lonely life had finally deranged him. When Devi described the charm and asked for someone to volunteer assistance, they were horrified.

"In other words, you want one of us to murder you," the eldest said. "That's what it would be: murder. You'd bleed to death in the sea, or the sharks would finish you off even quicker. You're totally mad, you know. Even if you want to die in some particularly awful way, Devi, you'll get none of us to do it."

Then up spoke Beersheba, who had been listening to every word. "I think it's rather sweet," she said, "to die for love. I don't know who his sea witch is, but when a man loves enough to throw his life away, he loves indeed."

"Silly girl, don't you understand?" the eldest fisherman said. "She's only his fantasy."

"She is not!" Devi cried hotly. "She's as real as you are, and lovelier than any woman I ever saw. If I die of her charm, so be it. I'd rather die than live without her."

"See, he wants to die for love," Beersheba said. "I think that's beautiful. So romantic." She gave a dreamy sigh.

"Fool," snapped the eldest fisherman. "He won't find himself a man-killer here. We only kill fish."

"I'll do it," said Beersheba.

Devi turned toward her, incredulous. "You aren't strong enough," he said.

"I am so. All day I heave kegs of beer and chop the heads off fish. My hatchet is sharp as a razor and heavy enough to go through bone."

"Do you mean it? " Devi asked. "Can I trust you?"

"Yes, I mean it."

The fishermen fidgeted uneasily at this sinister pact made before their eyes. They drank little, joked less, sang not at all, and went home early.

During the next three weeks, while Devi was sticking to his fish diet and daily swims, each man in turn tried to talk Beersheba out of her promise. To each one she said, "No, I've given my word and I won't break it. I think perhaps the cripple is more of a man than any of you, after all."

When the fatal day arrived, the fishermen gathered on a hillside overlooking the dock where Devi proposed to end his earthly life. They wanted to watch, and at the same time they didn't want to watch; so they compromised by watching from a distance. They saw Devi and Beersheba walk out to the end of the dock, she carrying a bucket and her hatchet. Devi lay down on his back and stretched out his arms to either side.

"It's a gruesome business, this," the eldest fisherman said. "We ought to be stopping it, instead of looking on." But no one moved.

"Look," said another, pointing out to sea. "There's a dolphin. Seems like it's alone. That's unusual."

There was indeed a lone dolphin swimming toward the shore. As it approached, the setting sun touched the horizon. Beersheba's hatchet rose and fell. The fishermen heard a shriek. The boards of the dock blossomed with red. Seconds later it happened again. Then Beersheba pushed Devi off the end of the dock. His body splashed down only a short distance from the swimming dolphin.

For a few moments, all was perfectly still. Then there were two more splashes. Beersheba drew up several bucketfuls of water to wash down the dock.

The eldest fisherman shaded his eyes and looked farther out across the water. "Now there are two dolphins," he said in a hushed tone.

All the fishermen looked. Sure enough, a pair of dolphins frisked gaily around each other, where there had been only one before.

None of them ever mentioned the incident again. Devi was gone. His cottage disintegrated in the winter storms. Local legend hinted that he had been taken away by the sea witch. Sometimes it was suggested that he may have lived happily ever after.

In later years, whenever a boat sank and a man was drowned, the fishermen would say that he had gone to visit Devi Jones.

FIFTEEN

PRINCE GIMME AND THE FAIRY OF THE FOREST

Some traditional fairy tales are morality dramas, designed to teach children that virtuous behavior earns rewards and vices will be punished. Such stories may depict naughtiness transformed into goodness by some physical trial, with a homily tagged on at the end to emphasize the point.

Prince Gimme is the protagonist of this morality play, representing the unfortunate consequences of hubris, greed, and frivolity. He is cured by female magic, with the mystic symbol of the Cauldron standing for spiritual transformation, and the Goddess's archetypal trinity shown in her ubiquitous white, red, and black. Hindus called these colors the sacred gunas of purity, passion, and darkness, sacred to the Goddess in her Virgin, Mother, and Crone forms as Maya, Durga, and Kali.* The feline familiars in this tale partake of the same color scheme. Fear of the familiars is part of the prince's trial, indicating that threats may be necessary to bring about sincere reformation.

---

*See Walker, Barbara G., *The Woman's Encyclopedia of Myths and Secrets* (San Francisco: Harper & Row, 1983), 358.

"Surely you are the Fairy of the Forest," he said.

*O*nce upon a time there was a little prince who was his parents' only child, born after years of waiting. Nothing that he wanted was ever refused him, and thus he grew up haughty and spoiled. He had only to say "Gimme," and the object of his wish was instantly given by his indulgent parents, courtiers, or servants. Consequently he said "Gimme" so often that it became his nickname. His real name was Percival George Oliver Aloysius Ferdinand Alexander von Hardtstrucken-Wittenheim.

Because Prince Gimme was so greedy and asked for so much, his life was a continual round of banquets, concerts, theatricals, carnivals, games, dances, royal hunts, ingenious toys, and other frivolous entertainments. He liked to play, but he showed little interest in affairs of state. His parents began to fear that his future reign would deplete the resources of the kingdom without strengthening the government.

When Prince Gimme came of age, his elderly mother and father began to talk of arranging a marriage for him. Dozens of eligible princesses sent their portraits for his approval, but the prince only glanced at each one, declaring "She's not beautiful enough."

The king and queen feared that their only son would never marry and their line of succession would end with their deaths. The king tried to reason with Gimme, pointing out that intelligence and kindness are more desirable qualities than beauty. The queen tried to appeal to the sense of filial duty, insisting that she could never die in peace unless she had grandchildren growing up around her. But Prince Gimme listened only to his courtiers, who all agreed that no human woman could ever equal the legendary beauty of the Fairy of the Forest. The prince declared that he would have her and no other as his bride.

This was one request that his parents had no power to grant. They were in despair. The prince, denied something for the first time in his life, grew ever more obsessive in his determination to wed the Fairy of the Forest. He sent criers throughout the kingdom, promising great rewards to anyone who could show him the way to her abode. No one responded except a little-known witch woman who sent a message, saying that she would help the prince if he would come to her cottage on the border of the forest.

Prince Gimme immediately ordered up a magnificent entourage of knights, horses, courtiers, and carriages, and set off for the witch's house with much drum-beating and horn-blowing. Lest he should become bored on the long road, he arranged for tumblers, clowns, and horseback acrobats to perform outside his carriage windows; silk-clad ladies to stroke him and feed him grapes; and musicians and singers to fill his ears and drown out the rough noises of travel.

When they arrived at the witch's house, they set up colorful tents and spread out a lavish picnic of rich food and wines. A footman went up to the witch's door and knocked, to invite her to join the prince at his feast.

The company waited apprehensively for the witch to open her door, expecting a fearsome hag with the evil eye. They heaved a collective sigh of relief when the witch proved to be no such hideous ogress but a slender young woman who was even quite pretty. She was dressed as a peasant, and a little black cat leaned against her leg.

"What is all this hubbub?" the witch demanded.

Glittering in his cloth-of-gold uniform, Prince Gimme stepped forward and bowed graciously. "I am the prince, here in person to honor you with my presence and to find out the way to the Fairy of the Forest, my intended bride. I have brought chests of jewels for your payment. Mistress Witch, do sit down and have a glass of wine with me."

The young witch laughed. "I don't want your chests of jewels or your wine," she said. "And I don't want all those fancy fritillaries cluttering up my yard and trampling my herb garden. Get rid of them at once, Prince, and then perhaps we'll talk, just the two of us alone."

"Unthinkable!" cried the captain of the guard. "The prince can't be left alone outside of the palace. Royal persons never go anywhere without attendants."

"Suit yourself," said the witch. "If the prince won't visit me alone, he won't visit me at all." She went back into her house and shut the door.

Prince Gimme would not have his will thwarted by a matter of precedent. Shoving aside the captain of the guard, he ordered the whole entourage to pack everything up and go away, leaving nothing behind except the prince's white charger for him to ride home on. The courtiers obeyed, though they feared the king's wrath when they returned without Gimme.

After they were gone, the prince went up to the witch's door and knocked on it again with his own royal knuckles. The witch looked out and saw nothing but Gimme and a white horse with gilded hooves, wearing a golden saddle, a gem-studded bridle, and ropes of pearls in its mane and tail.

"Put that creature in my stable, next to the mule," she ordered. "Be sure to give him plenty of water, fresh hay, and a measure of oats. And take off that silly jewelry tack."

Never having been ordered around by anyone before, the prince found it momentarily amusing. He obediently led his horse to the stable. He took a long time to figure out how to remove the saddle and bridle, how to pitch the hay, and how to fill the water trough from the well, but eventually he did it.

Upon his return, the witch removed his crown and sword, strapped a heavily packed knapsack to his back, and shouldered a traveling bag of her own. Then she walked into the forest, beckoning Gimme to follow her.

"Where are we going?" Gimme asked.

"To the Fairy's sacred grove," said the witch. "It's a long way. Your shoes don't look any too sturdy, but I suppose you can make it."

Prince Gimme soon discovered that his jeweled dancing slippers were not sturdy enough for tramping over rough ground. They soon began to rub and pinch, creating oozing blisters on his feet. Some of their jewels fell off in the mud. Gimme protested at the witch's pace and demanded a rest, but she paid no attention. She slogged steadily onward, apparently tireless. He tried dropping behind to ease his sore feet for a few moments, but then he had to run to catch up with her before she passed out of his sight. After several hours of walking, he was hobbling painfully, and the pack straps seemed to be cutting his shoulders to pieces. Still, the witch tramped on. He followed, gritting his teeth.

It was nearly dusk when they reached the sacred grove. There the witch told Prince Gimme to collect dry wood for a fire, while she spread out her paraphernalia and some food for a frugal supper. The grove was large, floored by soft grass and walled by tall whispering pines. In the center an ancient standing stone presided over a broad altar table and a stone-lined fire pit, where the witch soon had a merry fire going. The prince sank down exhausted and drank deeply from the flask that she handed him.

After they had eaten, she made a dense, sweet smoke by casting some herbs on the fire. She went around the periphery of the grove, laying charms. She placed several mysterious objects on the altar table, speaking words in a language that Gimme had never heard before. She gave him something to drink in a curiously wrought copper goblet. Then she pricked his arm with what he thought was a very sharp thorn. His consciousness began to fade.

Deep within his mind, he was seized by a sudden panic. He realized that he was being drugged and wondered if the whole elaborate charade was nothing more than a method of kidnap and murder. Suddenly he saw the foolishness of having isolated himself in the midst of the great forest with this strange woman.

But it was too late. Already he was unable to move or speak. Gently, slowly, his mind spiraled down into utter darkness.

He didn't expect to awaken, but he did. When he opened his eyes, the grove was empty. The fire was out. The witch was nowhere to be seen. The first silver beams of dawn were sifting down through the trees. Prince Gimme arose stiffly and looked around.

There was a path he hadn't noticed before, prettily bordered with harebells, leading away to a clearer space among the trees. He followed the path and soon came to a beautiful chapel of snow-white marble roofed with silver, flashing in the early sunlight like a crystal.

"The witch didn't deceive me after all," Gimme said to himself. "Surely this is the abode of the Fairy of the Forest." He entered the chapel.

Inside, everything was white, illuminated by the early sunlight slanting down from high windows of translucent mother-of-pearl. On a silver throne in the center of the hall sat an extraordinarily beautiful maiden in a white satin gown, wearing a diamond crown. Her hair was cream white, her eyes so pale a blue as to seem nearly white also. A white leopard, wearing a diamond collar, crouched beside her.

Greedy and spoiled though he was, Prince Gimme knew his manners. He knelt graciously before the maiden and raised his clasped hands. "Surely you are the Fairy of the Forest," he said. "I salute your loveliness

BARBARA G. WALKER   135

and humbly beg leave to present myself as your suitor, though I may be un-worthy to touch the hem of your garment." He extended a hand. The leop-ard growled, and Gimme snatched his hand back rather hastily.

"I don't know whether you are unworthy or not," said the maiden, "but you are mistaken. I am not the Fairy of the Forest. I am the princess of purity."

"Forgive me," said Gimme. "I naturally thought no human lady could be as beautiful as yourself. Can you tell me where to find the Fairy of the Forest?"

"You might find her if you follow the track of my beast. Are you brave enough for that?"

"I will do anything you bid me to do, fair princess."

"Then follow," she said. A silvery mist arose around her throne and concealed her. The leopard leaped up and set off through the pillars of the chapel, out to the woods, and along a smaller path leading deeper into the forest. Prince Gimme followed, hurrying on his sore feet to keep the ani-mal in view. Despite his best efforts, the white leopard's easy lope soon outdistanced him, but he kept to the path.

About midday he came upon another clearing. In the center stood a castle of red sandstone, with blood-red banners floating from its battle-ments and a tall gate of carved copper studded with garnets. Gimme wearily approached the gate and rang its copper bell. The portals slowly and soundlessly opened before him.

He saw no one in the courtyard, so he passed on to the great hall be-fore him. There he found a tall, majestic woman seated by the fire on a throne of bright red marble, wearing a red velvet robe and a crown of ru-bies. Her hair, too, was red—not carroty orange but a deep, rich ma-hogany red. Beside her lay an enormous red-maned lion.

"Surely," Gimme said to himself, "this is the Fairy of the Forest." He bowed low before her, politely introduced himself, and explained his mis-sion. "Great lady," he said, "please be indulgent toward your most faithful and adoring suitor. My heart tells me that you must be the Fairy of the Forest."

The woman parted her red lips and smiled. "Your heart is mistaken," she told him. "I am not the Fairy of the Forest. I am the mater gloriosa."

"Forgive me," said Gimme. "I naturally thought no human lady could be as gloriously beautiful as yourself. Can you tell me where to find the Fairy of the Forest?"

"You might find her if you will follow the track of my beast," said the lady. "Are you brave enough to do that?"

"I will do anything you bid me to do, glorious queen."

"Then follow," she said. The fire suddenly roared up and spread a curtain of flame across the hall. Though Prince Gimme felt no heat, it seemed that the entire castle was enveloped by flames in a single moment. The whole illusion disappeared, leaving him in the clearing face-to-face with a huge, snarling lion. Gimme trembled but stood his ground, futilely wishing that he still had his sword.

After lashing its tail and showing its teeth at him in a most intimidating manner, the lion turned haughtily away and stalked off, as if to say Prince Gimme was not worth any more of its time. It paced deliberately into a very small path leading deeper into the forest, sliding smoothly and stealthily through the undergrowth, occasionally looking back at him with a brief growl.

Gimme followed, taking care to keep a respectful distance away from the creature. He was feeling much less sure of himself, lost and worried by forces beyond his control, such as threatening lions and spooky disappearing castles.

This path was narrower and darker than the others. The tree canopy overhead was so dense as to shut out most of the daylight. The path was often choked by clawlike brambles studded with sharp thorns, or it fell into puddles of black, stagnant water. Gimme couldn't keep up with the lion, which vanished among the trees. It was all he could do to follow the path through thickets and marshy places. Soon his fine clothes were tattered and muddy. His jeweled slippers hurt his feet so much that he threw them away and proceeded on dirty bare feet. He was ragged, smudged, and disheveled, a most unprepossessing sight.

Toward evening he came to another clearing that contained a rude domelike hovel built of black stones, overgrown with creepers and weeds. It had a dark iron door, like a prison cell. As Gimme approached, the door opened with a rusty creak. A figure emerged from the dark, ill-smelling interior. It was a bent, withered old woman in fluttering black rags, her skin as dark and wrinkled as an ancient mummy's, and seemingly smeared with soot. Instead of the white hair that might be expected on so old a person, her head was covered by frightful night-black coils that seemed to writhe with a life of their own, like snakes. Beside her, a black panther glowered at him with malevolent amber eyes.

Suppressing a shudder, Prince Gimme drew himself up and saluted the crone respectfully. "Excuse me, madam," he said, "I am searching for the dwelling of the Fairy of the Forest. Can you show me the way?"

"It is here," the old woman croaked.

"I beg your pardon?"

"It is here," she repeated. "I am the Fairy of the Forest."

The hag is wandering in her wits, Gimme thought. I must be diplomatic in extracting information from her. He forced a smile and said, "I have been told that the Fairy of the Forest is the most beautiful creature in all the country. In your wisdom perhaps you can explain this tale to me."

"You have eyes but do not see," said the crone. "You foolishly enter the fairy land, which is a land of illusion, and you have no understanding of illusions. You are stupid."

Suddenly she thrust a filthy claw toward him. The black panther sprang upon him with a rattling snarl, knocked him down, and crouched on his body. He was pinned to the ground by its heavy talon-studded paws on his chest. Its vicious yellow fangs slavered, an inch from his throat.

Prince Gimme lay perfectly still and stared into the feline face of death.

"In order to understand illusions," said the woman, "you must pass through the Cauldron and come forth reborn. "Are you willing to give up your pride of life to find the fairy you seek? Are you brave enough for that?"

Gimme didn't know what she meant, but he was unshakeably convinced of his own sincerity. He nodded.

"Death is the final understanding," said the crone. "No man knows his muse until he knows her as his destroyer. Come with me."

The panther released him and crouched growling beside him as he arose cautiously. The crone beckoned. He followed her into the black stone hut, the panther following closely. When his eyes adapted to the darkness, he saw in the center of the hut an immense black iron Cauldron sitting on a bed of charcoal. The vessel was as high as his waist and large enough to accommodate a whole side of beef.

"Climb in," the crone ordered him.

"What, into the Cauldron?" Gimme cried. "You must be joking."

"Do you want to learn the illusions of the fairy realm, or do you want to die right here? The cat is ready and able to rip out your throat."

"Listen here, you," cried Gimme, finally exasperated. "I've had it with all these illusions. I've been robbed of my servants, forced to do the work of stable hands and woodcutters, drugged and diddled and dagged and dragged through a damnable wilderness on sore feet, threatened by lions and panthers, and now I find the object of my gallant quest is not the beautiful fairy princess I expected but a dirty old woman who wants to boil me alive. Enough! I don't care if I never marry anybody. I just want to go home, take a bath, have a decent dinner, and forget the whole thing. Call off your cat and let me out of here."

The crone laughed. "Well, you're showing a little spirit at last," she said. "But what you demand isn't possible. Among all the other humbling lessons you have to learn is the lesson of responsibility. Once you've set events in motion, you must see them through and accept the consequences. Your greed brought you here. Now you must support your own decisions. That's an essential quality of rulership. No prince worthy of the title backs away from what he has brought on himself. A prince must be brave."

"What, brave enough to commit suicide? That's not brave. That's stupid."

"Stupid is a man who would prefer being mauled by large feline claws to being bathed in magic and shown the true fairy vision. My pet thinks so too."

At this, the panther stretched a forepaw toward the prince and unsheathed its thick, shiny claws, which were several inches long, wickedly curved, and sharp as needles. The animal's face seemed to wear a sweet anticipatory smile. Its pink tongue gently licked its fangs. "Hm, hm," it said, purring.

Prince Gimme's heart sank into his feet.

"All your life you've been selfish," the woman said severely. "Before you can be a king, you have to learn to take responsibility for others and also to listen to others. Now, dear prince, listen to what I tell you. If you don't get into that Cauldron right this minute, the cat is going to spring up at your face, bury its claws in both sides of your head, wrestle you down to

the ground, and shred you from top to bottom in long, thin strips. Take
your choice."

"Since you put it like that," said Gimme, "I will do what you bid me to
do." He threw one leg over the side of the Cauldron. It was filled with a
warm liquid that tingled his skin rather pleasantly. He climbed all the way
in and immersed himself to the neck.

Suddenly the liquid seemed to harden like glue and to suck him under
like quicksand. At the same time, it grew unbearably hot. Prince Gimme
tried to scream, but his mouth was filled with choking fluid. He sank down
into the Cauldron, thinking in despair that this was a lonely, pointless way
for the great prince of Hardtstrucken-Wittenheim to die.

His consciousness continued, however, into strange, terrifying dreams.
First, he thought all the flesh was boiled off his bones, reducing him to a
skeleton. He stood up in his naked bones and walked into a vast river of
blood. He floated to the farther shore, which was lined with beehive-
shaped tombs. Living corpses in various states of putrefaction walked,
stood, or sat among the tombs. Drifting through the air like a wind-blown
leaf, he was carried past them.

He came to a broad meadow and fell on the ground. Soil began to
cover his bare bones. It turned gradually into flesh, until he felt muscles
once more able to move his limbs. He stood up and found himself a whole
man again, though he was as naked as the day he was born.

He was standing up in the black iron Cauldron in the dark hut. The
crone and her black panther stood before him.

"I'm not dead, then," Gimme exclaimed in surprise.

"Of course you're not dead, you idiot," said the crone. "You are no
more dead than I am the ancient dark one, may her name be spoken with
awe. But you are changed. You know a little more about the meanings of
importance and unimportance, reality and illusion. To know the Fairy of
the Forest as your destroyer is to know nature's complete cycle. See here."

The crone removed her snaky-haired mask, threw off her black rags,
and stood revealed as the young witch woman, accompanied by her little
black cat. The Cauldron, the hut, and the weed-choked clearing disappeared. Gimme realized that he was standing at the altar table in the sacred
grove. The sun was just rising over the treetops.

"You!" he cried. "You are the Fairy of the Forest!"

"I told you so," she said.

"Then it was all a magical dream, an illusion dwelling only in drugs?"

"Not quite," said the fairy. "Illusion comes from yourself, not from magical potions alone. You've been changed in ways necessary to the fulfillment of your life. I could never marry the childlike popinjay that you were. He who occupies high rank should learn the lesson of humility. He who accepts the fact of death is most reverent toward life."

"Mistress Fairy, you are wise indeed," said Gimme, seizing her hand. "Marry me and be the guiding spirit of my reign."

The Fairy of the Forest accepted, and gave him a smock to wear. He led his charger from her stable while she saddled her mule, and together they rode to the palace. The king and queen loved the practical little fairy at once, and her black cat—a very wise animal—soon became the palace pet.

After the old king and queen died, the fairy became queen and guided her husband wisely and thriftily. His kingdom prospered. His nickname was changed from Gimme to Giver, and he lived happily ever after.

SIXTEEN

THE ORACLE

In the old parable of the blind men and the elephant, one who holds the tail says the beast is like a rope, one who touches the leg says it is like a tree, one who feels the trunk says it is like a snake, one who feels the ear says it is like a fan, and so on. The same parable applies aptly to men and their deities. Since there is no objective, external creature to be felt, each man projects his own notions onto the concept of the sacred. Thus men create God, and women create Goddess.

This story is about understanding, especially the interpersonal rapport obtainable among women who follow their own "star." The star often symbolizes the soul, as shown by our very language: It is the astral (meaning "starry") self. In the Major Arcana of the tarot deck, a naked Goddess called The Star bathes both earth and water in streams of enlightenment.

The oracular pilgrimage center in this story is based on old tales of the Delphic sybils, whose underground serpent shrine was founded by the Goddess's women long centuries before Apollo's patriarchal priests usurped the site in the name of their deity. Even so, the shrine continued to be administered and staffed by women, and dedicated to the muses, without whom Apollo had no real power.

Four pilgrims were on their way to the oracle . . .

Once upon a time there was a famous oracle, so ancient and holy that folks came on long pilgrimages from distant countries to visit it. The oracle was located in a large cave on a precipitous mountainside, overlooking a deep, wild valley where a rushing stream poured out of a cleft in the sacred mountain. It was claimed that the water of this stream had magical and medicinal properties, because of its origin in the mountain of the oracle. Some of the oracle's temple attendants filled little crystal vials with this water and sold them to ailing pilgrims. The water never cured anything, but it brought in a great deal of money, which helped to keep the temple and its personnel in comfortable affluence.

The road up the sacred mountain was dotted with inns for the pilgrims. The innkeepers also made a great deal of money, because their rooms were nearly always filled, all year round. On any given day at any one of these inns one might find pilgrims discussing the exact nature of the oracle. Even those who had already visited the holy cave and had seen the shrine with their own eyes disagreed about what they had seen. Every individual's story was different.

One day four pilgrims on their way to the oracle found themselves seated together in one of the inns, discussing oracular phenomena. They were a diverse assortment. One was a hulking giant of a man, half again as tall and twice as broad as the average, hardly able to squeeze himself into the inn's biggest chair. The second was a dwarf, not much higher than the giant's knee, requiring a built-up chair to see over the tabletop. The third was a handsome young prince, richly dressed, sporting a gold-hilted sword and a cloak of royal purple. The fourth was a gray-haired woman in a plain black robe, wearing no jewelry except an amulet on a silver chain around her neck.

The giant introduced himself as the leader of his king's guards, a professional warrior esteemed for the invincible reach and power of his sword arm. The dwarf introduced himself as his king's jester, beloved by the whole court for the originality of his antics. The prince introduced himself as his king's son, unfortunately not the heir to the throne because his father

143

had somehow neglected to schedule a wedding ceremony for his mother; nevertheless, he lived well at court and was generally thought as much a prince as the legitimate heir.

Having introduced themselves, the three men turned to the woman in black and paused expectantly. She said quietly, "I don't belong to any king, or to any man for that matter. I'm a witch. I come to the oracle to study the art of prophecy as it is practiced here."

The prince asked, "Then you believe that prophecy is an art, rather than a gift of the divine?"

"Of course," said the witch. "A true prophet reads the nature of his hearer better than he reads the future."

The dwarf said, "Surely you can't be suggesting that holy men and women learn and practice their revelations, just as I learn and practice jokes and gestures to make people laugh?"

"Yes, I'm suggesting that," she answered. "Most people have a great desire to believe. Even when the mundane sources of their miracle tales and psychic readings are plainly explained to them, they think it must be dissembling, to obscure the true magic."

"Do you want to destroy people's beliefs?" growled the giant. "If you were not a woman, I'd invite you to step outside and defend that suggestion. There must be magic and divine powers in the world, or we wouldn't want to go on living."

"I rest my case," said the witch.

The prince urged, "You yourself make use of predictions, spells, and charms. You practice magic every day."

"It's a living," the witch shrugged.

"Don't argue with her," counseled the dwarf. "This oracle is the greatest and holiest in the world. It will certainly show her, and all of us, the true vision of the divine. After all, we're here to learn, not to quarrel."

"All the same, witches should be taught not to have opinions," grumbled the giant.

"If you want to make the first opinion of the oracle," said the witch, "I suggest that you be the first of us to enter the Holy of Holies, as we must go one at a time. Such a strong warrior as yourself is best qualified to face any dangers that might threaten. You can come back at the end of the day and reveal the true nature of the oracle to the rest of us."

Failing to hear the irony in her tone, the giant immediately agreed that he was most qualified to face the unknown first. The others concurred. Early the next morning they went together to the forecourt of the temple, under a beetling cliff, to see him off. He waved to them cheerily as he followed a silent, white-robed, lamp-bearing attendant into the sacred cave.

He walked for a long time through black tunnels, without any illumination except his guide's lamp. Finally he saw a gleam of light ahead. He came to a spacious cavern, rich in translucent flowstone formations, all aglow with the warm light of lamps placed behind them. In the center of the floor stood a golden altar bearing a single crystal cup of dark-colored liquid. Beside the altar stood a beautiful lady in white. She lifted the cup and held it to his lips, keeping it there until he drank all the liquid. It was a peculiar sort of wine, with a bitter undertaste.

Then his guide took him through a long gallery with many pictures painted on the rock walls, seeming to dance and sway in the flickering light as he passed. Here and there were deep niches in which mysterious figures stood, clothed in glittering gems, apparently alive, making cryptic gestures. Strange odors wafted from burning censers along the way, making a haze in the dark air. The giant began to feel dizzy.

At last he was halted before a high doorway curtained with cloth of gold. The guide drew aside the curtain and motioned him through. He entered alone into the chamber of the oracle.

It was a high-ceilinged cavern carved from native rock, hung with rich tapestries. Torches burned in sconces around the walls. In the center stood a huge black marble throne, on which sat a giant of truly awesome dimensions, big as an elephant. His ponderous head seemed to reach the roof of the cavern. His limbs were like tree trunks, his hands the size of breadboxes.

The pilgrim giant fell on his knees and worshiped the oracle, feeling his own individuality dissolve in a torrent of reverence and wonder.

The oracle bent toward him and handed him a small bronze medallion, on which was carved a five-pointed star. The mighty lips opened, and the creature said: "Every man must follow his star. Every star must sink below the face of the earth. As in the beginning, so in the end. Be as wise as you can. That is what I have to say to you."

Then the oracular giant raised his chin very high, closed his eyes, and became still. The pilgrim felt himself dismissed. Clutching the medallion, he backed toward the door and rejoined his silent guide, who led him by a tortuous route out of the caverns. All the way his head was buzzing strangely. He felt that he had experienced something significant, that he had been told something deeply meaningful, but he had no idea what it was. He resolved to ponder the oracle's words later.

When the giant returned to his fellow pilgrims, he told them that the total experience was indescribable, but the oracle was definitely a giant man, like himself but much, much bigger.

The next morning, the dwarf entered the temple, waving to the others as he followed the silent guide. He also was led to the golden altar and given the mysterious drink. He also traversed the picture gallery with buzzing in his ears, and stopped at the cloth-of-gold curtain. He also entered the chamber of the oracle. But instead of the giant he expected to see, there was a miniature chair in the center of the cavern, occupied by the smallest of men, only as high as the dwarf's waist. This wee man was old, with silvery white hair, a long white beard, and a little wrinkled face like a dried apple.

While the dwarf knelt in awe of such perfection of smallness, the tiny man reached up and handed him a small bronze medallion on which was carved a five-pointed star. He said, in a piping voice: "Every man must follow his star. Every star must sink below the face of the earth. As in the beginning, so in the end. Be as wise as you can. That is what I have to say to you."

Then he closed his eyes and put his little hand before his face, palm out. Interpreting this as a dismissal, the dwarf backed toward the door and was led away, back to the daylight, feeling sure that he had been given a message of profound meaning, if only he could grasp what it was.

When the dwarf returned to his companions, he said the experience was awesome and unforgettable. But the oracle was no giant, after all. On the contrary, he was a dwarf, like himself but much, much smaller.

The next morning, the prince entered the temple, giving the others a jaunty salute as he disappeared in the wake of his guide. He too went to the golden altar and drank the strange wine. He too walked the picture gallery, feeling peculiar tingling sensations throughout his body and a certain muzziness in his head. He too went through the cloth-of-gold curtain. In the chamber of the oracle he saw neither a giant nor a dwarf but a normal-sized king in splendid robes, a crown of gold and jewels on his head, a diamond-studded scepter in his hand. He was seated on the most magnificent throne imaginable, with purple velvet cushions and rich carvings inlaid with precious stones. The prince bowed low, hardly daring to raise his eyes to such royal splendor.

The kingly personage reached out with a benevolent gesture and handed him a small bronze medallion on which was carved a five-pointed star. He spoke in mellow tones: "Every man must follow his star. Every star must sink below the face of the earth. As in the beginning, so in the end. Be as wise as you can. That is what I have to say to you."

Then he stood up and crossed his arms on his bemedaled chest, indicating that the interview was over. The prince humbly backed out of the chamber and was led back to the light of day, certain that a sacred king had given him an unparalleled key to enlightenment, if only he could divine its mysterious meaning. Ponder as he would, the meaning remained obscure.

When the prince rejoined the others, he said that he was in possession of a world-shaking secret. But the oracle was neither a giant nor a dwarf. He was the king of the whole earth, a noble gentleman like the prince himself, but much, much greater.

On the fourth day, it was the witch's turn. She left her companions in the temple forecourt and followed the guide through the black tunnels. When she approached the golden altar, the white-clad lady looked into her eyes and graciously bowed her head, saying, "Welcome, sister. Blessed be."

"Blessed be," the witch responded, taking the crystal cup in her hand. She drank the wine. She followed the guide through the picture gallery, looking at the pictures with understanding. She had seen their symbols before and knew their significance. She spoke to the mysterious figures in the niches and received their answers.

When she passed through the gold curtain into the chamber of the oracle, she stopped in her tracks for a moment, then slowly smiled at what she saw.

Facing her in the torchlight was a full-length mirror, with two women standing beside it: a young maiden on the left, a white-haired crone on the right. The maiden reached out her right hand to the witch, and the crone reached out her left. The witch took their two hands and stood joined with them to create a triangle, facing the mirror.

"So, it's the inner self that speaks, after all," the witch said. Both women nodded.

"Deep in the earth, we know where we have begun," said the maiden.

"Deep in the earth, we know where we will end," said the crone.

"I understand," said the witch. "The guiding star is the inner spirit."

From the crone's hand she received a small silver medallion on which was carved a five-pointed star. She kissed both women and left the chamber to follow her guide back to the open air.

When she sat with the three men in the inn that evening, she said nothing at all until the prince asked, "What of the oracle? What did you see?"

"I saw nothing that I do not see every day," answered the witch. "I understood nothing but what my very bones have known since my birth. I felt nothing but the blood in my veins, the clothes on my body, and the ground beneath my feet."

"How materialistic," sneered the giant. "Obviously you are a woman of worldly and limited perceptions."

"How ordinary," said the dwarf. "Have you no sense of the sacred, no capacity for awe, no reverence for the profound?"

"How plebeian," sniffed the prince. "Surely you must lack the advantage of a cultivated and refined taste."

The witch looked at them all and smiled. "How manly you all are," she said. "Do you think your experience here will affect your future lives to any significant degree?"

"Certainly," said the giant.

"Of course," said the dwarf.

"Without a doubt," said the prince.

They parted amicably enough and went their separate ways.

Finding themselves unable to apply the oracle's mysterious words to their daily lives, the three men soon forgot about their pilgrimage. They left the bronze medallions put away in odd places and ceased to remember them. They went on with their usual activities in their usual ways and sometimes described the process as following their star.

The witch, however, thought deeply and long. She meditated on the silver medallion with its five-pointed star like the five projections of the human body. She learned more about herself, and in so doing learned more about others. She became a highly successful witch, consulted by many affluent people. So she prospered and lived happily ever after.

SEVENTEEN

LILY AND ROSE

White and red sisters are well known in fairy tales, such as the story of Snow White and Rose Red. Here the sisters are transformed into husband and wife, for the benefit of a matricentric or female-governed nation.

The villain whose heart or soul resides outside of his body is also a convention of fairy tales, based on that most primitive of human beliefs, that a person may be hurt through magical aggression against a detached body part, such as hair, spittle, blood, fingernail clippings, and so forth. Many primitive cultures held that the placenta or umbilical cord was a newborn infant's other self, external soul, or blood-rich vital spirit, and great care must be taken with it. Such objects were ceremonially disposed of with assiduous charms to preserve the child from harm. Similarly, fairy tale monsters are often attacked by magic, through destruction of something external to their bodies. Such details indicate the true antiquity of the folklore embedded in these stories.

*Lily went to work with her ax and soon cut through the
thick trunk.*

*O*nce upon a time there was a poor peasant girl who was named Lily because she had lily white skin and silver blond hair. She was the only child of a woodcutter living in the deep forest; Lily's mother died when she was quite young. Her father taught her to work felling trees, and cutting, trimming, splitting, trussing, and stacking wood for market.

Her father was a hard taskmaster, but his training made Lily stronger and stronger as she grew up. By the time she was full grown, she was well able to wield the heaviest ax, to chop trees or split kindling for hours at a time without tiring, or to carry a hundredweight of firewood on her back ten miles to the market town. She also learned to shape and carve wood and became a skillful artisan.

Lily might have been content with her rough but peaceful life, were it not for two disadvantages.

The first was her beauty, which Lily saw as a problem because it attracted all the rowdy youths for miles around. They teased her incessantly, waylaid her on the road to market, stole her wood, plucked at her clothes, pulled her hair, held her down and mauled her, and played dozens of crude tricks that they seemed to think would force her to pay attention to them, even to like them. In fact, they made Lily increasingly angry. Once or twice she lost her temper altogether and attacked her tormenters in earnest. Though outnumbered, she fought so effectively that she left one with broken teeth, another with a broken nose, a third with a broken arm (clubbed by a length of firewood), and two more internally injured from kicks in the belly. Naturally, this only escalated their malice.

Then came her father's misfortune. One day the woodcutter's right arm was caught and mangled by a falling tree, and he was unable to use it anymore. Thereafter, Lily had to do all the chopping and other heavy work. In his loneliness, frustration, and constant pain, the woodcutter took to drink. He spent half of their scanty earnings on liquor while Lily struggled alone to do the work of two woodcutters. Despite her best efforts, she and her father became poorer.

As time went on, her father became more subject to drunken rages, stupors, and fits of madness. He would berate Lily for not working harder, or he would accuse her of bewitching him. Sometimes he would wander away and not return for days or even weeks. Thus Lily's young womanhood became little more than incessant sorrow, backbreaking toil, and nagging irritations. She saw herself as unlucky and often wished she could be someone else.

One day while chopping, she noticed a warhorse in full regalia standing all alone in a forest stream, looking uncomfortable and puzzled. Lily waded into the water to investigate. She found that the horse was tethered by his rein to the hand of a dead knight-errant, who lay under the surface of the water. Lily guessed he had been wounded in a battle, had perhaps fainted, and had fallen from his horse into the stream, where, weighed down by his suit of armor, he had drowned in water only waist-deep.

Lily detached the horse from his master's corpse, led him out of the stream, and tethered him on the bank. Then she dragged out the knight's body. While she was wondering what to do next, the horse whinnied and gave her a nudge with his nose. Suddenly she understood that the horse was telling her to take the knight's place. Without hesitating to think, she set about doing so.

With difficulty she extracted the dead knight from his armor and clothing and gave him back to the stream in pristine nakedness. As he drifted away, she found a fortune indeed, in a well-filled purse tied to his belt. She left her own clothing by the stream and dressed herself in knightly armor, which fitted her tolerably well. The metal suit was so clumsy and heavy that she couldn't mount the horse until she found a huge boulder to climb on first. Once mounted, however, she felt transformed, more powerful than her former self. She said to the horse, "I shall call you Fortune."

Lily arranged her weapons, slinging her big woodsman's ax across her back, and settled herself in the saddle. "Go, Fortune," she said to the horse, and they rode out of the forest.

At first Lily had thought to go home and share her luck with her father. But then she reflected that he would only drink it all away. Moreover, what if she was suspected of having robbed and killed the knight? She would go to the gallows. Impelled by these thoughts, she rode by her father's cottage without stopping and threw down on the doorstep enough money to keep him in food and drink for a year. Then she set out to travel and see the world.

On the road to town, Lily encountered the same lads who were accustomed to tormenting her. Her heart sank. "They will report me," she thought desperately. Then she remembered that she was fully covered by the armor. The visor concealed her face. If she didn't speak, they would have no way to identify her. So she rode toward them boldly.

To her surprise, all the lads bowed down and obsequiously tugged their forelocks as she approached. She smiled inside her helmet. To the largest youth, who had manhandled her most rudely in the past, she gave a buffet with the flat of her sword that rolled him over in the mud. He hastily scrambled up to his knees, babbling, "Yes, sir! Thank you, sir!"

Again she smiled. "Now I am Sir Lily, respected by the country louts," she said to herself. "Cowardly toadies that they are, what different faces they show to a bearer of weapons!" She began to like the idea of masquerading permanently as a knight-errant.

She camped for several weeks in the hills and practiced using her weapons. With the sharp dagger, she chopped her hair short. She taught herself to speak in a low, masculine-sounding voice. During her leisure hours, she carved a lily out of wood and placed it as a crest on her helmet. When she felt ready, she rode forth in search of adventure.

One day she came to a castle that was still and silent. There were no knights on the battlements, no workers in the fields, no merchants passing in and out of the gate, no flags flying, no cattle or other animals. The only living thing to be seen was a pretty red-haired maiden penned in an iron cage beside the castle gate. She was weeping bitterly.

"What's the matter?" Lily asked her.

"Oh, Sir Knight, I am the most unfortunate creature in the world," wailed the maiden. "I am Princess Rose, the king's daughter. My parents have been taken hostage by a terrible ogre, who holds them captive in the castle and makes me live in this cage until I consent to marry him. I'll die first. He is hideous and cruel. He has killed all my father's knights and many of our servants. No one can fight him. The ogre is invulnerable."

"Why?" Lily asked.

"He has grown a huge magical tree in the castle courtyard. At the top of the tree is a chest, and in that chest the ogre's heart is hidden. As long as his heart is safe there, nothing can harm him."

"We'll see about that," said Lily, who felt that she had had enough of bullies to last her a lifetime. "I am Sir Lily, and I know how to deal with trees. Is there a secret way into the castle?"

Princess Rose told her of a waste pipe on the north side of the castle that led into the underground dungeons. "I used to play there as a child, until I was caught and forbidden. But surely a noble knight like yourself wouldn't enter a castle by so ignominious a route."

"Nothing that accomplishes its purpose is ignominious," Lily said.

Under cover of darkness, she rode around to the north side of the castle, tethered Fortune, and removed her armor. Carrying only her dagger and her ax, she crawled through the waste pipe and made her way into the castle courtyard. There stood the magic tree, huge and black against the night sky. Lily went to work with her ax and soon cut through the thick trunk. The tree tottered and fell with a tremendous crash.

The ogre, roused from sleep, came roaring out of the castle with a torch in each hand. He was a nightmarish creature, twice as tall as a man, with one eye in the middle of his forehead and long tusks sticking out of his mouth. He lunged at Lily, who deftly eluded him and darted to the fallen crest of the tree. There she found a wooden chest wedged among the branches. With one blow of her ax she broke the chest, exposing the ogre's heart, which was beating wildly. Lily plunged her dagger into it. Just as he was reaching out to seize her, the ogre pitched forward on his face and lay still.

Lily took a bunch of keys from the dead monster's belt and went off to free Princess Rose from her cage. When she was released, the princess threw her arms around Lily and kissed her. "You are my noble white knight, valiant Sir Lily," she cried. "You must come into the castle. My parents will want to meet you and make a celebratory feast for you."

The king and queen were released from their prison and reunited with their daughter amid much rejoicing. The dead ogre and his tree were cleared away, and all was made ready for a great feast. Additional servants were hired from neighboring estates. Soon the castle was a hive of activity, as preparations were made to celebrate the destruction of the ogre, who had oppressed the whole countryside for a long time.

The grateful king and queen presented Lily with a new velvet cloak to wear to the feast, and Princess Rose with her own hands embroidered a golden lily on it. At the banquet table the king arose and made a speech, praising Lily as the kingdom's bravest knight, even though "still a beardless youth." He went on to say that, true to kingly tradition, he intended to give Sir Lily half his kingdom and the hand of his daughter in marriage.

Lily choked on her mouthful of roast goose and had to drink a few hasty swallows of wine.

"My handsome white knight is becomingly modest," said Rose, kissing her tenderly.

Quite taken aback, Lily hardly knew what to say. She managed to rise to her feet and thank the king graciously enough. But after she sat down, she leaned over and whispered in Rose's ear, "We have to talk."

When they met together in a private room, Lily told Rose that she was a woman and revealed the whole story of her false knighthood. Princess Rose sat in silence for a few minutes. Then she began to laugh. She laughed and laughed, so infectiously that Lily had to join in.

"It's the best joke ever," Rose said, wiping her eyes. "All those proud warriors, outdone by a woman who chops wood. Lily, I love you anyway. We'll be married, you and I. It will be for the great good of the kingdom, which has been needing an efficient government for a long time. Eventually we'll be king and queen. I'll keep your secrets, and you'll keep mine."

Lily said doubtfully, "I'm not sure I can carry off this deception forever."

"Nonsense. You're adventurous, or you wouldn't have done what you did in the first place. Don't doubt yourself now. We'll have fun with this, you'll see."

In the end, Lily agreed. She was married to Princess Rose in a gorgeous ceremony, and they settled down to live together. The servants said they seemed very happy, because they always laughed a lot in their private apartments, behind closed doors.

When Lily and Rose took over rulership of the country, their subjects came to honor and love them very much. King Lily often rode among the people on his noble horse, Fortune, to visit with them in person and listen to their troubles, which he usually put right. Queen Rose was greatly praised for her common sense, her benevolence to the poor, and her many good works.

There were occasional whispers about their sexual proclivities, which were not always strictly orthodox. It was said that the queen took lovers from time to time, and so did the king when he was traveling abroad. It was even said that the king took male lovers, as had several other kings recorded by the histories. Unlike those others, however, King Lily chose men who had never showed homosexual tendencies before, nor did they afterward. It was puzzling. Nevertheless, not one of them could be induced to gossip about the king's sexual tastes.

Lily and Rose governed well and were beloved by their people. They raised two children, who were trained to govern after King Lily. On the whole, they lived happily ever after.

In the deep forest far away, a small bag of money was anonymously left once a month on the doorstep of a crippled old woodcutter, who soon used it to drink himself to death.

EIGHTEEN

THE GARGOYLE

It is puzzling that Gothic cathedral builders chose to decorate their "houses of God" with a plethora of demonic figures, even more than divine ones. Presumably, the idea was to make common folk visualize devils clearly enough to fear the possibility of spending eternity in their company. One might suspect, however, that the stonecarvers simply enjoyed creating gargoyles, just as modern moviemakers, toy designers, artists, and special-effects wizards enjoy creating monsters.

During the age of cathedral building, churchmen seriously believed that many women revered demons, who protected them. Therefore, there would have been nothing too bizarre in the idea that a woman could be under the protection of one of the church's own demons. All women were suspect anyway, in the eyes of a church that held them responsible for the very existence of sin and death, and whose official inquisitorial handbook declared their carnality the sole source of all witchcraft.

*She would bring small offerings for the gargoyle and sit
and talk to him.*

$\mathcal{T}$he gargoyle crouched on a corner pinnacle of the cathedral and gazed down over the city. His stony wings were folded over his back, his chin in his hands, his tongue sticking out between his fangs. Day after day, year in and year out, he crouched there in all weathers, watching the humans below.

What the humans didn't know was that gargoyles sometimes left their posts by night and flew about in the darkness. The few people who saw them usually supposed that they had experienced a nightmare.

The gargoyle on the corner pinnacle often flew to a certain row house in the quarter just below his taloned feet, to watch a maiden named Marie. He had watched Marie ever since she was a small gamine growing up in the streets around the cathedral. She had been a remarkably pretty child and had developed into a beautiful young woman.

The gargoyle was quite in love with her. She, however, loved the boy next door, a lad her own age named Pierre. Marie and Pierre had been school-children together, had played together and protected each other from all the dangers of the streets. Now they were sweethearts, planning to be married.

The gargoyle was jealous of Pierre in a distant, stony sort of way, just as he was jealous of the more favored indoor statues in the lower parts of the cathedral, the statues that looked more like people and always had candles burning at their feet.

"Why should they get all the attention, while we sit up here cracking in the cold and breathing chimney smoke?" the gargoyles grumbled to one another. "We are statues too. We also deserve to stand indoors and receive gifts and adulation."

But the gargoyles had noticed that the indoor statues didn't seem to have any power of nocturnal locomotion, even though some of them had wings. So they thought themselves superior because of their wilder, freer life. They called the indoor statues cream puffs, sissies, namby-pambies, house pets, and altar potatoes.

The gargoyle on the corner pinnacle had a wider view of the cityscape than others, so he often described various happenings for those farther along the walls, out of the line of sight. The gargoyles were interested in accidents, altercations, crimes, fires, wars, and mob movements. They told one another stories about what they had witnessed during historic events, like the Great Revolution. Those had been exciting times! Ordinary, everyday life generally bored the gargoyles because they had seen so many centuries of it.

Nevertheless, the corner gargoyle did enjoy watching Marie grow up and go about her life. He was fascinated by the sweetness she maintained in her sour environment, like a flower blooming on a city dump. Pierre also seemed to appreciate her good qualities. They were a fond couple, happy in each other's company.

One night the gargoyle flew to Marie's bedroom window and perched on the windowsill, hoping to watch her asleep. Unfortunately, she was not asleep and saw the gargoyle looking in at her. She screamed in terror, rousing the whole household.

The gargoyle withdrew in some embarrassment. He popped up over the eaves, out of sight. He heard Marie's parents come rushing into her room. He heard her hysterically pouring out her impression of what she saw. She called him a devil.

"Hush, it was only a bad dream," her mother said soothingly.

"No, no, I was awake, I *know* I was awake," Marie insisted.

Her father leaned out the window and announced that there was nothing there. Marie was comforted and calmed until she was able to return to the business of sleeping, but not before the window had been closed and locked, and the curtains drawn over it.

Because gargoyles never closed their eyes to sleep (indeed, they had no eyelids to close), they saw nearly everything that went on in the streets, night and day. One of the sidewall gargoyles announced to his fellows that there was a very evil person living on the street below, a solitary man who preyed on women. He had raped and murdered three and still was not caught. The gargoyles watched him with some interest, as they considered themselves aficionados of true-crime stories.

They perceived that when this man chose a victim, he would stalk her for several days or even weeks, and then devise ways of entering the victim's house. The corner gargoyle was appalled to discover that the evil man had begun stalking Marie, who was quite unaware of him.

One day Marie's parents came out onto the street with baggage made ready for a journey. The gargoyle realized that they were going on a trip, and Marie was not going with them. They gave her the house key and kissed her good-bye. She waved cheerfully as they set off. Only the gargoyle saw that, just around the corner, the evil man was watching them.

As night fell, the gargoyle never took his gaze from Marie's door. Around midnight, the evil man appeared and worked for a while at the lock. The door opened, and he went into the house. The gargoyle bounced agitatedly up and down on his pedestal as he wondered what to do.

"Go and save her," said the next gargoyle to the left.

"How can I? She thinks I'm a devil."

"So much the better if the man thinks so also," said the next gargoyle to the right.

The corner gargoyle took his companions' advice and flew down to Marie's window. It was locked but uncurtained. Through the glass he saw the evil man kneeling on Marie's bed, pinning her down and holding a knife to her throat. She was wide-eyed and whimpering with fear but not daring to scream because he was threatening her.

The gargoyle danced about on the windowsill in some indecision. Then the evil man began to rip off Marie's nightgown. "Oh, God help me!" she wailed.

The gargoyle thought, "God won't help you, but I will." He gave a mighty lunge and crashed through the window, his hard body shattering the glass into a thousand fragments. Before the man could do more than turn his head, the gargoyle's stone claws were around his neck, squeezing.

He dragged the man off the bed and onto the floor, still squeezing. The man's body went limp as a rag. He threw the man's knife out the window. Marie sat up, stunned. Holding the evil man with one hand, the gargoyle picked up Marie's hand and passed it over his own head, soliciting a pat. In a dazed sort of way, she patted him. Then he flew happily through the broken window, carrying his victim. Just before settling down on his corner pinnacle, the gargoyle casually tossed the man down into the street.

The broken body was found the next morning. People wondered how a fall from the parapet above could have inflicted so much damage to the neck, which was squeezed as if by a garrotte. Some officials came up to the parapet and poked around for clues. The gargoyle calmly watched them, his tongue sticking out between his fangs. They didn't notice his slightly bloodstained claws.

The priests of the cathedral soon solved the mystery by declaring that the man had been attacked by devils and fought valiantly against them while he was striving to reach the safety of the cathedral; but unfortunately one of them managed to choke him to death before he got to the door.

A day or two later, Marie herself came up to the parapet. She went from one gargoyle to another, gazing earnestly into each stone face. She carried a wreath of flowers and a small candle in a cup. When she came to the corner gargoyle, she draped the wreath over his head, laid the cup at his feet, lighted the candle, and sat beside him. She looked down on the roof of her house. The window was being repaired.

Marie fell into the habit of visiting the parapet every few weeks. She would bring small offerings for the gargoyle and sit and talk to him. The gargoyle was delighted.

One day Pierre followed her, unseen. From behind a pillar he watched her place a bouquet of daisies in the gargoyle's lap, pat his spiky shoulder, and settle herself beside him. Then Pierre jumped out of hiding and seized Marie's arm.

"Marie, what are you doing?" he cried. "Have you become a worshiper of devils?"

Startled, Marie turned to face her lover. She drew herself up, shook off Pierre's hand, and said, "I don't think that's any of your business, Pierre."

"My business? Of course it's my business! You are to be my wife. I must be concerned if my wife has taken to devil worship."

"This is not a devil. He's just a gargoyle. But most important, he saved my life. I owe him some recognition as my savior."

"Marie, what are you saying? This is blasphemy, madness, delusion. The image of your savior is downstairs behind the altar."

"Sorry, Pierre. That's not so. *He* never did anything for me. Here is the one who saved me." She put her hand on the gargoyle's folded wing. "I know, Pierre, because I was there and you were not. I misjudged him when I first saw him, and thought him a bad dream. Now I know better."

Pierre embraced her with tears in his eyes. "My poor sweetheart, your dreadful experience has unhinged your mind. I fear the church fathers will hear of it and accuse you of witchcraft and devil worship. You know what would happen then, Marie. It's so terrible, I don't even want to think about it. I couldn't bear to lose you, especially not that way."

"What do you think, then? Have they put images of devils all over their holy building to entice people to worship devils?"

"I don't know why the church fathers do any of the things they do. Ours is not to reason why, Marie. The point is, they have the power to break your body and burn your soul if you question them. Please stop bringing offerings to this little devil here, before they catch you. I'm so afraid for you."

Marie snorted. "I think there's something very wrong with a world where rapists and murderers are not caught but harmless women are. I know you have physical courage, my dear, but I fear you haven't much courage of the mind. I like my gargoyle. I feel comfortable here, looking at the view with him. That's all anyone has to know. Let it be my private place, Pierre. I won't give it up for anyone, not even for you."

Pierre hesitated. "You know the church burns women to death for less than this," he said. "You know you must never seem to say anything irrational or . . . or different."

"I know," said Marie. "Let it be our secret."

Pierre kissed her and agreed, though he still looked worried. Marie gave the gargoyle a final pat and a wink behind Pierre's back. Then the two lovers walked away, arm in arm.

The gargoyles envied their corner colleague, who was actually liked and defended by a real human. They assured him that he was now superior to the indoor statues who had done nothing to deserve the honor.

Marie did take up a few simple procedures of white witchery that somehow came into her head while she sat beside her gargoyle. A few neighbors very quietly came to know her as a healer and wise woman, but the church fathers never heard anything about her. Presently, Marie and Pierre were married in the cathedral. A few days later, Marie brought the gargoyle a tiny piece of her wedding cake.

Marie and Pierre lived happily ever after and had children who grew up in the same street under the gargoyle's eye. He enjoyed watching their games and pastimes. Sometimes he seemed to wear a smile around the tongue that stuck out between his fangs.

NINETEEN

LITTLE WHITE RIDING HOOD

The three generations of women in this story wear the traditional colors of the trinity of Virgin, Mother, and Crone—the gunas, white, red, and black. Since little Riding Hood is the maiden, her color is white and she is called the daughter of our familiar fairy tale heroine Red.

Today's new earth-consciousness necessitates a new view of the hunter. He, representing man's destructive exploitation of the wilderness, is not the hero but the villain of the piece, replacing the wolf, who represents the spirit of the wilderness itself. Wolves are not known to eat living people. Thus, the old tale's version of wolfish appetite for human flesh is another canard, probably created to make children fear and loathe the dogs of the forest because of their possible impact on pastoral economics.

She stood up and grabbed a stout stick.

Once upon a time there was a little girl called White Riding Hood because she always wore a snow white hood when she went out riding or walking. She lived with her mother, Red Riding Hood, in a cottage on the edge of the great forest.

White Riding Hood's grandmother (who always wore black) lived in another cottage deep within the forest, a long way from inhabited and cultivated lands. Nevertheless, people often traveled the winding forest road to visit White Riding Hood's grandmother, because she was known far and wide as a powerful witch who could cure diseases, set broken bones, deliver babies, give sound advice, and create charms for love, good luck, abundant crops, and clement weather. She could communicate with spirits of trees and wild animals. Her cottage was surrounded by pens where she kept an ever-changing assortment of convalescent forest creatures whose injuries she healed.

One day White Riding Hood's mother made up a basket of staples—salt, flour, honey, cheese, dried lentils, and other foodstuffs—for White Riding Hood to carry to her grandmother. She would stay for several days, bringing the basket back later with various herbs and roots that the grandmother gathered. White Riding Hood was happy to obey, because she loved to visit her grandmother. The forest cottage offered birds and animals to observe and play with, and it smelled richly of the herbal concoctions that her grandmother brewed. There was always something interesting going on there.

White Riding Hood's grandmother had taught her many things about plants, stones, stars, winds, and waters. She also taught her granddaughter to respect the wild creatures. She was especially fond of the shy forest wolves, whose habits she had studied by long and patient observation.

She insisted that the wolves were not the ferocious vermin that some people claimed they were, but highly intelligent, loyal, noble-hearted dogs, gentle with their own kind and even with humans who didn't threaten them. The grandmother had cured several wolves of sickness and healed injuries inflicted on them by hunters or by trappers who set the vicious leg-hold traps. She had earned the trust of these wolves, and they came back occasionally to visit her. She had learned how to behave nonthreateningly in the presence of a wolf pack, so she would not be attacked. She taught White Riding Hood the proper attitudes that the wolves could recognize, and made her realize that if she behaved appropriately, she had nothing to fear from these forest dogs. Therefore, White Riding Hood never felt nervous in the forest, even when she heard the wolves' eerie howling as they organized their hunts.

Fresh morning light sparkled brightly on the dewdrops as White Riding Hood set off on her errand, carrying her basket and whistling cheerily in response to the birds. She walked several miles into the woods and then sat down beside a stream to drink and rest. As she sat there, a pair of hunters came along, carrying a large dead wolf slung from a pole between them.

White Riding Hood was horrified to see that the wolf was a mother whose distended teats suggested an orphaned litter of pups somewhere, and that her left hind leg had been trapped and chewed away up to the hock.

"Hey there, little girl," the elder hunter said. "See what we caught for you? One less wolf to worry about."

"I don't worry about wolves," White Riding Hood responded. "And that's a terrible thing you did, making a mother die in agony, chewing her leg because she was trying to get back to her children."

Suddenly angry, the hunter said, "You've a nasty mouth on you, little girl. Maybe we ought to take some time to teach you proper respect for your elders."

The other hunter giggled and shuffled his feet, a vacant expression on his face. "Look, Will, she's old enough, isn't she?" he coaxed. "She's old enough to do it to, isn't she? Hey, Will, let's do it to her. Can we, Will? Can we?"

White Riding Hood's mother had warned her about the hurtful intentions of certain men toward little girls. She stood up and grabbed a stout stick.

"Hey now," growled Will, "you wouldn't want to try fighting a couple of big strong men, and get yourself all beat up and dirty, and that nice white hood spoiled, just because you don't show enough respect. You wouldn't want anything to happen to you like what happened to this here wolf, would you?"

"You mean you'd put me in a trap and hack my leg off?" White Riding Hood said. She planted her feet apart and held her stick ready to strike.

She was too angry to feel afraid, even though she knew her position was dangerous and if the men chose to fight her, she would inevitably lose.

The weak-minded one giggled again at her words. "Go on, grab her, Will," he snuffled.

"Don't you touch me, or I'll tell my grandmother on you," White Riding Hood threatened. "She's the witch of the Great Forest, and she'll put a spell on you to make your feet turn backwards and your ears fall off. You'll be sorry."

"I've heard about her," Will sneered. "She's a devil who can turn herself into a wolf. If that's your grandmother, you've got evil blood in you, girl."

"Go on, Will, grab her, grab her," the younger one said again.

Will hesitated, then turned away with a contemptuous gesture. "She's not worth a scuffle," he blustered. "And we've got to get to the rest of the trapline. Forget it, Rollo."

"Aw, come on, come on, Will," Rollo whined. "She's old enough, isn't she? Come on, let's do it to her."

"I said no, Rollo," the older hunter snapped, and his companion cowered. They turned and marched away, leaving White Riding Hood to her own devices. She dropped her stick, picked up her basket, and ran to get away from the hunters as fast as possible.

When she arrived at her grandmother's cottage, she told her grandmother about the two hunters. "I know that pair," the grandmother said. "They're as mean as can be. I know how we can foil them, but it will have to wait for tomorrow. Right now, we should go out and see if we can find those orphan cubs before it's too late."

So White Riding Hood and her grandmother went out to check the various wolf dens that the grandmother knew. Sure enough, in the third one they found four very hungry infant pups crying for their mother. White Riding Hood wrapped two in her cloak, and her grandmother took the other two. They carried the pups back to the cottage. The grandmother showed White Riding Hood how to feed them with warm goat's milk from small bottles with leather nipples. They seemed to digest it well enough, and soon they were sleeping contentedly in a straw-lined box near the hearth.

White Riding Hood was so enchanted with the baby wolves that she didn't get around to looking at the other animals until the next morning. This time her grandmother had a fawn with a fractured leg, a hawk with a broken wing, and a raccoon who'd had three toes pulled off by a trap and was recovering from an acute infection.

After tending to these creatures, the grandmother took tools and set off with White Riding Hood to visit the hunters' traplines. She carefully sprang each trap and then broke it, throwing away the springs and leaving behind only scattered pieces of metal. One trap she left intact and carried home. She concealed it and set it at her front doorstep, saying to White Riding Hood, "Now we'll see what we catch. I know those fellows will be coming by here when they find out what happened to their traps."

Her prediction came true early the next morning, when Will and Rollo showed up, enraged, at her gate.

"Come on out of there, old witch," Will roared. "I know it was you who broke our traps. Come on out and take what's coming to you."

"Come and get me if you dare," the grandmother called. She wrapped herself in a bedsheet and put over her head a grotesque mask carved and painted to look like a huge wolf with bared teeth. It had a long, purplish-red tongue that she could push in and out between the big teeth by using her own tongue.

Holding his gun in readiness to shoot, Will charged up to the door with Rollo following. He raised his foot to kick the door open, but at the same time his supporting foot was seized by the trap that sprang up from under the carpet of leaves. He fell heavily on his side. The gun went off, blowing some twigs off a maple tree, and flew out of his hands.

The grandmother threw the door open and appeared in her wolf mask, a hatchet in her hand. Yanking fruitlessly at the trap, Will began to scream. Rollo stuttered, "Wh-what b-big teeth you have, Grandma!"

"The better to eat you with!" the grandmother shouted, and neatly split Will's skull with her hatchet. Rollo turned and ran as if all the devils in hell were after him. He was never seen in the forest again.

Later the grandmother chopped up the hunter's body into manageable pieces and strewed them in the forest for the wolves to eat.

Little White Riding Hood went home the next day. When her mother asked her what she had done at Grandmother's house, she said, "Well, we helped feed some wolves."

TWENTY

HOW THE SEXES WERE SEPARATED

This story is a retelling of two myths. The first is the Greek myth of Zeus's attack, out of his resentment of their godlike bliss, on the hermaphrodites of the Golden Age. The second is the Babylonian myth of the jealous god punished by the Great Mother's rainbow, barring him from earthly altars for his crime of having instigated the Flood—a myth whose discovery threw a rather different light on the derivative biblical tale of Noah.

The Old Testament god's self-proclaimed jealousy might have been based on the same sexual envy made plain in the older myths, since he "separated" Eve from Adam. Rabbinical tradition held that these purported parents of humanity had formerly lived as an androgynous single-bodied couple, in which case the alleged purpose of providing Adam with a companion would have no weight. Earlier scriptures spoke of a primal couple, Adamu (male) and Adamah (female). The Hindu Yab-Yum or Ardhanarisvara are other versions of this primal hermaphrodite, whose English name is formed of the mythical union of the god Hermes and the goddess Aphrodite. Their combination into a single entity was a Greek symbol of love between the sexes, which patriarchal religions came to regard with uneasy suspicion.

His angry voice would roar like thunder . . .

*I*n the beginning, the Great Mother commissioned the double-sexed Primal Androgyne to create human beings in its own image. The first people had two sexes in the same body and lived in a state of continual delight. Together with other red-blooded animals, humans were hermaphrodites who felt each of their halves constantly pleasuring and responding to the other half. As a result, their world was blissful, peaceful, and loving. They lived and died in perpetual ripples of joint ecstasy, unaware of loss, loneliness, or evil. This was their Golden Age.

A deity calling himself Sky Father, however, became very jealous of the happy, completed humans. Because of his own emptiness, he wanted to be loved and worshiped to the exclusion of everything else. Obsessed by his jealousy, he brooded to himself in a dark clouded corner of the heavens, becoming more and more surly, disgruntled, and resentful. Sometimes his anger would flash out of black clouds toward Earth as a streak of destructive lightning. His angry voice would roar like thunder, and the terrified humans would run and hide, not knowing why the god menaced them. He became even angrier when he saw how they tried to avoid him.

On several occasions, Sky Father poured furious fire on the humans' towns to teach them to stop ignoring him. He killed a great many of them. Once he even sent so much rain from his thunderclouds that Earth was flooded, and millions of innocent creatures drowned. The Great Mother and the Primal Androgyne punished him for that. They put a rainbow across the heavens to bar his way to Earth's altars, so he could no longer eat the delicacies that humans offered their deities.

This made Sky Father even more jealous. He began to hate the Primal Androgyne for having made humans in its image. He wanted to take credit for creating them in *his* image. He thought and thought about this until it occurred to him that there was something he could do, after all, to claim the title of creator. He could make some radical modifications in the original hermaphroditic plan of red-blooded creatures. He would make them more like himself.

Accordingly, Sky Father waited until other deities weren't looking, then slid down to Earth on one of his own lightning bolts and began to tear apart all the male and female halves of red-blooded creatures. The humans shrieked at this desecration and called upon the Great Mother to save them, but she was occupied on another planet at the time and didn't hear their pleas.

There were a great many hermaphrodites to be separated before he should be discovered, so Sky Father worked fast. In his haste, he tore apart the males and females carelessly. A little piece of flesh that belonged to each female was pulled out from between her legs and left sticking awkwardly to the lower belly of each male. The humans later determined that this was the reason for the periodic bleeding of the female in memory of her loss, and for the fact that each male's extra piece of flesh is controlled not by himself, but by its former owner, the female body.

Sky Father told the male human beings that they were now created in his image, because he had taken female bodies out of them. Their Golden Age was over. He told them that he was a jealous god, and they must worship no other gods before him. He demanded servitude, hard work, and perpetual praise. He insisted that all sacrifices on all altars must be dedicated to him alone. He wanted abject obedience in all things, and threatened the disobedient with terrible punishments, preparing an underground realm of torture where they would suffer agonies forever. Most of all he commanded the males never to mourn for their lost female halves and to never show the slightest hint of femaleness anymore.

When the Great Mother returned to Earth, She was infuriated at the newly wretched condition of her favorites, the red-blooded species. She cursed Sky Father up, down, and sideways. All the deities witnessed his public disgrace. This did no good; it only added to his hatred of the Great Mother and all other deities who might remember his shame. He vowed that someday he would get rid of them all and reign in the heavens alone.

Meanwhile, the humans and other animals remained irresistibly compelled to seek reunion of their male and female parts, cruelly torn asunder. The two sexes continued to desire coupling, to restore the male's appendage to its proper female place, and to taste again a few moments of the bliss that they used to enjoy always. None of Sky Father's threats or punishments could prevent this. The humans—if not the animals—could be made to feel guilty about it, and to despise themselves for their natural desires, but even they couldn't be made to stop coupling. Much later, in a place called Rome, they even gave it the name of *religion,* which means "re-linking."

Men tried to assuage their guilt by assuring themselves that they, made in the image of their own creative god, were superior creatures to women. Women remained unconvinced, because they knew who really controlled the piece of flesh that men thought essential to their manliness. Still, as Sky Father enforced new rules, the women were increasingly oppressed by their former other halves.

The Great Mother took pity on the women. She reasoned that if the men were going to be jealous like their god, they might as well have something to be really jealous of. She gave females exclusive right to the enviable powers of birthgiving and nurture. Men could only watch, generation after generation, while women brought forth new life out of their bodies and formed with each new life the closest bonds known to human experience. The men tried everything they could think of to control this awesome magic, but they never quite understood how it was done.

Sometimes, groups of men decided to seize control of the other end of the life cycle, death. Their inner selves reasoned that if they couldn't create life, at least they could destroy it, and that felt like power. Quite a few of them eventually came to spend their whole lives in the pursuit of that kind of power, and even to think it an honorable way to live.

Thus the world staggered on into the age of Sky Father, with the formerly compatible sexes more and more at odds. In their pain and rage, many humans listened to Sky Father's admonitions against the Great Mother and other deities, adopting the bloody sacrificial customs that he required of them, sometimes even killing one or more of their own kind to win his goodwill. He often promised that when this was done, he would lift the burdens of sin and punishment; but somehow he never did.

The Great Mother was distressed by this new world. Like any mother, she said of the humans that they were going through a phase. "They are endowed with the capacity of reason," she explained, "and sooner or later they will abandon Sky Father because he is unreasonable." She expected that eventually, if they didn't destroy themselves in the meantime, humans would mature in attitude and purge themselves of their hatred and destructiveness.

Meanwhile, she continued to speak to the ones who were ready to hear her, to inspire them to create, to hope, and to love. Although Sky Father did his best to diabolize her, many humans went on seeking her. They gave her thousands of different names, including Nature, Earth, Mother of Gods, Queen of Heaven, Lady Luck, Fairy Queen. She was never quite forgotten.

And that is why there are two separate sexes of humans who continually try to rejoin each other and yet have so much difficulty ironing out their differences that each generation produces barely half of them who succeed. Nonhuman animals have made somewhat better adjustments to the situation, either by keeping the sexes apart most of the time or by instinctively mating for life and making the best of it. Humans want to join their other halves and live happily ever after, but they sometimes frustrate their own true desires and die unsatisfied.

That's why they are forever telling each other stories about true love that overcomes all obstacles and joins two persons together as one. They keep trying for the only heaven that's known to be attainable.

TWENTY-ONE

THE LITTLEST MERMAID

Generations of readers have loved Hans Christian Andersen's little mermaid, who sits to this day on a rock in the Copenhagen harbor in the form of a statue by Edvard Eriksen. Nevertheless, as a child I was too distressed by her sufferings to enjoy her company. I thought she shouldn't have to sacrifice her own bodily comfort for the sake of love. Love should not hurt. Perhaps it was a masculine idea that women must endure pain in order to be worthy of love. But what was the prince enduring? He got it for free.

Therefore, the littlest mermaid here is given a more caring and sympathetic prince, and then relief of her pain. Her healer-wizard, Sklepio, is based on the old god of medicine, Asklepios to the Greeks, Aesculapius to the Romans. His own princess runs away to wed a commoner, not the usual course for fairy tale princesses, who were generally supposed to be rooted, like flowers, in the hothouse life of fantasy and privilege without any opportunity to make their own choices.

The mermaid went down into the abyss . . .

Once upon a time there was a mermaid known as Littlest, because she was the youngest and smallest of her sisters. She was small-boned and dainty, and quick and agile enough to slip out from the edges of the nets that the fishermen threw. She would pick up sharp pieces of coral rock and cut open the nets to release the dolphins, turtles, and fish. The fishermen would curse and scream, while she laughed at their discomfiture, flirted her tail at them, and swam away.

Littlest lived in the coral palace of her father, the sea king, who had been left a widower several years before when his queen was accidentally skewered by a nearsighted harpoonist. After that, the sea king avoided all contact with the terrestrials and their ships. He advised his daughters not to sing to sailors, sit combing their hair on exposed rocks, or play in the wakes of galleons.

Nevertheless, the littlest mermaid often flouted her father's advice because she enjoyed teasing the terrestrials. She would swim close enough to a ship to allow the sailors to catch tiny glimpses of her. On dark nights she would sing them sweet songs just barely audible above the whisper of the waves. She liked to cut anchor ropes and plug up tillers with seaweed. On one occasion she was even bold enough to rise up under a swimming sailor and yank his pantaloons down around his ankles.

The littlest mermaid also loved to play with the seals and dolphins, who were always ready for a game of somersault tag or chase-me. The sea king often deplored her frivolity and her choice of friends ("Those *animals*!" he would snort) and sometimes predicted that she would come to no good. But he made no serious effort to restrain her. Her elder sisters tried to interest her in useful crafts like pearl-stringing and coral-carving. Her attention soon wandered from these sedentary pursuits, and she was off again, with a twitch of her tail, to play belly-up with the sea otters.

One stormy evening the littlest mermaid was out riding the giant waves when she saw a ship in distress. Its masts were broken, its sails torn and dragging over the side. It was heeled over, drifting helplessly broadside-on to the seas, nearly swamped by every wave that broke over its decks. A few mariners, washed overboard, were struggling feebly in the plunging waters.

The mermaid came closer and saw the ship tilt down by the bow and begin to sink. At that moment she was bumped by a floating body. She turned and saw a richly dressed young man, unconscious, beginning to slip underwater for a final, fatal descent. The mermaid held him up and looked into his face, which she thought the handsomest face she had ever seen.

All night the mermaid struggled to hold the young man's head above water while she dragged his dead weight toward the distant shore. At dawn she managed to dump him on a beach, then she returned exhausted to the cushioning waters. As she swam slowly home, her tail muscles aching with exertion, she was haunted by the memory of the young man's face. She realized that she must be in love with him.

A few weeks later she saw him again, standing at the rail of a splendid ship flying the royal ensign from its masthead. He was alive, well, and even more richly dressed than before. He looked so beautiful that the sight of him seemed to squeeze her heart. She hung around the ship until she heard someone speak his name, which was Prince Aquam. The littlest mermaid decided then and there that she would never rest peacefully again until she could be Princess Aquam.

When she told her father, he was outraged. "I told you nothing good would come of fooling around with terrestrials," he growled. "If you had the brains of an oyster, Littlest, you'd know that mermaids can't marry footed earth-crawlers. Do you want to spend the rest of your days humping around on your belly on dry land, like a walrus?"

"Maybe I can be footed too," the mermaid suggested. "They say the sea witch can make feet for mermaids."

"Bah! Backstairs babble," said the sea king. "Forget all this nonsense and grow up, girl. The sea witch is dangerous, and I forbid you to go anywhere near her."

So, of course, the littlest mermaid immediately planned a visit to the sea witch, who lived in one of the deepest abysses. Hiring a couple of lanternfish to show her the way, the mermaid went down into the abyss, where the pressure made her ears ring. She found the sea witch cooking her dinner in a cauldron set atop a bubbling hot-gas vent over a volcano.

The sea witch was huge, wrinkled, blue-black, and crowned with sharp spines.

"What do you want, girl?" asked the witch, clashing her long fangs in a menacing way.

"I want to have a pair of feet like the terrestrials," the mermaid answered timidly. She was more frightened of the witch than she cared to show, for she remembered certain whispered servants' tales about deep-sea witches who ate human flesh.

"Hah! Your great-great-great-aunt once came to me for the same reason," the witch said. "She had some stupid obsession about a terrestrial boy, of all things. I told her it would come to no good, and I was right. What's *your* reason?"

"Well, I . . ."

"Never mind, I know. It's the same idiot notion all over again, isn't it? You think you're in love. I'll never understand the charm of those silly crippled earth-crawlers. And here you are, wanting to be like them. Well, it's no sand in my craw if you want to make yourself into a lame duck. I can give you feet, but there's one great drawback."

"What is it?" the mermaid asked.

"You have to pay with pain. Every time you take a step on these new feet, it will feel like you're walking on the points of knives."

"I don't care," said the littlest mermaid. "I want to be Princess Aquam. After I marry the prince, I can have myself carried around in a golden litter with curtains of silk."

"All right," sighed the witch. "It's your choice. Come on into my cave."

For the next few days Littlest underwent a series of magical operations, some of them extremely uncomfortable. In the end, her shining muscular tail was replaced by a pair of slim white legs and delicate feet so tender that she could hardly bear to touch them to the rocks.

"Now, the last thing is to remove your gills and make you an air-breather," said the witch. "That will have to be done on the beach. And you can't swim that far anymore. Arnold, my shark, will tow you."

The mermaid shuddered slightly. Like all mermaids, she feared sharks and didn't like to trust even a tame one. She had seen Arnold, a monstrous thirty-five-foot great white with sandpaper skin and a formidable mouthful of teeth. Still, having no other option, she plucked up her courage and allowed herself to be hitched onto Arnold's dorsal fin, while he weaved restlessly back and forth in the mindless, threatening manner of sharks.

"You're sure he knows what to do?" Littlest asked nervously.

"Of course he knows," the witch snapped. "The only thing you need to worry about is not to let him go into a feeding frenzy; I can't answer for his behavior then. Your eyes are much better than his, so just steer him away if you happen to see any clouds of blood in the water. As soon as you get to the beach, take the two pills I've given you and lie down. You'll sleep for a while, and when you wake up you'll look just like any other earth-crawler, more's the pity."

She slapped Arnold on the tail and off he went. They swam for many miles. Arnold paused occasionally to snap up a small fish or two, but fortunately the mermaid spotted no clouds of blood in the water. She released the shark ten yards from the shore and walked through the surf to the beach, astonished by the knifelike pains in her feet and the weak, clumsy movements of her legs. She felt crippled indeed.

Exhausted, tense, and hurting, she lay down under a palm tree and took the witch's pills, which plunged her into a dreamless sleep. When she awoke, her nose was breathing air and her skin felt unpleasantly sticky, salty, sandy, and for the first time in her life, dry.

She got up and turned toward the town, where she knew the prince's palace was located. She found walking so painful that she frequently had to sit down by the roadside. While she was sitting, a horse and wagon came by with a fat man on the driver's seat.

"May I ride to town in your wagon?" the mermaid called. "My feet hurt and I can't walk very well."

The man halted his horse and looked at her. "You've got more wrong with you than sore feet, little lady," he snickered. "Do you often go around stark naked in broad daylight on the public roads? Are you simpleminded or what?"

"I don't own any clothes," the mermaid said. "But I'm going to be a princess soon, and then I'll be dressed even better than you. I'm going to Prince Aquam's palace. Will you take me there?"

The fat man laughed. "Well, you're crazier than a coot, but an original, that's for sure. Climb on up here, little lady, and we'll see how far we go."

She climbed up on the wagon, wincing as she did so, and sat beside the driver. He immediately slipped his hand between her thighs and pinched her, asking in suggestive tones, "How are you going to pay for the ride, little lady?"

"I have no money now," she said, wriggling uncomfortably, "but I'll pay you well after I become a princess."

"I'd rather have the payment now," he leered, "and I don't mean money. Just lie down there in the back of the wagon and spread your legs, and we'll call it square."

"No, I won't," said the mermaid, finally catching his drift. "I am to be the bride of the prince, and I don't want any attentions from an ugly ruffian like you. Let go of me."

"Oh, yes?" snarled the driver, clutching her more tightly. "Suppose we just make it an order, hey? What are you going to do about it?"

"This," said the mermaid, plucking the buggy whip from its socket and ramming its butt into his stomach. Though her new legs were weak, her arms and shoulders were immensely strong from a lifetime of swimming. Her blow was powerful enough to tumble the man from his seat onto the ground. The mermaid then reversed her grip on the whip and snapped it over the rump of the horse, which sprang into a startled gallop. The wagon vanished down the road in a cloud of dust, leaving the driver shouting curses and dancing up and down in a fury.

The mermaid realized that her nakedness provoked unpleasant reactions from male terrestrials, so she stopped the wagon by a clump of broad-leaved bushes and contrived herself a garment of intertwined leaves. Then she drove the wagon sedately into the town and up to the palace gates. She told the guard, "I have come to see the prince."

The guard's eyes bulged as he looked her over.

"What name shall I give, milady?" he asked with heavy irony.

"Just tell him his rescuer is here."

The guard was somewhat intimidated by her bizarre appearance and her authoritative manner. Behind his hand he whispered to the assistant gatekeeper, "I don't know, maybe she's a fairy. Better not take a chance. Go tell the prince." The fellow ran off, and the mermaid waited calmly.

After a while, a pageboy appeared with the message that the leaf-clad woman was to be conducted to the audience chamber. There she found the prince sitting on a ruby-studded throne, nibbling boiled shrimps and picking his teeth with a golden toothpick. He looked her over lazily.

"What do you mean by saying you're my rescuer?" he asked.

"More than one moon's cycle ago, you were in a shipwreck," she said. "I kept you from drowning and brought you to the shore."

Prince Aquam's eyes widened. "It's true that my ship sank," he said. "Everyone said it was a miracle that carried me so many miles to the shore. I remember nothing of it. You're a frail young woman; how could you possibly swim so far out to sea?"

"I am an expert swimmer," the mermaid said. She described the storm, the condition of the ship, and even the clothes the prince had been wearing at the time, to convince him that she really had been at the scene. Eventually the prince believed her.

"Apparently, then, I owe you my life," he said. "You must be an angel, or a water sprite, or a powerful fairy. If you've come for repayment, tell me what you wish."

"I wish to be your princess," she said bluntly.

The prince dropped his jaw, as well as a shrimp that he had been lifting to his mouth. "But that's not possible," he said. "I'm betrothed to the princess of Estuaria. Our wedding is to take place in three weeks' time. Ask me something else—anything."

"I wish nothing else," said the mermaid.

The prince began to sweat. He had been trained never, under any circumstances, to offend a powerful fairy. "Please be my guest for a while," he offered, "and perhaps some other course will present itself. My palace is at your disposal. When you have rested and refreshed yourself, we'll talk again."

The mermaid was conducted to a sumptuous apartment. Soft rugs caressed her pained feet, and there was a huge four-poster bed and a closet full of richly embroidered dresses. A maid came to help her bathe and arrange her hair. A butler brought platters of fruit and other foods strange to her taste. She ate and took a nap and afterward felt better despite the constant soreness of her feet.

Later a servant came with the prince's invitation to join him at dinner. She was taken to a private dining hall where she and Aquam were entertained by musicians and dancers while the food was being served. He told her about his forthcoming marriage to the heiress of Estuaria, a necessary political alliance with a more powerful nation. He had never met the princess but had been given to understand that she was intelligent and likeable. "You must realize that we royals can't always govern our own lives," he said. "Some think we have nothing to do but pleasure ourselves. That's not so."

"I don't care," said the mermaid. "You must marry me because you owe me your life."

The prince was much troubled by this. He answered her evasively and did his best to be a charming dinner companion. After dinner he taught her to play chess. At the end of a pleasant evening by the fire, she went off to her big four-poster bed.

Then the prince hurried to another wing of the palace to visit his mother the queen, whom everyone regarded as a witch because she was so wise. Aquam laid the problem before her, and she soon suggested a solution.

"If the girl is as naive as you say," the queen told him, "you may arrange a false wedding ceremony and let her believe she has become your princess. In three weeks' time, you can say you are called away on a journey. Go to Estuaria and celebrate your real nuptials. Then you will have to arrange to spend time with each bride alternately, until a more permanent solution suggests itself."

"By 'permanent,' I hope you don't mean anything violent," the prince said. "I'm very much attracted to this girl, or fairy, or whatever she is. Besides, I owe her my life."

"Don't worry, son," said the queen. "These things have a way of sorting themselves out."

The prince went to bed somewhat reassured. The next day he arranged a private, false wedding ceremony to make the littlest mermaid think she was his princess. They lived together happily, although his bride's obviously painful foot condition distressed the prince. In less than a week he found himself so deeply in love with her that the idea of his political marriage to the unknown princess of Estuaria grew increasingly repugnant.

Nevertheless, being a dutiful soul, he invented an excuse to travel when the time came, and left his faux princess with many tearful kisses and protestations of undying affection. The mermaid suspected no duplicity because she was blindly, deliriously in love with her prince and was sure he would never deceive her about anything.

When the prince arrived in the capital of Estuaria, the king and queen greeted him nervously. He saw no sign of the princess. After the welcoming ceremonies, he ventured to ask where she was. Her parents blushed and stuttered a bit, and then the king confessed that they didn't know where she was just at the moment, but they were sure she would be found soon. Somewhat aggrieved, the prince accepted their invitation to stay a few days at the palace while the hunt for the princess went on.

During the next night he was awakened by a hurried, frantic knocking at his window. He arose from bed, opened the casement, and looked out. A small figure was dangling from above on a rope.

"Who are you?" asked Aquam.

"Shh! I'm the princess of Estuaria. Help me in the window."

He reached out a hand and drew her into his room. She was a small, wiry, knobby girl with a pointed chin, snapping black eyes like a gypsy, and a mop of rather greasy curls. He thought her unattractive. "Are you really the princess?" he asked.

For answer, she held out her hand and showed him the royal signet ring. "I've come to ask a favor of you," she said. "You seem like a decent fellow, but I don't love you and I never could. I'm in love with a commoner whom my parents will never permit me to marry. So I'm going to run away with him tonight. I don't want to be a princess anymore anyway. I've come just to ask you to go away in peace and don't think of starting a war or anything against my parents over this. Will you agree?"

The prince was rather taken aback by her abrupt manner, but he thought of his pseudo bride at home, whom he truly loved. He smiled on the knotty little princess.

"Rest easy, Your Highness," he said. "I don't think I could love you either. I'll work it out somehow with your parents. I wish you joy with your commoner. Who is he, anyway?"

"A great magician and healer named Sklepio," she answered. "Someday you'll meet him, and you'll be glad. Thanks for your help and understanding. You're a good man, Aquam."

She kissed him on the cheek and sprang up to the window to reach for her rope. As he leaned out to watch, she was drawn up to the roof—by Sklepio, the prince assumed—and disappeared.

The next day he made preparations to return to his home. He assured the king and queen of Estuaria that he bore them no ill will and that he had enjoyed his stay with them. He promised that their two countries would always maintain friendly relations and said he would be happy to come back if the princess should be found. He was fairly certain that she would not be.

The mermaid greeted his homecoming with delight. She was even more delighted when he suggested a second, public, ceremonial wedding to be attended by the whole court and to accompany her official coronation.

During Aquam's absence, the queen had become better acquainted with the mermaid and had grown quite fond of her. She regretted having advised her son to mislead such a loving and lovable girl, so she was glad to make amends with a genuine wedding. She threw herself into planning the most magnificent ceremony ever seen at court. With her own hands she placed the crown on the head of her new daughter-in-law, then publicly hugged and kissed her.

The mermaid heartily returned the affection of her royal mother-in-law. During the next few years the women became very close. The mermaid's untimely loss of her own mother was effectively healed by the warm relationship with her mother by marriage.

When the old king died, Prince Aquam became king and assumed the duties of government, with the help of his mother and his wife. The mermaid led a mostly happy life, though she continued to be plagued by chronic pain in her feet. No physician had been able to cure her, though many tried.

Finally, one day, a famous healer named Dr. Sklepio came into Aquam's kingdom, accompanied by his gypsylike little wife. They visited the palace and met the royal couple. King Aquam and the healer's wife exchanged a secret glance, and both smiled.

Dr. Sklepio looked at the young queen's feet. "This is no disease, but an enchantment," he said. "Perhaps I can reverse it."

After three days of elaborate spells, the healer was able to remove most of the pain from the queen's feet. He prescribed daily exercises, foot baths, and sea swimming to restore full walking strength. In a few months, the mermaid was walking and even running as well as if she had been born with legs.

King Aquam rewarded the healer and his wife with a grant of land and a small castle. The two couples became friends and lived happily ever after.

A year or so later the mermaid bore a baby daughter who would become heir to the throne. The child was born with webbed toes. All the soothsayers hastened to pronounce this an exceptionally good omen for the future ruler of a maritime nation. The little princess grew up strong, intelligent, and pretty. And from her earliest years, she proved to be the best swimmer in all the land.

TWENTY-TWO

CINDER-HELLE

This version of the Cinderella story may be traced back to religio-political allegory, satirizing the feudal church and state (Ecclesia and Nobilita), and recalling northern Europe's indigenous worship of the Goddess Helle, or Holle, or Ella, or Hel. In one of the original German versions, the gift-giving fairy godmother was a sacred tree grown from the grave of the heroine's mother, obviously a former pilgrimage shrine. The story touches on the uneasy truce between the urban political power of medieval Christianity and the spiritual power of pagan (meaning "rural") cults of the old Goddess—who was doubly underground when the primal netherworld earth mother survived to become a heretical secret, and her worship went underground.

Cinder-Helle's use of menstrual blood in her charm is one of the oldest and most durable notions about witches' magic, dating from that remote prepatriarchal time when women's moon blood was considered the source of every life, the foundation of all family blood bonds, and the essential medium of spiritual power. Patriarchy regarded it with horror, and its extraordinary taboos perpetuated many absurd superstitions about the capacity of such blood to defy the will of male gods.

The scepter in the shoe is an ancient symbol of sexual intercourse or sacred marriage, dating all the way back to the Eleusinian Mysteries sacred to Demeter in ancient Greece. Its unconscious survival even today may be sought in various kinds of shoe fetishism.

*The pumpkin became a splendid golden coach with elegant
fittings inside.*

nce upon a time, the ancient Underground Goddess was known as queen of the honored dead and ruler of the foremothers. She had many priestesses on earth. Her priestesses established the ethical system, gave advice, kept records, mediated quarrels, prescribed medicines, delivered babies, kept the peace, and performed a thousand other physical and social services that held the world in balance. The people loved them and their Goddess and worshiped their own ancestors as spirits residing in the Goddess's depths.

But then along came armies led by male priests, who converted by the sword. That is, they gave people a choice between accepting their new male god or having their heads sliced off. For most it wasn't a difficult decision. The king officially abolished the Goddess's temples, even though many of the priestesses continued her worship in private, out in the open fields and woods, or in the homes of the secretly faithful.

One of these priestesses married a wealthy man and bore a beautiful little daughter. They named her Helle, one of the Underground Goddess's many names, which referred to the hidden chambers deep in the earth where the Goddess received the dead and recycled them to be born again on earth as new children. Therefore it was a name of great holiness (or hellness). The priestess mother hoped it would bring her daughter lifelong blessings.

Unfortunately, this didn't seem to be the case. The priestess died while Helle was still a child. Her father then married an arrogant, greedy woman named Christiana, who had two grown daughters, Nobilita and Ecclesia. Helle's stepmother and stepsisters mistreated her, forced her to dress in rags, do all the housework, and wait on them hand and foot. Helle's father hardly noticed or cared. He was often away from home, traveling on business, and was always preoccupied with his own affairs. He needed to earn a lot of money for his new, highly avaricious family.

Nobilita put on many airs, dressed herself in the best silks, satins, and ermines, and spent her days giving commands. She also carried weapons— whips and daggers—to enforce her commands. Ecclesia eschewed weapons and pretended a pious modesty, but she was just as fond of finery as her sister was, if not more so. She was clever, with a broad streak of sadism, and punished Helle's "sins" with such imaginative cruelty that the poor girl came to prefer Nobilita's routine abuse.

As Helle grew into a beautiful young woman, out of jealousy her less-than-beautiful stepsisters oppressed her more than ever. They often rubbed ashes and soot on her face and into her hair to conceal her beauty, so they called her Cinder-Helle. "Your fires are out," Ecclesia said to her. "Your mother was a witch, your old Goddess is dead, and you're nothing but a cinder-maid."

Sometimes, when she had a few minutes to herself, Cinder-Helle went to her mother's grave and talked to it, pouring out her troubles. A graceful willow tree had grown up from the grave, and when its branches gently rustled in the wind, Cinder-Helle imagined that the mother-spirit was speaking words of comfort to her.

One of the old Goddess's major harvest festivals honoring the fore-mothers, Hallow Eve, was still celebrated with a ball at the king's palace. One year it was a particularly great occasion, because the handsome young Prince Populo announced that he would choose his bride on that evening. She would be crowned Hallow Eve Queen and later would become his real queen.

All the well-to-do maidens coveted invitations to this Hallow Eve ball. Therefore Cinder-Helle's stepsisters were delighted when a herald brought an invitation to their house. They began at once to plan their festive costumes. Cinder-Helle asked timidly, "But what shall I wear?"

"You!" exclaimed Nobilita. "You'll wear your rags, as usual, and stay home as usual among the cinders. You can't go to the ball."

"But the invitation is addressed to all the young ladies of the house," Cinder-Helle protested.

"You're not a lady. You're a servant."

"I'm as much a lady as you," Cinder-Helle declared. At this, both sisters set upon her with slaps, pinches, and hair-pullings, finally shoving her out of the room. "Go back to your cinders, witch-spawn!" Ecclesia shrieked. "You can't go to the ball, and that's final!"

As the great day approached, the stepmother and stepsisters forced Cinder-Helle to fit and sew their costumes for them. Sitting alone in her garret room, sewing, she often watered the thread with her tears. The sisters berated her if she seemed to do anything better for one of them than for the other. They jealously craved to outshine one another. Each wanted to be crowned Hallow-Eve Queen and to marry Prince Populo. Nobilita insisted that her queenly bearing and pride made her the obvious candidate. Ecclesia claimed that she alone embodied all the virtues, and if the prince failed to choose her, he would be damned.

On the appointed evening, Cinder-Helle's stepmother and stepsisters entered their turreted coach together and departed for the ball. Left alone, Cinder-Helle sadly made the harvest charm as her mother had taught her, hollowing out a pumpkin shell and putting a candle inside it to represent the glowing orange harvest moon. Then she took the pumpkin as an offering to her mother's grave. Sitting under the willow tree, she wept as she told her troubles to the mother-spirit.

Then she distinctly heard the voice of the tree speaking to her. "Don't cry, daughter Helle," it said. "You shall go to the ball. You are in your moon time, and therefore you have magic. Listen to my directions. Only remember one thing above all: Fairy gifts dissolve at midnight."

Cinder-Helle nodded and dried her tears, all rapt attention as the voice continued. "Now, take your Hallow Eve pumpkin back home, and blow out the candle. Put into the pumpkin two cobwebs from the barn, two dewdrops from the eaves, a lump of coal from the grate, an earthworm from the garden, a mouse from the trap, and six beetles from under the hearthstone. Then sprinkle them all with your own moon blood, and see what happens."

Cinder-Helle followed these directions faithfully and was astonished by what transpired. The pumpkin grew and grew and sprouted wheels, axles, doors, and windows, becoming a splendid golden coach with elegant fittings inside. The cobwebs turned into a beautiful ball gown and matching cloak of silver gray silk, lavishly sewn with sparkling rubies that congealed from the drops of blood. The dewdrops turned into well-fitting, dainty crystal slippers, also decorated with rubies. The lump of coal shattered into small bits that strung themselves together and became a necklace of black pearls. The earthworm became a golden bracelet in the form of a serpent with ruby eyes. The candle became a golden tiara glorified by rubies the size of walnuts. The mouse turned into a pompous periwigged coachman in a rich gray velvet jacket with scarlet buckles. The six beetles grew into six magnificent black horses, as well matched as peas in a pod, harnessed to the coach with traces of gold and deerhide set with carnelians and red garnets.

Cinder-Helle was delighted with these transformations. She hastened to remove her rags, wash herself, and dress in her fairy finery. Then the mouse-coachman drove her to the palace, where her entrance created a sensation. When she swept through the ballroom doors all eyes turned in her direction.

Prince Populo gallantly hastened to welcome her and to kiss her hand. He was so smitten with her, in fact, that he would dance with none other for the whole evening. If she sat out a dance, he insisted on sitting with her, talking to her, admiring her jewels, fetching her sherbets with his own hands. He begged her to reveal her name, but she would not. She was too ashamed of her everyday life.

Like many others among the ladies, Nobilita and Ecclesia were enraged at the advent of this beautiful stranger who monopolized the prince's attention. They watched helplessly, grinding their teeth, as Prince Populo announced that this unknown maiden was his choice for Hallow Eve Queen.

When the time came for the mock wedding, Cinder-Helle was asked to remove one of her dainty crystal slippers so the royal scepter could be inserted into it, as a symbol of union. Just as this was done, the clock struck midnight. Suddenly she remembered her mother-spirit's warning about fairy gifts dissolving at midnight.

She fled from the ballroom, leaving her slipper in the prince's hands. As she ran out toward her coach, it shrank into a pumpkin. The coachman dropped down on all fours and scampered away, a mouse once more. The horses shriveled into black beetles and scuttled off. Cinder-Helle felt her silken ball gown dissolve into cobwebs, leaving her naked body sprinkled with drops of blood, which were all that remained of her jewels. Her bracelet became an earthworm and dropped from her arm. Her pearls turned into coal. Her remaining shoe was now nothing but a wet spot.

She ran into the cover of the woods and hurried home by hidden paths. She was back in her old rags, sitting by the fire, when her stepsisters returned from the ball. They could talk of nothing but the mysterious stranger who had enchanted Prince Populo and then vanished. "Just think," said Nobilita, "he has no mate now except that silly little shoe, his symbolic bride. Surely that play wedding will never be considered binding, for the bride will never be found."

The stepsisters didn't reckon on Prince Populo's determination. He kept the crystal slipper, which had been preserved by the magic touch of the scepter and had not dissolved along with its mate on Cinder-Helle's other foot. He announced that all the maidens in the kingdom would be tested by this slipper. He would marry the one whose foot it fitted, because they were already married by the ritual of the scepter.

Accordingly, the prince went forth in person with the slipper, day after day, to visit every house in which a young woman of marriageable age lived, to try the slipper on her. He found no foot dainty enough to fit it.

When he came to Cinder-Helle's house, the stepmother and stepsisters bustled about to make him comfortable, to offer him refreshments, to show him their best possessions. Nobilita brought forth an album of portraits of illustrious members of her family. Ecclesia enumerated for him her charitable works and spiritual accomplishments. Both tried to impress him with their erudition, their cultivated tastes, and their patronage of the arts.

The prince was not especially impressed. In the last few days he had looked at a great number of maidens. These two seemed no better than average, perhaps even less interesting than most. Nevertheless, he offered the slipper to their feet. Nobilita and Ecclesia pushed and twisted, but neither could force her large foot into it.

While they were trying, Prince Populo noticed Cinder-Helle sitting in her usual place by the hearth. Her face, though disguised by dirt, rang a faint bell in the depths of his mind.

"Who is that?" he asked.

"A nobody, a scullery maid," said Nobilita. "A lazy, dirty servant," said Ecclesia.

"Still, her feet seem very small," said the prince. "Let her try the slipper."

"Impossible, Your Highness," cried the stepmother. "The girl is nothing but a slatternly peasant, nowhere near as suitable as these two lovely maidens here." Both stepsisters simpered ingratiatingly.

"Let her try the slipper," the prince commanded.

Cinder-Helle was brought forward and seated in an armchair usually forbidden to her, while Populo himself applied the shoe to her foot. It fitted like a glove.

"This is my bride," he declared, recognizing her features under the soot and smudges. Cinder-Helle happily kissed him and smeared his face also. They looked at each other's dirty faces and laughed.

The formal wedding was celebrated at the earliest possible date. When Cinder-Helle became Princess Helle, she reestablished the temples of the Goddess. She founded a chapel and pilgrimage shrine at her mother's tomb and declared the willow tree sacred. She made Nobilita a secretary-companion to the wealthiest duchess in the kingdom, who was also the toughest, crudest, bluntest, most hard-riding, foul-mouthed, rough-hewn woman in six counties. Eventually, Nobilita abandoned her affectations and became something like a real person. Princess Helle also made Ecclesia live up to her pretenses of piety by taking a vow of poverty and ministering to the sick. Eventually, Ecclesia learned to feel useful in this life and became a sincere, almost saintly person. As for Christiana, she died unsatisfied.

And of course, Prince Populo and Princess Helle lived happily ever after.

TWENTY-THREE

HOW WINTER CAME TO THE WORLD

Here Persephone or Kore (Corey) and her mother, Demeter (Dea Mater), are presented without a dominant Father Zeus, and with a mythic understanding of the seasons.

Persephone means "Destroyer" and was originally applied to Kore's underground crone form, completing the Demeter trinity of Virgin, Mother, and Crone. Apparently Persephone was another name for Hecate, queen of the ghost world, long before patriarchal writers invented a new myth to account for her presence underground. Pluto, "Abundance," was another name for the Goddess herself. Although the name was commonly applied to the dark god, Greek myth still speaks of a female Titan named Pluto. Titans, like giants, were the elder race that preceded the divine pantheon, and Shakespeare still understood that the fairy queen's true name was Titania.

Pomegranates were sacred to the underground Goddess and were primary womb symbols, with their uterine shape, red juice, and many seeds. In classical antiquity, the gates of the dead were guarded by the three-headed dog Cerberus, who passed into Christian lore as one of the gatekeepers of hell.

Princess Corey spent much time dancing and picnicking . . .

$\mathcal{O}$nce upon a time there was a beautiful fairy princess named Corey, daughter of the great fairy queen Dea Mater, also known as Titania, the Titaness. At that time the fairies ruled all of nature. Their songs and dances caused flowers to bloom and fruits to ripen, breezes to blow, stars to glow, streams to flow, and earth to grow good things. It was a golden age of eternal summer. There was delightful weather all year round.

Princess Corey, the apple of her mother's eye, spent much time dancing and picnicking with her maidens on a hillside where pomegranates grew wild. They were especially fond of pomegranates. Queen Dea Mater was always busy keeping the winds warmed, spacing out the rains for maximum crop growth, and otherwise looking after the weather. She saw to it that her daughter's favorite hillside was always bathed in the brightest sunlight or moonlight (for the fairy maidens loved to do ring dances under the moon).

At that time there were no trolls on the fairies' earth. All the trolls lived in caves deep underground, in a gloomy realm of eternal night. Their function was to draw down the dead from the upper world and rule over the nations of ghosts.

Pluton, king of the trolls, resented this state of affairs. He wanted to acquire some of the light and sweetness of the upper world for himself. Trolls are very acquisitive by nature. They clutch their hoards of gems and precious metals or seal them into the rocks to discourage thievery. They are miserly, always wanting more of everything. Thus Pluton brooded over the thought that the fairies might have more of something than he had. To him Princess Corey embodied the advantages of the upper world, which he coveted.

In Princess Corey's favorite hillside there was a cave, whose small mouth was concealed by some bushes. Behind it, a passage led to the lower world. King Pluton sometimes went there and peeped out at the dancing maidens. He saw the beautiful princess encouraging flowers to bloom and fruits to ripen, breezes to blow, stars to glow, streams to flow, and earth to grow good things. He resolved to kidnap her and make her his bride.

Then, he thought, he would be able to control much of the enviable light and sweetness of the upper world and bring some into his own realm.

King Pluton made careful plans. He prepared a cave palace for his unsuspecting bride-to-be and stocked it with a choice selection of gems from his hoard. He chose the best and brightest ghosts to be her servants. He had his smiths and stonecarvers create a throne of the finest multicolored jasper for her, a crown of silver set with rubies, a platinum scepter topped by an immense diamond, a dining-table of polished rainbow obsidian, and a bedstead of mauve jade. He had her chambers walled with slabs of malachite and floored with snow-white marble. He furnished them with exquisitely carved ornaments of beryl, agate, amber, chalcedony, and opal, created by the lapidary trolls whose skills were unmatched anywhere in the cosmos.

Looking around these rich apartments, Pluton felt confident that his bride-to-be would find the underworld more beautiful than the upper world, since he had spared no expense to dazzle her with the bounty of his kingdom. "Flowers are all very well," he muttered, "but they fade in a day, whereas the glory of a sapphire or a tourmaline is forever. Surely the girl can't be such a fool as to prefer the ephemeral to the eternal."

When all was ready, he went to the cave mouth on the hillside and waited for Princess Corey and her maidens. When they appeared, he leaped out of the cave with a great crackling and booming of broken rock, seized the princess, and charged back into the cave with the princess slung over his shoulder. The maidens screamed at the sight of his looming black figure and his craggy face. They ran away to tell Dea Mater that a huge, hideous troll had kidnapped Princess Corey and carried her underground.

Pluton installed Corey in the palace he had prepared for her and was chagrined to find that she didn't like it. "It's dark," she complained, "and chilly and damp, and there are no flowers." In vain he called her attention to the malachite walls and marble floors, the jasper throne, the silver crown, the beautiful ornaments. In vain he offered her necklaces of gold and topaz, bracelets of lapis lazuli and garnet. She only sighed and pined day after day. She ate and slept little. She paid no heed to her splendid jewels or her ghostly servants who came and went so silently and deferentially. She became thin and pale. Her hair hung in dirty strings. Her eyes and nose were red from weeping. Pluton began to think that her beauty was like that of the flowers, subject to early fading.

Meanwhile, on earth, the fairy queen was so distraught at the loss of her beloved daughter that she stopped all activity and sequestered herself in her palace to grieve. No longer did the flowers bloom or the fruits ripen. The breezes stopped blowing, the stars stopped glowing, and the streams stopped flowing. No more did the earth grow good things. Dark clouds gathered in the sky, shutting out the light of the sun and the moon. Trees dropped their leaves. Grass turned brown and died. Streams were choked with ice. Birds no longer sang. Seeds no longer sprouted. Animals and people began to starve. The first winter fell on the land.

In vain the fairies told Dea Mater of all these terrible things happening on earth because of her neglect. She didn't care. She only wanted to be alone with her sorrow.

At last the fairies realized that something would have to be done before the earth withered away altogether and left them without a home. Fearing that their own sun-powered nature magic wouldn't work underground, they sent a delegation to an old elf named Zooz, who claimed to be the greatest magician in the world. They begged him to go down to the underworld and rescue Princess Corey, before the earth was completely destroyed.

"What's my reward?" Zooz asked the fairies.

"If you succeed," said their leader, "we'll give you a castle in the sky and make you a king of heaven."

"Done," said Zooz, who knew a good offer when he heard one. He packed up his kit and set off to visit King Pluton. He knew a nearby cave reputed to be a main entrance to the nether world.

At the entrance to the cave, Zooz noticed a pomegranate tree with pitch-black limbs. He cast a communication spell and addressed the spirit of the tree. "What manner of tree are you, with strange dark skin?" he asked.

"I bear the fruit of the dead," said the spirit. "Souls come to me thirsty and hungry, and I offer refreshment. Once they have taken a single seed of my fruit, they are bonded to the nether regions and can't return to earth."

"Then I won't eat your fruit," said Zooz, "because I am destined to become a king of heaven, and I wouldn't want to stay forever underground."

"Suit yourself," said the tree spirit. "Underground isn't so bad, once you get used to it. Not every good thing is found only on the earth's surface.

Without my strong roots underground, I'd fall over in the next storm and die."

"May your roots never wither," said Zooz politely. He passed the pomegranate tree and entered the underworld. He found himself facing a fearsome gatekeeper with three heads, each with the face of a savage dog, and a thick body with three doglike tails. "You're not dead," snarled the gatekeeper. "What's your business here?"

"I've come to see King Pluton," said Zooz.

"The king doesn't see live folk," growled the gatekeeper. "Go away."

"He'll see me," said Zooz. "I'm in a position to offer him something valuable."

The gatekeeper snorted contemptuously. "King Pluton already owns every valuable object, every gem crystal, every vein of precious metal, every important rock. What could you possibly offer him?"

"Something nonmaterial, so valuable as to have no price," said Zooz. "Let me in, and I promise you your king will reward you."

"You're a bold rogue," said the gatekeeper. "Enter, then. If you're not telling the truth, you'll soon become a living ghost. Believe me, there's little pleasure in that."

"May your tails wag forever," said Zooz politely. He passed the gatekeeper and proceeded toward the king's dark palace. On the way he passed crowds of pallid, half-transparent ghosts wandering aimlessly, some bewailing their fate, others stolidly resigned or simply blank. Trolls worked in groups here and there, digging in the rocks for crystals or panning the streams for gold. Oily black lakes and stalagmitic columns dotted the landscape. The air was stagnant but chilly, with a claylike odor. "I can well understand why Princess Corey doesn't want to live here," said Zooz to himself.

When he arrived at the dark palace, he announced that he had an important offer to make to the king. Eventually he was conducted to the throne room, where Pluton sat on a black onyx throne, with his counselors standing by in black robes of state. Zooz bowed, and Pluton waved a hand toward him, saying, "Speak, earth dweller. You have five minutes of my valuable time, no more."

"I've come to offer you a kingdom beyond Your Majesty's wildest dreams, sire," said Zooz. "Half of the world, in fact. A land of the dead so huge that you will be known, honored, and feared by every human on the earth, which one day will be virtually overrun by humans in inconceivable numbers."

"Big talk," sneered Pluton. "Who is to make all this happen? You? Don't make me laugh."

"Yes, I will do it," said Zooz, "because I am destined to become king of heaven. When that happens, I will seize power over everything else, since, as everyone knows, all things are controlled by the stars—even your underworld, great king. When I become the ruler of heaven, I will divide the cosmos with you. I will rule the sky and the lands of the living. You will rule the nether regions and the lands of the dead, forever. And as death carries away more and more individuals of all species, your kingdom will grow exponentially, without limit."

"And who is going to make you king of heaven?" asked Pluton.

"The fairies will, at first. Then the humans will worship me, and as their numbers increase, I will grow greater and more powerful with each passing year."

"Why should the fairies exalt the likes of you?"

"Because I will bring Princess Corey back to them," said Zooz. "That will be your payment to me for your own future exaltation. The fairies have promised me the heavens as a reward for persuading you. As you know, fairies always keep their promises."

"Yes, but do sly elf magicians with ulterior motives keep their promises?" Pluton asked. "Counselors, what do you think?"

The counselors consulted among themselves, buzzing with opinions and assessments. They agreed that an exponential augmentation of the earth's human population would benefit all of Pluton's ministers, as a corresponding expansion of the underground realm would mean more authority to be delegated and more power to go around.

Finally their spokesman addressed the king: "We advise that Your Majesty accept the offer. It can only lead to enhancement of your magnificence. Even if something goes wrong, no real harm is done and little is lost. Your Majesty does not need the fairy princess."

"It's true that she has been a disappointment," Pluton mused. "Her beauty and her creative powers have languished, and she's no fun to have around. Very well, wizard, I accept your offer. Take the wretched girl back with you, but you must leave me one of your eyes as evidence of good faith. You can have it again when you have fulfilled your part of the bargain."

Zooz was understandably reluctant to leave one of his eyes in the dark king's keeping, but he had no choice. A court barber-troll quickly performed the extraction and lined the empty eye socket with silver to preserve its latent powers of vision. After that unpleasant ordeal, Zooz was conducted to the princess's chamber.

He found Corey sitting sadly on her mauve jade bed, looking pale and ill. She gazed at him without interest, but she perked up when he said he had come to take her home. She took his hand and allowed him to lead her through miles of caverns to the main entrance. No one interfered with their passage. Even the three-headed gatekeeper stood aside to let them pass, though he showed his three sets of fangs menacingly.

On the way out, Corey saw the tree of pomegranates, her favorite fruit. Hopeful joy had made her really hungry for the first time in months, so she snatched one of the pomegranates from a branch. Before Zooz could prevent her, she tore open the skin and popped one of the sweet red seeds into her mouth. Zooz lunged at her, crying, "No!" But it was too late. The pomegranate seed was eaten.

"Oh, Princess, what have you done?" he wailed. "Now you belong to the underworld because you've eaten its magic fruit. Yet you also belong to the upper world because King Pluton promised to release you. I foresee that you will have to belong to both worlds."

"I want my mother," said Princess Corey.

When mother and daughter were reunited, there was dancing and feasting throughout the fairy realm. The fairies rejoiced, and the world rejoiced with them. Green buds sprang from apparently dead trees. The clouds dispersed; the sun shone. The air grew warmer. Once again breezes could blow, stars could glow, streams could flow, and the earth could grow good things. Flowers bloomed. Fruits ripened. Mass starvation was averted.

Queen Dea Mater gave Zooz his promised reward, dominion over the heavens. But before setting out to his castle in the sky, he warned her that Corey was still bonded to the underworld on account of having eaten its magic fruit. "There is no antidote to that charm," he said. "She will have to dwell in Pluton's kingdom for half of each year. But you may look forward to her return every spring."

Dea Mater didn't like this, but she agreed that not even powerful fairies could resist the charm. She took another way around the difficulty. She began to train Princess Corey to accept her fate with equanimity and to turn it to her advantage. Instead of spending her time underground helpless with despair, Corey was to exert herself to gain power over Pluton and make herself the undisputed queen of the kingdom of the dead.

Dea Mater trained her well. When Princess Corey was forced to return to the underworld at the end of half a year, she no longer sighed or pined. She greeted the dark lord with grace and confidence. She joined him at the state banquet and ate heartily. She admired and appreciated his jewels. She asked questions about the operations of his government and about the trolls' mining activities. Gratified by her attention and delighted to see that her half year aboveground had restored her beauty, Pluton fell in love with her. Soon she had him so totally besotted that he could deny her nothing.

Following her mother's good advice, Princess Corey became the true queen of the dead, whom she treated with kindness. She took the name of Queen Crone and the title of Lady Death. When earth people felt death coming on, they appealed to her because she seemed both more powerful and more merciful than the king of the trolls. Little by little, year by year, she moved herself onto Pluton's throne and became the most feared and adored of underworld spirits.

During her annual absence, Dea Mater grieved and the earth languished. Winter returned. But each year Princess Corey came back to visit her mother, and the fairies' festivities brought life back to the world. So the years were divided into winters and summers, with transitional seasons of anticipation in spring and melancholy in the fall.

Since the fairies kept their hold on the earth for half the year at least, King Pluton considered that Zooz had not fully kept his part of their bargain and refused to give back his eye. He sent a message to the new lord of the heavens, saying, "I have only half the dominion of the earth and must give up my queen for half the year. Therefore you deserve only half the faculty of vision."

Zooz was furious. He ranted about the perfidy of underground folk, calling Pluton names like Father of Lies, Great Deceiver, Adversary, and

Evil One. He taught the humans to fear and hate the underworld and its denizens, even the ghosts who were their own ancestors. He turned against the fairies because of their half-and-half pact with Pluton, and he even dared to describe Dea Mater as a mother of devils.

Zooz envied the awe that humans accorded the powers of the nether regions. He tried to turn it onto himself by claiming sole responsibility for earthly deaths, rebirths, punishments, rewards, rules, and regulations. He became increasingly conceited and autocratic. He abused his human slaves by visiting arbitrary punishments on them, forcing them to make war on one another over trifling differences of opinion about his worship. He commanded them to despise some of the few things that made their lives worth living, such as love and physical pleasures. In the end he became quite irrational, but he gained enough power to force the fairies underground along with their Queen Crone and to have them identified in many human minds with powers of darkness.

Ironically, Zooz's manipulations actually did expand the lands of the dead exponentially, as the humans died in inconceivably large numbers and joined the ghost population. Death began to be so commonplace in the human world that the people even got used to Zooz's seemingly insane directive to inflict it on fellow members of their own species. Some of the most violent among them were those most devoted to the lord of heaven.

Still, some of the humans remembered that it was Dea Mater and not Zooz who brought the earth its annual flowering, who caused the breeze to blow, the stars to glow, the streams to flow, and the earth to grow good things. Some remembered the fairies as beneficent spirits and sought contact with them. Some worshiped King Pluton and Queen Crone, on the ground that death was inevitably stronger than life, and deities of the dark, solid earth were closer to human affairs than those of the thin airs of heaven. Moreover, they never ceased to yearn for the trolls' treasures or to dig into the rocks in search of unfading jewels and mineral wealth.

As rulers of the ever-growing realm of ghosts, King Pluton and Queen Crone became famous and powerful. The king even learned to feel gratification when his resourceful queen returned to her maiden form each year, transformed herself into Princess Corey, and made the earth smile again. To some extent he became reconciled with her mother, Dea Mater, who learned to respect his true and deep love of nature's hidden but enduring aspects, the dark rocks and soil containing the minerals of which all life is formed. They realized that cooperation was better than alienation and made alliance in order to live happily ever after.

But Zooz would have no part of their detente. He remained eaten up by rage and jealousy. He never got his eye back. It stayed in the underworld and ignited undying fires there. Some of the earth people remembered him as the one-eyed god and made up absurd stories to account for his loss and his eternal anger.

TWENTY-FOUR

THE EMPRESS'S NEW CLOTHES

In Andersen's tale of the emperor's new clothes, every character is male, ignoring centuries of female intimacy with all matters of dress and fabric arts. This version makes all the important characters female, with a resulting surprise ending that allows the two protagonists to stay alive and even to prosper. The empress is credited with more common sense than that emperor, and she shows a better grasp of how to earn the loyalty of her subjects.

Page 214

"But she's naked! Mommy, the empress is naked!"

nce upon a time, during the reign of the last empress of Cathay, two clever sisters who were dressmakers devised a plan to make themselves rich. They pretended to have the world's most exquisite and expensive silk, to which they attributed the magical power of distinguishing between virtuous and sinful people. They said the magic silk couldn't be seen or felt by people whose consciences bore any burden of guilt or immorality, whereas innocent folk could perceive it clearly. They sold, for enormous sums, many empty bolts to foolish customers who dared not admit that they could see nothing on them.

Word of the magic silk eventually came to the ears of the empress herself, just as she was planning a great procession in honor of her own birthday. She insisted that she must have new clothes made for the occasion out of this wonderful material. Not the least of its advantages, thought the empress, was its capacity to sort out the blameless from the dishonest among her own courtiers. She sent for the two dressmakers, promising them a reward of riches beyond their wildest dreams.

The younger sister was frightened by the summons to the imperial court. "We'll be discovered, arrested, and executed," she said. "This is the end of the game, and the end of us. Oh, why did I let you talk me into this scam in the first place?"

"Stop whining," the older sister snapped. "We'll get away with it, I tell you, if we don't lose our nerve. Our fortune is made forever if we succeed in dressing the empress in her birthday suit—ha ha. Just be bold, and remember, they're not going to be able to admit that they can't see it."

"But the court is full of the empire's best and wisest," wailed the younger sister. "Nobles, scientists, seers, legislators, educated people. Surely we can't pull the wool—or silk—over their eyes."

The elder sister snickered. "Trust me, they're the worst hypocrites of all," she said. "Relax, sister. We'll get away with it. After we've made our fortune, we'll leave the country and live in luxury as far away from here as we can get."

They traveled to the imperial court. The elder sister tried to keep up her younger sister's spirits by reminding her of the good life that would be theirs—the fine clothes, the servants, the parties, the best food and wine, the eager suitors.

On their arrival, they were ushered immediately into the presence of the empress, who demanded to see the magic silk at once. The sisters showed several empty bolts and made a great pantomime of unrolling yards of material at the empress's feet.

"Look at the golden shimmer of that one, Your Imperial Majesty," said the elder sister. "Light as a cloud it is, too. You can hardly feel it on your skin. And this one—Did you ever see such a rich violet shade in all your life? And such exquisite patterns. Like spider silk woven by fairies."

All the courtiers proceeded to ooh and aah, pretending to see and feel the delicate silk. Each one was secretly appalled to find it indistinguishable from empty air and began to think back over his or her past crimes with unaccustomed shame and fear of discovery.

The empress herself was much chagrined at her own inability to see the magic silk. She smiled and said nothing, inwardly recalling various immoralities of her past and some of the ruthless measures she had been forced to take to secure her position on the throne. She looked around the audience chamber and saw all her attendants and counselors loudly exclaiming over the beauty of the magic silk. "Am I the only evildoer here?" she thought nervously. "They must never know!"

In subsequent weeks the two dressmakers were installed in a gorgeous suite with a fully appointed workroom and were given everything they requested. They pretended to be sewing industriously, day after day. They gave the empress several fittings. In pantomime, the sisters dressed her in undergarments that they praised as the world's most beautiful, then in a golden gown that they said shone as brightly as the sun, then in a cloak that they claimed was fit for a goddess. All the while, the empress stood naked while her courtiers looked on and murmured flatteringly about the dazzling loveliness of her clothes.

Seeing how easily they had bamboozled the courtiers and even the empress herself, the younger sister began to feel that their deception might succeed after all. Yet she was apprehensive. When the great day of the procession dawned clear and fine, she suffered a sudden failure of nerve. She clutched her sister's arm.

"We can't do it," she cried. "We've got to run away, right now."

"What do you mean, we can't do it?" said the elder. "Don't quit on me now, little one. We're almost home free. Don't you want to live in luxury for the rest of your life?"

"Yes, but I especially want there to be a rest of my life, even if it's not luxurious," said the younger sister. "Listen, she's going to go out there in broad daylight, in front of thousands of people, and parade around without a stitch on. Nothing that humiliating has ever happened to an empress. Don't you understand? Somebody in the crowd is sure to see the truth, and we'll be drawn and quartered before tomorrow's sunrise."

"We've gotten away with it so far, haven't we?" said her sister. "Hang on, everything will be all right. Guilt is universal. There's not a person in the whole empire who doesn't have a secret shame."

"Yes, I know. I have one myself," said the younger sister gloomily. But she swallowed her fears and went with her sister to the empress's apartments to dress her for the great occasion.

While pretending to put on the clothes, the elder sister pantomimed a thousand careful adjustments. "Your Imperial Majesty should remember to hold her head high, so as not to crumple this dainty stand-up collar," she said. "And the train must be swept to one side when Your Imperial Majesty makes a turn."

"Like this?" said the empress, turning.

"That's exactly right, Your Magnificence," cried the dressmaker. "You honor us by wearing our clothes with such grace."

"We are told that grace is Our birthright," said the empress. "But then, imperial persons are always told such things."

The procession started out with much rolling of drums and blaring of trumpets. Preceded by heralds, knights, and courtiers in their most splendid costumes, the empress walked forth into the sunlight, clothed with nothing but her dignity. Her assembled subjects raised a great cry of admiration and homage, its volume only increased by their anxiety to conceal their surprise.

The procession had passed nearly all of its appointed route when a small child peeped out from behind her mother's skirt to see the empress pass by. During a pause in the imperial music, the child's voice rose loud and shrill into the clear morning air: "But she's naked! Mommy, the empress is naked!"

The empress turned her head abruptly toward the sound and made a small gesture. The procession halted immediately. Guardsmen seized both the child and the mother and brought them before the empress.

"What did you say, little girl?" the empress asked.

"You're naked," the child replied, while her mother wrung her hands and writhed with fear.

"Please forgive her, Your Imperial Majesty," the mother cried. "She's only a baby. She doesn't know what she's saying."

"On the contrary," said the empress, "We think she knows very well what she's saying. She is too young to have crimes to repent. Guard, let them go, and give Us your cloak."

Weeping with relief, the mother fell on her knees to thank the empress for her mercy, but the empress paid little attention to her. Swathed in a guardsman's cloak, she finished the processional route and returned to her palace.

The dressmakers were arrested at once and dragged in chains to the throne room.

"You two have diddled Us in grand style," said the empress to the trembling sisters. "You've proved beyond a doubt that everybody in Our court and even in Our imperial city is basically dishonest, except for one small child. Should you be rewarded for heroism or executed for treason?"

"Neither, please, Your Mercifulness," begged the elder sister. "Only let us go in peace, in your infinite compassion, and we will never trouble anyone again. We are most heartily sorry for our crime and can only plead for Your Imperial Majesty's indulgence."

"What have you to say for yourself?" asked the empress, turning to the younger sister.

"Dear Majesty, I can only say that I didn't expect to get away with our scheme, and now my worst fears have been realized. We have done you wrong, and if you think we deserve death, that's your decision to make."

"Well spoken," said the empress. "You may deserve death indeed; but you have outwitted Our best counselors and even Our imperial self, and thus proved yourselves too clever to be discarded. Never let it be said that

We have not sufficient sense of humor to appreciate the joke of a lifetime on Ourselves. We forgive you. We have decided to reward you instead of condemning you. You shall be appointed official dressmakers to the empress and privy counselors on matters of morality and ethics. Guard, remove their chains."

The two dressmakers became the empress's personal attendants, fashion stylists, and intimate advisors. The empress learned to trust both their tailoring skills and their needle-sharp perceptions. For the following year's birthday procession, they created a costume of real silk that was widely admired as the most beautiful ever seen. Enjoying the empress's confidence and a permanent sinecure, they lived happily ever after.

TWENTY-FIVE

THE THREE LITTLE PINKS

The story of the three little pigs is a frivolous fairy tale, and this one follows suit. Bottom-of-the-garden fairies constitute a reference to the famous hoax perpetrated on Sir Arthur Conan Doyle by means of fairy pictures cut out of a book, propped up on a bush at the bottom of his garden, and photographed. He wrote excitedly about his conviction that they were genuine nature spirits.

No one seems to know when pink was declared the official feminine color. It may have had something to do with the combination of Virgin and Mother, symbolized by white and red respectively. But it is a curious fact that only very recently have a few men become bold enough to wear pink.

Page 223

He puffed up his chest and blew.

*O*nce upon a time there were three fairy sisters, of the type known as Little People, whose job it was to paint flowers pink. As you may know, most fairies look just like human beings, but the flower-painting or bottom-of-the-garden fairies are very tiny and have transparent wings. They don't look like full-sized human beings at all. Perhaps you have seen some of them fluttering by and mistaken them for moths or butterflies.

These three flower-painting sisters, Pearl, Shell, and Candy, had pink hair and were known as the three little pinks. They worked in the queen's gardens. Pearl was in charge of painting the most delicate tints, verging on white. Shell applied rosier pinks, coral, tea-rose, and flesh colors. Candy painted intense hot pinks and deep raspberry shades. They all believed that some kind of pink is the best possible color for any flower.

Unfortunately, their opinion was not shared by the queen's head gardener, Florian Wolf, who detested pink as a "female color." Florian Wolf didn't like anything female, except the queen, who paid his salary. He put up with the fairies who painted flowers red, yellow, blue, and purple because the queen liked to see a lot of color in her garden. But Florian didn't want any pink fairies at all.

One day when he found the three little pinks going about their business among the roses, he threw a tantrum. "I told you three to knock it off!" he yelled. "I ordered white, red, or yellow roses only. Now you get some new colors or get out."

"You can't throw us out," said Candy defiantly, in her piping voice. "We've lived in this garden for nearly three centuries. It's our home. We were painting flowers pink here when your pink baby bottom was still in diapers. Just who do you think you are?"

"I'm her majesty's head gardener, that's who," Florian Wolf snarled. "And this garden is going to be what I say it's going to be, no more and no less. You'll find out that it doesn't pay to talk back to me."

With that, he swatted the fairies aside and proceeded to pull up all the pink-tinted roses by the roots. He threw them on the ground and stamped on them.

At first the three little pinks stood still, watching this desecration with horror. Then they recovered their wits and acted. Each one snapped a thorn off one of the rosebushes. Buzzing with anger, they flew at Florian Wolf's face and scratched him with all their might. Whenever he batted one away, the other two kept up the attack.

As last Florian retreated, bleeding from a dozen little scratches and roaring with rage. From the safety of the greenhouse doorway, he shook his fist at the fairies, dancing up and down in his fury.

"You pinks will be out of this garden by tomorrow's sunrise," he shouted. "If I find one of you, or one pink flower anywhere after that, I'll net you, pull your wings off, and feed you to the pigs. You'll make nice morsels for them, all right."

The fairies were appalled. "What a violent person!" Pearl exclaimed.

"I don't know how the flowers can tolerate him," said Shell.

"Of course we're not going anywhere," said Candy. "We'll find a way to solve this problem." They clustered, discussing the situation.

"Should we ask for help from the fairy queen, or the mortal queen?" Shell asked.

"Neither," said Candy. "We can fight our own battles. But first we have to move our sleeping places. He knows where our cobweb hammocks are. We have to leave them and build ourselves some houses for protection."

"What a good idea," Pearl cried, clapping her hands. "I've always wanted to build a house."

"Let's separate and build houses in new spots," Shell suggested. "Then we'll meet at midnight by the big oak."

"And then," said Candy, "we'll paint everything in the garden pink. That'll show him."

Giggling with mischievous delight, they flew off in different directions to establish their new homes.

Pearl went to the oriole, whose nest she admired, to ask about materials and construction methods. Flattered by a fairy's request for advice, the bird cocked her head up and down in order to look wise. Then she said, "By far the best building material is straw. You can find plenty of it in the hayloft of the royal stables." So Pearl flew off to collect straws. She began to build her house on the lowest branch of a large dogwood tree that bore pale pink flowers.

She didn't know that she was observed by Florian Wolf's pet rat, Racer, who lived in the stables. Racer was kept well fed on table scraps, because he was a champion runner. He had won a lot of money for Florian when the gardeners, stable hands, and other servants bet on rat races.

Because rats know everything, Racer knew about the altercation between his master and the pinks. And because rats are adept at concealment when they want to be, Racer easily kept out of sight when he followed Pearl to find out what she was doing with the straw. He watched as she worked busily, humming as she wove the straws and happily saw her house grow. It seemed to her the most beautiful house ever. It needed just one more touch to make it perfect: to be painted pink all over. This was soon done.

Shell went for building advice to her friend the beaver, who said, "The best building materials are twigs. A house of twigs will trap other debris and will soon become watertight." So Shell gathered piles of twigs and built her house under a pink rosebush, where she felt protected by the thorns. She colored most of the twigs pink to match the roses above.

Candy consulted the mud wasps, who were always constructing houses. They said, "Bricks made of clay are the only good building materials. Interlock the bricks in your walls. If the clay is well dried and bonded, not even the heaviest rain will wash it away."

So Candy toiled very hard, blistering her tiny pink hands, to build a brick house next door to the mud wasps. She chose a spot by the stump of an azalea bush that Florian Wolf had cut down because he disliked its brilliant hot-pink flowers.

When the three fairies met at midnight, they first visited one another's new houses, admiring the pink straw and pink twig houses especially. Candy was a bit crestfallen because her house was not pink, but she explained that making and laying bricks was extremely hard, slow work, and she had not had time for cosmetic considerations. At least her house was sturdy.

"Now," said Pearl, "we'll really go to work."

The three pinks explained their situation to all the other flower-painting fairies, who already knew most of the story anyway, and obtained their permission to paint every single flower in the garden pink before the rising of the sun. They even pinkened a quantity of leaves for good measure. When Florian Wolf awoke that morning, his eyes were greeted by a blaze of pink as far as he could see.

Florian's face grew even pinker than the most vivid verbena. He stormed out of his door, flinging it back so hard that the hinges cracked. "I'll kill those little pink pests," he growled, setting off toward the grotto where he knew they hung their cobweb hammocks.

On the way, he met the queen, taking her early morning constitutional around the garden. "Why, Florian, what a good idea," she remarked, as he dropped to one knee before her. "It's fun to have an all-pink garden for a change, isn't it?"

"Yes, Your Majesty," Florian said through clenched teeth.

"I like it, Florian. Let's keep it this way for a while."

"Yes, Your Majesty."

"Perhaps next month you can change the dominant color to purple. For royalty, you know."

"I'll try my best, Your Majesty."

"All right, Florian. Dismissed."

She walked on, and Florian Wolf was left kneeling in the path, bristling with suppressed wrath. "I'll kill those conniving fairies anyway," he muttered. "Defy my orders, will they? We'll see about that."

He burst into the fairies' grotto and found it deserted, the cobweb hammocks tattered and useless. "All right, where are they?" he asked himself. Then he noticed Racer weaving back and forth between him and the door.

Racer understood human language fairly well, but he knew Florian didn't understand rat language at all; so he had to resort to broad pantomime, like a theatrical dog, to get a meaning across to his master. He finally made Florian Wolf realize that he could find the missing fairies. "Go on, then," Florian commanded, indicating that he was prepared to follow Racer and proud of himself for having comprehended the crude sign language of a dumb animal.

The rat led him to Pearl's straw house, whose pink color shone brightly against the bark of the dogwood tree. "Come out of there, you nasty little pink popinjay," Florian yelled. "Here comes big bad Wolf to say it's time for you to feed the pigs."

"You can't make me come out," Pearl shouted defiantly. "This is my house."

"Oh, yeah? I'll huff and I'll puff, and I'll blow your silly house away," Florian cried. He puffed up his chest and blew. Straws began to flutter and then slipped away one by one. Holes appeared in the walls, revealing a terrified Pearl crouching within. As her roof disappeared, she made a sudden galvanic leap and flew straight up, out of Florian's reach. Then she set off as fast as she could go, to the house of her sister Shell.

Racer was fast enough to keep up with the fairy's flight, so he followed and found the twig house under the rosebush. He saw Pearl knock at the door and enter and heard the two fairies barring the entrance with stout sticks. Then he raced back to his master, to repeat the I-know-where-to-go pantomime until Florian understood.

Led to the twig house by Racer, Florian shouted, "Look out, fairies! Here comes the big bad Wolf to turn you into pig meat! Now come on out before I stomp that ramshackle little mess you call a house into kindling!"

"Just you try, big bad Wolf," Shell called back.

Florian tried, but the thorny stems of the rosebushes grew so thickly over the twig house that he couldn't reach it. So he desisted, and snarled: "I'll huff and I'll puff, and I'll blow your house away." He puffed up his chest and blew until his eyes popped and his cheeks turned cyclamen pink. Sure enough, the twigs blew apart and the two fairies were revealed, clinging together in fear.

"Quick, make for Candy's house," Shell whispered to her sister. The fairies flew up, barely escaping Florian's quick snatch. Again the rat followed them and discovered the location of Candy's house. Again he raced back to Florian Wolf and led him on the path.

When Florian came to Candy's brick house, the mud wasps were buzzing around it in such numbers that he dared not reach toward it with his hand. One of Florian's chronic problems was an acute allergic reaction to wasp stings. He tried to conceal this, regarding it as a weakness. Nevertheless, he gave wasps a wide berth. So he contented himself with threats and demands that the three fairies give themselves up.

"Get lost, big bad Wolf," Candy shouted from within. "You can't make us do anything we don't want to do. This is our garden, not yours. You work with the fairies or you don't work at all, lamebrain."

Enraged, Florian screeched, "I'll get you yet, all of you! I'll huff and I'll puff, and right through your wasp army I'll blow your house down."

Again he filled his chest and blew such a hurricane that the wasps were hurled back against their own clay walls. Nevertheless, no matter how hard he blew, the little brick house stood firm. In his rage he failed to notice that the wasps were becoming very irritated indeed.

At last the wasps reached the end of their patience and passed the attack signal among themselves. Flying under the whistling wind stream from Florian's mouth, they charged at his arms, hands, legs, shoulders, torso, and neck. In seconds he was covered by buzzing, venomous tormenters. His roars of rage turned to screams. He writhed and rolled on the ground, crushing some of the wasps, but others persisted. Not until he was reduced to a huddled, whimpering lump did they leave off and return to their nests. The three little pinks came out of their brick house and waved gaily as the wasps came home one by one, dipping their wings in passing salute to the fairies.

Florian Wolf managed to drag himself back to the main garden shed before he collapsed, swelled up like a sausage and turned bright pink all over. The queen's own physician attended him and barely saved his life. The doctor ordered him to give up gardening forever, because one more wasp sting would undoubtedly kill him.

Florian went to work indoors, for a seed-catalog company. He was replaced in the royal gardens by his former apprentice, a clever young man who understood the advantages of working with the fairies. The royal flower beds flourished, more colorful than ever, with pink represented as well as any other color.

Pearl, Shell, and Candy kept busy at their usual jobs. They found that they enjoyed living together in Candy's brick house, so they stayed there. During the following spring they added two new wings and painted the whole exterior pink.

TWENTY-SIX

FAIRY GOLD

Mythic traditions the world over speak of man's best death as a consummation to be found in the arms of the Goddess. In India the dakinis or death priest-esses comforted the dying with loving embraces. Scandinavian Valkyries seem to have been similar Goddess surrogates, as were Persian houris, giving rise to the Islamic belief in sexual angels whose love would eternally reward warriors killed in battle. Roman philosophers longed for a death in "coming to Venus." During the Middle Ages, classical statues of the old Goddess were sometimes viewed as deadly to young men, especially monks.

Fairy gold was another name for vain hopes, or false treasure found by the cold gray light of dawn to have evaporated or turned into worthless tinsel. In this new story, however, the treasure is as real as the hero's immolation. Both, in a way, turn out to be blessings.

*He saw the figure of a nude woman, sculpted of marble and
painted with rich, lifelike colors.*

*O*nce upon a time there was a poor shepherd lad named Winsom, who lived with his widowed sister, Lissom, and her two children in a cottage on the wild fells. Brother and sister had always been close, since they had been orphaned at an early age and had been raised in a workhouse, where their only protective support was each other. Lissom had married a good man, but soon after the birth of their second child he had been "taken by the fairies."

In the fells country, "taken by the fairies" meant a special kind of death. Not far from the shepherd's cottage was a steep, deep ravine known as Fairy Gorge. It was so narrow that a long-legged man might jump across the top if he dared. At the upper end, a stream plunged down a drop of more than a hundred feet into the dark depths of the gorge. Some people professed to hear prophetic fairy voices in the waterfall's echoing roar.

The banks leading down to the gorge were slick and slippery, especially in damp weather. Quite a few sheep and cattle and even some people had ventured too near the drop and had slid down into the depths. Their bodies usually were found washed up on a bank far downstream. That was the fate of Lissom's husband.

Winsom was careful to pasture his sheep well away from Fairy Gorge, but one day he lost a lamb that wandered in that direction. It was a special, perfect lamb, born of the herd's finest ewe. Winsom and Lissom were sure that it would grow up to be a prizewinner, and Winsom was determined to recover it.

On approaching the gorge, he thought he heard the lamb's bleating above the noise of the water. He cautiously leaned over the edge and peered down. Yes, the lamb was bleating down below, apparently *in* the waterfall. Its cries were loud and lusty, so Winsom assumed that it was not seriously hurt.

He hurried back to the cottage to fetch a long rope and to tell Lissom what he planned to do.

"Oh, my dear," she said, clasping her hands nervously, "not the Fairy Gorge! I don't want to lose another loved one to that awful place!"

Winsom quickly kissed her cheek and told her not to worry. He hurried off with his rope. After putting knots in the rope at intervals, he tied one end to his waist and passed the other end around a tree near the top of the waterfall. He let himself down into the gorge, finding small footholds in the rocks as he went. The lamb kept bleating below, apparently behind the curtain of falling water.

Near the bottom of the gorge, Winsom found a flat rocky platform that extended through the waterfall. He untied his rope and walked through the water, following the lamb's cries. He found himself in a natural cavern. A dim light filtered down through crevices in the rocks, revealing to Winsom something in the cavern that was not natural.

First he saw his lamb, standing in a small rivulet, apparently unharmed. Then he saw behind it the figure of a nude woman, more than life sized, sculpted of marble and painted with rich, lifelike colors. She stood in a white flowstone grotto, on a marble dais with mysterious carved lettering around its rim.

Winsom couldn't read, but even if he could, he wouldn't have understood those letters, from the alphabet of an ancient, long-dead language. But what they said was: "All Hail to Our Holy and Blessed Goddess, Mother of the Universe, Bride of God and Man."

Winsom thought her the most beautiful thing he had ever seen. He approached in awe and reached out to touch the delicately peach-tinted marble arm. He thought he saw a flicker of motion in her lustrous painted eyes, a shift in the wavy golden locks that fell over her shoulder, as if a breeze had lifted her hair. He saw her finger pointing to a hollow behind the dais. Had that finger been pointing before? He wasn't sure.

He looked into the hollow and saw an ancient chest, its weathered, punky wood still bound by straps of tarnished brass. Through crevices in the wood he saw a glint of gold. He lifted the creaking lid and sat back amazed at the sight of the treasure within: goblets, plates, bowls, vases, rings, chains with medallions, all carved in gleaming, imperishable gold.

He took one gold ring to prove to Lissom that he had discovered this untold wealth. He returned to the beautiful statue and knelt before her, pressing his forehead to her hand. "Thank you, lovely queen," he said. He thought her hand grew warm, like living flesh, at his touch.

As he clasped the marble hand, the gold ring slipped down over his finger and stuck fast.

Reluctantly tearing himself away from the luminous painted gaze of the Goddess, he wrapped the lamb in his cloak, tied it against his body, and returned through the waterfall to make the arduous climb out of the gorge. Several times he thought he might lose his grip and was glad he had had the foresight to tie sustaining knots.

He hurried home to restore the lamb to its mother and to tell Lissom about his wonderful discovery. Her eyes widened at the sight of the glittering gold ring on his finger.

"We're rich, dear sister," he cried. "Rich beyond our wildest dreams! The fairy queen herself has given us a golden treasure that will keep us for the rest of our lives."

Lissom found his story hard to believe at first, but the gold ring on his finger convinced her. "Winsom, we must hide this ring and not tell anyone where you found it," said Lissom.

He tried to pull it off for her, but it refused to pass over his knuckle. "That's odd," he said, "because it slipped on very easily."

"Never mind," said Lissom. "Just keep your gloves on, or your hand in your pocket, if you meet anyone. Now we must plan how to remove the treasure and how to sell it gradually, piece by piece, according to our needs."

They set about constructing a rope ladder that could hang from the tree above the gorge. They roped up a basket that Lissom could lower from above, to haul up the gold objects. The next day their sheep stayed home, tended by the children, while the brother and sister carried out their plan.

Lissom's eyes grew wider and wider as she saw the rich artifacts coming up out of Fairy Gorge. The old chest yielded a wheelbarrow load of shining objects, virtually priceless not only because of their precious metal but also because of the historical value of their rare, archaic design. Winsom and Lissom took them home and carefully stored them in a locked cupboard in their root cellar, to be taken to market over the course of future years, whenever a new infusion of money was needed.

They had their leaky roof repaired, extended their property lines, built a larger, improved sheepfold, bought a fine purebred ram for their herd, and sent Lissom's children to a prestigious private school. They gave parties and invited neighbors to share their good fortune. They gave generously to local charities. Soon Lissom found herself courted by a handsome young squire, whose company she began to enjoy.

Lissom hired a maidservant, and Winsom hired two helpers to take the sheep to pasture every day, so they were relieved of much of their toil. Nevertheless, Lissom noticed that even though her brother didn't need to attend the sheep, he often disappeared from home for many hours at a time. She asked him where he went.

"I visit the fairy queen in the grotto," he admitted rather ruefully. "She looks so beautiful standing there in her nakedness. I feel extraordinarily comfortable just being in her presence. I'm sure she loves me, Lissom. She is cold when I'm not there, but she turns warm when I touch her. Sometimes I think she moves, or changes her position on the dais."

Lissom felt a chill touch her spine. "Surely you're mistaken, brother," she said. "Your imagination works overtime. You are too much alone. You should go into town and meet a real woman, someone kind and cheerful who might love you and bear your children someday."

"There's no real woman as perfect as the fairy queen," said Winsom. "I don't want any lumpish peasant girl. The queen of my heart lives down there in Fairy Gorge."

"Oh, Winsom!" his sister cried. "It has always been said that the one who finds fairy gold will go mad. Is this happening to you, that you think yourself beloved by a statue?"

"She is more than a statue," Winsom answered solemnly. "You haven't seen her and you don't understand, Lissom dear, so please don't tax me with it. It's a harmless habit that gives me pleasure. Let it go at that."

Lissom held her peace, but as the months went on she noticed that Winsom's absences became longer and longer. Sometimes he stayed away from home all day, and then even overnight. He usually took along a basket of food, but Lissom thought he never ate anything. He seldom ate at home. He grew thinner and thinner. Strangely, though his fingers were thinned down to mere claws, his gold ring never became loose enough to slip off. His eyes took on a hectic brightness, like one who was looking into a glowing world beyond the sunset that no one else could see.

Then Winsom began staying out several days and nights in succession. Lissom became so worried about him that she went to Fairy Gorge and climbed halfway down the rope ladder, calling his name in the direction of the waterfall. Soon he came through the water curtain on the platform below, wildly waving his arms at her.

"Go back!" he cried. "Don't come here, Lissom! Not even you may come here! This place is mine, and mine only! Please do as I say! I promise I'll be home soon."

Lissom hesitated, clinging to the ladder. Her heart sank at the sight of her brother's wild, white face, so thin and bony, his hair plastered to his skull, his clothes sopping wet. He seemed so frantic, so out of control, that she gave in and climbed back up the ladder. She went home and waited.

When he finally returned, near dawn the next morning, he was staggering with weakness and obviously sick. Lissom put him to bed at once and brewed him some strengthening beef tea, but he couldn't keep it down. Over the next few days she tried desperately to get some food into him, but he seemed unable to eat. He became delirious. He muttered love words into empty space, as if he saw a beloved mistress standing before him.

Then one cold, misty morning, Lissom came into her brother's bedroom and found his bed empty. She searched the house, but he was nowhere to be found. She ran outside and searched the outbuildings. He was gone.

Choking down a surge of apprehension, she set out across the fells to Fairy Gorge. She climbed down the rope ladder and passed through the waterfall. As she stood in the cave, wet and shivering, she saw her brother's body in circumstances that she would never forget.

He lay across the marble dais, obviously dead, his skin gray, his limbs stiff. But on his face was a smile of the most delicious happiness. He looked not only peaceful but ecstatic.

The most curious thing was that the tinted marble statue of the Goddess lay with him, her limbs intricately intertwined with his, her hands gripping him in a way that seemed impossible. Lissom felt sure that Winsom had described the Goddess *standing* on the dais. With the statue's naturalistic color against his death gray, she seemed the more lively and human of the two. On one of her fingers was a gold wedding ring, matching the ring on Winsom's dead hand. Dim light filtered down through the rocks and bathed both figures in a silvery twilight that seemed to cover them with a cloak of timelessness.

Lissom backed out of the chamber, which flickered before her sight as her eyes dimmed with tears. The waterfall washed her tears away as she slowly climbed out of the gorge. At the top, she unfastened the rope ladder and threw it down into the darkness, to be lost forever. She walked home slowly, making up her mind to leave Winsom undisturbed in his natural tomb, and to say he had been killed by a fall into Fairy Gorge. Her grief was soothed by the thought that in dying he must have been happier than most human beings ever expect to be.

She never returned to Fairy Gorge. She married the young squire and lived happily ever after, in considerable affluence on the proceeds of the fairy gold. Her children grew up literate, cultivated, and wise, and became the joy of their mother's old age. They married well and brought her grandchildren to receive her blessing. In later years they told their own children stories about their mysterious Uncle Winsom, who had been taken in the bloom of his youth by the fairy queen, and who left a rich, benevolent legacy of fairy gold.

TWENTY-SEVEN

HOW THE GODS MET THEIR END

This story is a version of the Teutonic Götterdämmerung, featuring such deities as Odin or Woden (Wednesday's god); Thor (Thursday's god); Freya (Friday's goddess); Loki with his miraculous offspring, the eight-legged horse Sleipnir; the primal mother goddess Idun with her life-giving apples; and Baldur, the young prince of the gods. Odin (Wednes) was the northern god-king who hung on the World Tree to win magic powers for the gods.

   The serpent in the apple tree symbolized creation and ongoing life long before the book of Genesis was written. The Great Mother's magic apples were so ubiquitous in religious traditions from China to Ireland that they were assimilated into the Bible story even though the word apple never appears there. We still don't know what Eve's forbidden fruit was supposed to be. But Hera's land of magic apples lay in the west, as did the paradise of Celtic heroes, Avalon, which means "isle of apples." Ancient middle-eastern cylinder seals show the Goddess handing out apples to men or gods while her sacred serpent looks down from the apple tree. From such a scene the Bible story could have been mistakenly deduced, thus saddling all of Western civilization with a fairy tale that everyone was commanded to take literally.

Page 237

He slithered down from an apple tree . . .

*O*nce upon a time, a minor god named Lowkey became unhappy because his godlike powers were incomplete, and he complained to the king of gods, Wednes (whose day is still celebrated every week). "Consider, Lord Wednes," he said, "what is the most godlike power in the world? Why, the power to give life. Goddesses can do it; mortal women can do it; even female animals can do it. But we, the gods, can't do it. I demand that this situation be remedied."

"Ungrateful whelp that you are!" Wednes snapped. "Haven't I done enough for you? Didn't I give up the use of one eye, and go into the very womb of the earth to find her cauldrons of magic blood, and even hang myself on the Tree to win us the powers of the runes and of fatecasting? Can't you be satisfied with these accomplishments?"

"I can't feel really godlike unless I have the ultimate power to give life," Lowkey insisted. "If you can't help me, I'll find a way to do it myself."

"Good luck to you," Wednes growled ironically. "You presume too much."

"I think you're satisfied with too little, sire," Lowkey said. "Surely we gods should be able to do anything a mortal woman can do."

Wednes said no more but dismissed Lowkey with a rude gesture. Lowkey smiled to himself, thinking that he recognized impotence behind his ruler's anger. He devised a way to get what he wanted. He went to another god, the thrower of thunderbolts, Thurs (whose day is also celebrated every week). "Divine Thurs," he said, "next time you send a thunderbolt to earth, kill me a woman."

Thurs agreed to do so and soon delivered to Lowkey the fresh corpse of a young mother. Lowkey removed the woman's heart and ate it. "Now," he said, "I will have the power to give life and will be the most complete of all gods."

In a short time Lowkey proudly announced to all the deities that he was expecting and soon would be able to produce a life. The goddesses laughed, but the gods believed him and were impressed.

When the time came for Lowkey to deliver his offspring, they all gathered around to witness the miracle. Lowkey put on a great show, groaning and straining, making his body ripple and dance, generally creating a huge fuss. After he had gained enough attention, he finally produced a living creature.

To his chagrin, all the deities began to laugh. Lowkey looked at the creature, and his balloon of pride abruptly burst. At first he thought it was a spider; then he saw that he had produced an eight-legged horse.

King Wednes felt sorry for Lowkey in his embarrassment, so he tried to be comforting. "Never mind, Lowkey," he said. "I'll take the creature and bring it up, and when it's grown I'll ride it. Even an eight-legged horse can be useful."

The other deities followed Wednes's example and tried to comfort Lowkey, but he never forgave their laughter. Unlike a real mother, he rejected his poor offspring, which was named Sleepnever because it seemed not to need rest. Eventually it grew into a strong if odd-shaped horse, and Wednes made it his favorite steed.

In later years Lowkey became increasingly reclusive, sullen, and obsessively concerned with matters of life and death. He took to playing unpleasant, ill-humored tricks on the other gods, who endured his mischief indulgently enough because they felt guilty for having mocked him.

One day Lowkey discovered that the deep secret of the gods' ongoing life lay in the apples daily delivered to them from the garden of the Great Mother, Idone. The gods were fond of saying, "An apple a day keeps old age away." For them it was literally true. The Great Mother's red essence of life was inherent in her apple tree. The gods didn't want it to be generally known that their immortality depended on something external to themselves. Lowkey had never been told because they didn't trust him to keep the secret, but he discovered it anyway. A little bird, who nested in the sacred apple tree, told him.

Being an accomplished shape-shifter, Lowkey took the form of a serpent to wriggle into Idone's garden and steal all the apples. Without their food of life, the gods began to age. Their hair was speckled with gray. Their skin showed wrinkles. Their limbs became weaker. Wednes's favorite son lost all his hair and was known ever afterward as Baldy.

Lowkey compounded his offense by trying to give away the secret even to mortals, to whom most gods wished to remain forever mysterious. In his serpent form, Lowkey went to the land of mortals and offered the secret to a woman. He slithered down from an apple tree and told her, "The gods lied to you, saying that you would die if you ate apples. What they really fear is that you might become like gods, knowing the secret of life and death."

The woman believed him and ate the forbidden apple, sharing it with her mate. But the magic didn't work for them. It was only ordinary fruit from an earthly, mortal apple tree, unlike the fruit of the Great Mother's magic garden, which held the essence of her life-giving blood. The woman had some of that herself, without apples.

The gods were angry. Lowkey's attempt to betray them to their inferiors was the last straw. They were aging rapidly. Some had even become ill. They agreed that something would have to be done quickly if they were to preserve themselves from death. "If we can die," said Wednes, "we will be no better than humans, and of course that is unthinkable."

Thurs had tried to save them by engaging in a wrestling match with the spirit of old age, who took the form of a crone. He scoffed at her, saying that his great strength could certainly overcome an old woman. Nevertheless, she won the match. "Not even godlike strength can stand up against old age," she said.

King Wednes told them, "There is one way for us to put off death as long as possible. We must teach the humans to revere us, feed us with sacrifices, and continually sing our glory and praise, for these things give spiritual life. When the humans no longer recognize our divinity, we are dead indeed."

The serpent Lowkey sneered at this. "Don't forget that they can recognize us as devils just as easily," he remarked. "Humans are stupid, flighty creatures without much sense of continuity. Sooner or later they get all their stories tangled up and wrong. If the gods' immortality depends on human opinion, then the gods are doomed. Face it. The period of ascendancy is over for all of you. You are approaching your twilight."

Then up spoke the goddess Fria (whose day is also celebrated every week). She said, "We may be ascendant no longer, but we should remember—and Lowkey especially should remember—that even if the miracle of indefinite life extension has gone the way of fable, the miracle of giving life hasn't ceased. Even the humans and the animals know it. Perhaps it would be best if humans forgot all about the gods and their wrangling, jealousy, and warfare. Let the humans be content with revering the female force that nurtures and protects the life it gives. And if we join them in experiencing old age and death, so be it. They don't need us to keep up their race. They only need to develop their own intelligence and understand themselves. They're wasting their time trying to understand gods, who don't want to be understood. Someday, perhaps, there will be a new world with better principles out of which the humans can create better deities."

Somewhat abashed, Lowkey slithered over to Fria and rubbed against her hand. "You are the wisest of us all," he said. "Let the humans know that Lowkey the snake will be the Goddess's humble friend forever."

"They will know," said Fria. "They will misunderstand, as they misunderstand nearly everything, but they will know."

It is written that shortly after this, the gods voluntarily went into their twilight. The male deities engaged in a mighty battle and killed one another off, all except Lowkey, who remained a serpent and hid in the womb of earth. The goddesses also hid under other names in the psyches of humans, even when the humans didn't know it. No one lived happily forever after, because that is not the nature of things. But some lived happily enough, for a while, in a world without gods.

Some say the apples of Idone will grow again one day, and the Great Mother's gift of immortality will be bestowed on a new batch of deities. Others say this can never be. As in all questions concerning gods, it is strictly a matter of opinion.

TWENTY-EIGHT

THE WHITE GOD

This story could be entitled "How the Hyena Learned to Laugh," or "The Holy War on Animals." Africa has been one of the chief sufferers from the patriarchal god's directive to humans to "subdue" and "have dominion over . . . every living thing that moveth upon the earth" (Genesis 1:28). Therefore a trio of the African goddesses appears here to investigate and remedy the situation.

Something of this sort will have to take place if the unique heritage of African fauna is to be preserved into the next century.

"The white god is insane," all the animals said.

*O*nce upon a time the white god Yawalla came to the African land and began causing great trouble among the animals. He allowed his followers to kill them in such numbers that, for the first time in all the millennia, the animal nations grew smaller and smaller. The slaughter came to the attention of the three goddesses Oshun, Yemaya, and Mawu. They set out to investigate.

They first questioned Elephant Mother, leader of the largest, oldest, and wisest nation among the warmbloods. She was in deep distress over the ongoing massacre of her people. "The white god's men want only our big teeth," she complained, "but they slay whole tribes to get them. They pile up mountains of my children's teeth to be exchanged for money. They are insane creatures."

Oshun said, "We've heard that Yawalla insists on the superiority of killer males to nurturant females. What say you, Elephant Mother?"

"Only another example of insanity," said Elephant Mother, waving her long, muscular trunk in disgust. "Naturally, the life-giving sex is the only one important enough to need numerical upkeep. Most males are useless, except for breeding, and even then they are addlepated and foolishly destructive during musth. Our matrons are right to keep males out of the herds, where young calves are being protected. Our bulls know their place. They're wise enough to remember their mothers' teachings and to stay away from nursery herds."

The goddesses went next to Lion Mother, leader of the cat nations. She was constantly angry and growling over the destruction of cat people in general. "They take our skins for no apparent reason, except to exchange them for money," she snarled. "The mothers of leopard, cheetah, and ocelot tribes have almost no children left. These men are felicidal maniacs."

Yemaya said, "We've heard that Yawalla insists on the superiority of fighting males to hunting females. What say you, Lion Mother?"

The lioness gave a contemptuous snort. "Males, superior?" she sneered. "Another example of Yawalla's insanity. Males are good for nothing except to lie around in the shade sleeping, or to waste their time bullying cubs. Everyone knows that females raise every generation to maturity, bring home the meat, teach the children to hunt, and keep the murderous fathers away. Males are so indolent that they never lift a claw if they can help it. They are the laziest creatures on the veldt."

The goddesses went next to Hyena Mother, leader of the carrion eaters. Hyena Mother was less tormented than the others, because men didn't covet her people's skins, and hyenas had made a good living from the huge mounds of carrion that Yawalla's men abandoned on the plains. She said, however, that they were obviously insane, for what sane creature would make a kill and then walk away from the meat? Furthermore, the killing had been so extensive that the herds supporting the hyena population had become quite thinned out.

Mawu said, "We've heard that Yawalla insists on the superiority of males to females. What say you, Hyena Mother?"

Hyena Mother laughed and laughed, until all the hyenas in the world began laughing with her. "That's the best joke I've heard in all my days," she gasped, wiping her eyes. "Those little pipsqueak males, superior? Everybody knows that females are bigger, stronger, faster, smarter, sexier, and better equipped to make a living than males are. It has to be so, because we females bear the responsibility for birthing, nourishing, raising, and training every generation of our kind. No wonder Yawalla's men kill for nonsensical reasons and leave the good parts behind. They're completely crazy."

The goddesses went next to Rhinoceros Mother and found her in a state of near-collapse, so great was her sorrow over the decimation of her people. "They are destroying all my tribes for the most foolish reason in the world," she said mournfully. "They have ancient, silly tales that equate one-horned mythical beasts with sexual potency. Therefore, the white god's men eat rhinoceros horn in the absurd belief that it will cure their impotence and all other weaknesses. They won't even go to the trouble of capturing my children, removing the horn, and letting them go again. These men are lunatics, willing to kill and kill for their erroneous notions instead of learning the truth."

The goddesses went next to Gorilla Mother and heard much the same story from her. "They kill and kill my people, who only want to be left in peace and who cause no harm to any other creature," she said. "I think the men must be insane enough to want to destroy themselves. There seems no other reason for their lunatic slaughter of the gorilla tribes, other than the fact that gorillas look something like them; so they may be killing one another in effigy. Of course they also kill one another for real—an unthinkable act, in the view of my people. Obviously they are out of their minds."

The goddesses went next to Vulture Mother, leader of the great birds, widest-winged and keenest-eyed among all her kind. She bobbed her bald, wrinkled head and cackled that the humans had once had the good sense to revere her, three thousand and more rainy seasons ago. They gave her the name of Nekhbet and worshiped her as the symbol of every life's ending and rebirthing. "But I fear their males are born crazy from the egg," she said. "Perhaps the females also, to allow the males to neglect their primary duty, helping to nurture the young. Our bird brains are better than that."

The goddesses consulted all other animal leaders they could find and heard the same thing over and over: The men of Yawalla were crazy killers who didn't even wait for hunger, which was the only proper reason for killing. Even when fully fed, fat, and satisfied, they would go forth with terrible weapons and slaughter dozens of animals at a time, and eat none of them. "The white god is insane," all the animals said, "and he has corrupted his people. They no longer know how to behave in the world. They have become a pestilence."

Oshun, Yemaya, and Mawu realized that something would have to be done. They thought the only logical choices for their agents on Earth were the human females, who must be encouraged to control their males, as did the females of other species. On further investigation, however, the goddesses found that many if not all of the human females were greatly weakened by Yawalla's rules, which often mutilated their bodies, robbed them of their children, forced them into sexual slavery, and taught the men, who should have been helping them, to treat them instead with mindless hostility.

"This Yawalla is an abomination," said Mawu angrily. "He has even caused the women to forget Us, their images and preservers. The white god has got to go."

"Let Us teach the women to despise him, then," said Yemaya. "That's the first step. Show them that he has no spiritual power over them, let them believe it thoroughly, and then they will regain temporal power. After all, nothing can change the fact that they are the mothers."

"Let the mothers accept only men who show decent, rational, fatherly behavior toward children and other living things," said Oshun. "Then the brutes who are not accepted may die out, and their violent heritage with them. Will that be Our plan, sisters?"

The goddesses agreed and set to work to change the minds of women, one woman at a time. It was slow going. Most men opposed the goddesses in their mission, though a few of the more rational ones saw the sense of their arguments and began to help. Some of the men came to believe that it was wrong to hunt without hunger. Women learned to despise leopard-skin coats and ivory ornaments, to reprimand others still ignorant enough to crave such things, and to laugh at men still ignorant enough to think rhinoceros horn would cure their impotence. Women taught their children, and they taught their children, and they in turn taught their children.

In time, the white god faded and became only one more minor consort of the powerful goddesses. Then Africa and its animal nations—the ones that managed to survive the great slaughters—began to flourish again. They lived a little more happily ever after, because it was understood among them that the only killers were those who couldn't digest vegetable food and who needed meat for their own hunger and that of their children. The goddesses watched the white god closely and made sure that he never again seized the upper hand.